Chivalry

Kristie Higgins

Allegro Publishing
406 Holly Rd
Glen Burnie, Maryland 21061
AllegroPublishing@yahoo.com

Chivalry/ Kristie Higgins.
ISBN 978-0-9903715-0-2

ACKNOWLEDGEMENTS

To Sharon K. Miller, my first editor, for pointing me in the direction of books and websites, essentially teaching me to edit my own book even before she started editing. She stayed with me, guiding me over many months, answering questions, giving advice, teaching me like a *sensei*. It was hard work, I'm sure, editing a book for a first time author. Though, she never complained and always continued to encourage me, which I greatly appreciate.

To Courtney Wilson, my friend and second editor, for being so patient with me with all my changes and postponements. I am completely surprised she never gave up and walked away from this, as a few others had. I'm glad she didn't, because her attention to detail was amazing.

To Chrystal Vaughn, proofreader, for suggestions, encouragement and advice in addition to her work.

To my horse racing insider, Kayla Jarvinen, for checking my accuracy on the way things are on the backside at a track, for showing me the differences between regular riding and race riding, for editing and correcting, for being patient with me with all my changes. For putting up with all my seemingly strange questions.

To retired jockey, Frankie Lovato, Jr. and his **Jockey World** website, *jockeyworld.org*, whose mission is "*...to improve, promote and provide education health & safety into the world of horse racing!* Jockey World is a 501(c)(3) nonprofit educational organization dedicated to providing reliable information, tools, training, guidance and resources that include knowledge in health & safety to anyone who wishes to pursue a career or develop a better understanding of the horse racing industry. **Jockey World** is not a gambling related organization." Frankie and his **Jockey World** Facebook group have been a joy to talk to and learn from.

To my beta and second readers, Kayla Jarvinen, Kristi Lyerla, Dana Moritz, Shannon Mummey, and Karen Ross, who were honest and helpful to make sure my prose was fluid, there were no inconsistencies, and offered suggestions to make my book easy to read and entertaining. Their feedback has been invaluable to me.

To the female jockeys of the era in this book, the late 1960s and early 1970s, who worked hard despite multiple barriers in the industry, who have inspired many other females to pursue riding careers, who fought to do what they loved, not for the fame or notoriety, but for the love of horses and the adrenaline rush of the race.

Thank you!

Kristie Higgins

Once you choose hope, anything is possible.

– Christopher Reeve

CONTENTS

PROLOGUE

February 1969

"Guess I'll see you in a couple days. Enjoy your day off."

"Yeah. With ten drug addicts chasing me around the house? No, thank you. Hey, you sure you don't want me to walk with you?"

"Nah. It's only a block. Nothing's gonna happen," Rachel answered as she scoped out the area for danger. Having seen nothing, she waved to her friend, Candy, who also waved and went inside.

Though she had only been outside for the short walk from the movie theater to Candy's house, she thought the tip of her nose might be frozen. She covered her nose with her mitten-clad hand and breathed into the warmth, hoping to thaw it.

If she were in Florida right now, she wouldn't have to worry about the cold New York winter, snow, and ice. She cautiously padded over a frozen puddle, then continued along the sidewalk toward the subway station.

It must feel so good to be in Florida right now. There was a young woman, just two years older than Rachel, who was getting ready to ride in a horse race there tomorrow. Rachel desperately wished she could be there to see it in person. Instead, she would have to wait for the *Daily Racing Form* the next day, or, if she were lucky, they would talk about it on the six o'clock news. She wished she knew someone at Hialeah Park Race Track in Miami so she could call them and get the latest word on everything. That would be even better.

Lately, at least to Rachel, the biggest story in the world was the emergence of female jockeys breaking into horse racing. It looked as though the race was actually going to happen this time, too. In other races where females had tried to ride, every trainer had scratched his horses from the race to protest the presence of a female jockey. Not this time. Unless they chickened out last minute, it would be a good-sized field of horses.

Rachel was so excited, she could hardly contain herself as she leapt over a patch of ice. She hoped one day to get her jockey's license, too. If only her mother would let her. Her mother, a trainer at Belmont Park, had been adamant about keeping Rachel from the dangers of race riding. After all, her own father had been killed in a racing accident fourteen years ago. While no other jockey had died during a race at Belmont since then, others around the country had. The average loss was two jockeys per year to accidents on the track during races. It was a dangerous profession, and Rachel's mother did all she could to keep her daughter from it. She had tried everything from scaring her with horrible stories, to begging her not to do it, to flat out ordering her to resist the urge to apply for that license.

But that was fine. Rachel knew she would get it eventually. In the meantime, she focused on the other woman who was going to ride tomorrow at Hialeah. Diane Crump, just an ordinary girl who loved to ride horses, was about to make history.

Rachel knew beyond a shadow of a doubt that she could do the same here in New York.

"Hey, you need a lift?" she heard.

Rachel jumped, as she hadn't realized that a black van had pulled up behind her. There was no way she was going to get into a stranger's van, no matter how cold it was. She frowned at the man and kept walking.

"Hey, uh, it's not safe out here. Hop in. I'll take you home."

Rachel hurried her steps, but the van continued next to her with the man leaning down so he could speak through the open passenger side window. It did not take long for his coaxing to become more desperate.

"You look cold. Come on."

Rachel kept walking, ignoring him, and at the same time, trying to deny the fact that this was really happening. *Please go away. Please go. Please go.*

"I'm lost. I need help. Can you give me directions?"

He's not lost. Keep going. Just keep going.

"Does your boyfriend take good care of you? I bet I could do a better job. I'm pretty good, you know."

Oh, God. Where do I go? He's just going to keep following me.

"You'd better get in, or I'm going to pick you up and throw you in."

Her body chilled from the inside. *Run!* She stopped abruptly and turned around. He stopped the van, and she ran behind it and to the other side of the street. There were stores nearby, and if she could get to them, she might be able to find someone to help get rid of this pest. She hurried her steps as she heard the van's wheels squealing as he did a three-point turn in the middle of the road.

"Come on, baby. Let's go. I just want to get to know you."

As Rachel neared the one level buildings containing several different stores, her heart sank as she realized all the lights were off and no one was anywhere in sight. The streets were deserted. One block away was the main road and several cars whizzing by. It was too far to run, and she knew he would surely catch her by then. Instead of running all that way, she decided to lose him. Just ahead, there was an alleyway narrow enough so his van would not fit, and she ducked into the darkness.

She heard the van come to a stop at the end of the alley. Then, only a few steps into the darkness, she ran into a brick wall lined with bags of trash. *No, this can't be. This isn't happening. Please, no! There has to be a way out.*

As she mumbled curses to herself for turning down this alley, she searched for a door. In the darkness, she slid her hands along a wall until she came to a steel door without a door handle. She glanced at the end of the alley and saw him. He was coming for her, and her only hope was this door. She pounded with clenched fists, begging for someone to be inside the record store on the other side.

Only seconds later, he was there. He wrapped his arms around hers, pinning them to her sides. She kicked his legs, his groin, anything she could get to, but nothing seemed to faze him. She screamed, but no one came. He opened the van door with one hand, still holding her with the other. He tossed her inside as she screamed for help again. Now that his hands were off her for a second, she fought to slide back out of the van, but he stopped her and threw her against the inside wall of the van. The cold metal rang as her skull hit. She could hardly see straight, but she continued to scream for help.

"Shut up!" he yelled, then hit her on the side of her head until she was unconscious.

CHAPTER ONE

Rachel struggled to open her bloodshot, swollen eyes. She hurt so bad – her arms, legs, her head, even her insides. What little air she had was gloomy, musty, sour, cigarette smoke-filled, and she choked as she tried to remember where she was. A hairy man in a worn out black t-shirt smirked, a brown cigarette hanging precariously from his lip. "There's my girl," he growled.

She looked up at him, fearful and confused about why she was in this horrible place. "I thought you'd never wake up, my love," he said as he rose from the folding metal chair beside her bed. Her head ached as she searched the room. She found nothing familiar to her and yet this awful man was calling her "my love."

The bed had no sheets and the mattress was stained with dark blotches of sticky blood. Whose blood? Hers? The mattress sagged horribly even under her slight figure. Even as he stood there watching her, she managed to lift her throbbing head to see if she was hurt. Through the smoke, she saw several long cuts on her stomach and inner thighs. Fresh blood ran along thick streaks of dried blood and pooled in the hollow of her belly. What had he done to her?

A sudden, sickening smell hit her and dizziness and nausea swept over her like a wave. But her stomach was empty and twisted painfully with a dry heave. As she rolled and writhed from the pain, she tried to slide out of the bed, but he grabbed her shoulder. "Where do you think you're going?" Words clogged her throat and she squeezed her eyes shut, unable to face the evil enveloping her. She knew she had to get up and get out of there, sick or not. Turning over again, she tried to slide off the other side of the bed. She whimpered as he wrapped his hairy arm around her bony ribs once again and pulled her back to the middle of the bed.

"Rachel?" It was her mother's voice. Thank God, her mother was here. She desperately wanted to call out so her mother would know where to find her, but she was afraid the man would hurt her mother, too. She shook her head and whispered, "No. No," repeatedly, hoping her mom understood. The man laughed and turned toward her mother, now behind him. Just as he was about to reach for her, Rachel found her voice.

"No!" Her shriek of terror stopped him with his hand outstretched. He faced Rachel again, confused. "No!" she bellowed, this time louder.

"Rachel, please..."

Rachel's mother was at her side, pushing on her arm. She was too close! He might get her, too! "No! Mom! Go! Go!"

"What? Why? Rachel? Are you awake?"

Rachel knit her eyebrows as she tried to understand. Why isn't Mom running? Why is she still here? Why is she asking if I'm awake?

"Are you awake?" she heard again.

It hit her like a lightning bolt to her head. *Awake?* Was she awake? Yes. She was awake.

"Um, yeah," she managed to squeak. Her voice was dry, raspy, hoarse, and she tried to cough to clear her throat. Coughing sent shooting pains throughout her entire body and radiating from her abdomen. Crying out in pain, she winced until the electric zaps dissipated.

Even as she recovered from the sudden pain, she held her mother's hand, though tighter now, her grip loosening as the pain faded. But there was a different pain that was left behind and it was more than she could handle. Involuntary tears fell and she wiped them away with her other hand.

"Do you need medicine?" her mother asked.

Medicine? *You need more medicine*, she heard a man's deep voice say. For just a second, she pictured a giant syringe and needle being shoved into her hip. His medicine always made her feel better, forgetting where she was, and though it burned at first, the escape was worth it.

"Yeah," she finally admitted. Her mother attempted to let go of her hand to push the nurse's call button, but Rachel held on tight, not letting her go. With her other hand, her mother reached over Rachel's broken and frail seventeen-year-old body and pushed the button on the railing of the bed. Rachel's dark, curly hair fanned over her white, sweat-dampened pillow, still messy from thrashing wildly in her bed. Her green eyes were haunted, sunken into dark pits that nearly swallowed them.

As they waited for the medicine to arrive, Rachel kept her gaze on her mother's shadowed hazel eyes. She wasn't the same mom as before. She was much older now, with wrinkles. How long had she been away?

A nurse came in, interrupting her thoughts, and poked the needle into the IV. It confused Rachel to watch that happen, as she expected the needle to be stuck into her hip again. "But," she started as she watched the nurse leave the room. "What about the medicine in my hip?"

"Honey, this is the way they give you medicine here."

Rachel's jaw dropped as she tried to understand her mother's words. They made no sense at all.

Within seconds she felt relief and was able to breathe normally again. The sudden relief almost made her cry. She felt the familiar feeling of floating somewhere out there, as she grew more and more tired. Sleep was rolling in to overtake her. If only she wasn't terrified of sleeping now. Still, blackness fell over her once again.

In the distance, she heard the nurse talking to her mom. It sounded as if they were far away, yet she understood most of what they were saying.

"She's in so much pain because he kept her high with a sedative pain killer called Ketamine. She needs a good amount of Morphine to keep the pain under control because of her high tolerance. Fortunately, she won't experience withdrawal symptoms when she goes home." Her mother said something in reply, and then Rachel heard the nurse leave the room.

Her head started to spin and she moaned and squirmed in her bed. Nausea was setting in and getting worse by the second.

"Rachel," her mom whispered through her own tears. "Are you awake?" Rachel tried to focus but she was so drowsy her eyelids felt like lead weights. As she awoke, the nausea hit her like a tornado. Panic struck her as she tried to sit up, but something stopped her. Something was keeping her down. She tried to lean over the side of the bed and twisted her body under two straps.

"Sick!"

Her mom grabbed a trashcan, shoved it under her head next to the bed, and caught her sickness just in time. Mom pushed the call button and the nurse rushed back in.

"She's sick. The medicine made her sick, I think." Mom handed Rachel some tissues.

"Okay, I'll be right back," the nurse said, hurrying from the room as Rachel moaned.

"It's okay, sweetheart. She's going to give you some medicine to make you feel better." Julia pushed Rachel's long curly hair back behind her ears, out of her face, then handed her some more tissues. Rachel was trying to catch her breath again and still trying to lean over the side of the bed, but it was hard because of these straps around her waist and hips.

It was hard to move as she hurt like hell all over her body. No, not just *like* hell, she was *in* hell. She just wanted to die and escape this torture. However, there was no escape from hell.

Soon, the nurse was there giving her IV another shot. Again, the medicine instantly hit her, but this time made her nausea suddenly disappear. "Feel okay yet?" she asked.

Rachel nodded and flopped her head back onto her pillow, instantly falling asleep despite knowing what would happen next.

CHAPTER TWO

She tried not to cry or make a sound so he wouldn't hear her. Did he think she was dead? Would he be back? She had to get out of there, but the pain was incredible and her hands were tied together to a headboard. Her arms burned from being stretched over her head. Rachel ripped at the rope with her teeth. She had to get this off and fast, before the man came back. At first, it wasn't coming loose, but she kept trying and trying. Finally, it loosened as she bit desperately at the knots.

"Rachel! Stop! Wake up! You're going to hurt yourself!" she heard.

"Mom?" She looked down at her wrists. There was no rope there, but there were partially healed burns and cuts and a loose IV that she had ripped out and tangled around her arms. Blood and saline had splattered onto the white blanket and she shrieked a piercing scream that could only come from a teen-age girl.

The nurse rushed in, grabbing gauze from the cabinet, and pressed on the vein to stop the flow of blood. After taping the gauze to Rachel's pallid arm, she clipped closed the dripping IV and hurried to get another lead.

"Mom, what happened?" Rachel asked. Her emerald eyes were more awake today, set more in reality and less in the past. A week ago, reality was too horrible to deal with but the drugs had helped her escape temporarily.

She faintly remembered waking up in the hospital, terrified, not knowing where she was. Policemen stood over her, asking her questions about where she had been and who had attacked her. But she hardly remembered talking to them and had no idea what she would have said. She couldn't even remember exactly what had happened or why she was in the hospital. The nightmares, however, brought back the unfathomable memories bit by bit, revealing the dreadful events in pieces as her mind tried to make sense of the puzzle.

"Honey, you were having another nightmare and you tore out your IV, so the nurse has to get another one for you. She'll be right back, okay?" Julia said, checking the gauze for blood. Thankfully, the bleeding had stopped. "Are you in pain?"

"Yeah. I want more of that stuff they shoot into my IV. It makes me go numb." *Give me enough to kill me, please. Why does it hurt so bad? What happened to me? What did that man do to me?* Her face bore a bewildered stare as she tried to figure it all out. Something was blocking her memories, though, and she wasn't sure she really wanted to remember.

***

There was a knock and then the sound of the creaking door. "Hello?" called a man, softly. "Are we awake today?"

Julia narrowed her eyes as she rose out of her green vinyl chair to meet the man at the door and block his entrance. He was wearing a grey suit and holding a grey hat and a notebook.

The press? Julia went from puzzled to angry in a split second. She had thought the media frenzy was over and hoped they weren't bringing it up again but he spoke before she had a chance to throw him out.

"Good afternoon, ma'am. I'm Officer Ritter from the NYPD...'scuse me, *Detective* Ritter. Just promoted." He nervously shuffled his feet. "May I come in and ask your daughter a few questions? We need to get more information on the bad guy."

Bad guy? Who is this? Colombo? Julia tried to be polite despite her mood. "Um, yes, sir. She's been sleeping and waking periodically. You never know what's going to happen. She has nightmares, flashbacks, screaming, biting at her IV... it's horrible." Tears slipped down her cheeks. Before he could see them, she covered her face with her hands.

Normally, she was better at controlling her emotions. Being the only female trainer at Belmont Park, she had learned not to appear too emotional about anything to avoid scrutiny from the men. But controlling her emotions right now was impossible.

Detective Ritter nervously put his arm around Julia and ushered her further into the room. Rachel was lying quietly under a white blanket. The two straps crossing over her hospital bed belied Rachel's otherwise peaceful appearance. She was so petite for seventeen and he felt awful for everything she had been through.

Rachel stirred in her bed when she heard the detective's voice. Her stomach turned with fear, though she told herself this man was safe. He was a detective, after all. She was glad when he stood away from her, at the foot of her bed, and talked to her mother.

"Ms. McMahon, the doctor tells me she was drugged with Ketamine."

"Yes."

"You know that's a veterinary drug, right?"

"Of course. I give it to my horses sometimes for pain relief."

"I suspect whoever used this drug on her either stole it from the vet's office or works as a vet there at the track."

Julia was silent as she drifted deep into thought, wondering who could have done this.

"Mom?" Rachel asked.

Julia came back to the present, moved closer to Rachel, and took her hand. "Rachel, this is Detective Ritter from the police department. He's come to ask you some questions about the, um, case. Do you think you'll be able to talk to him? Can you stay awake for a few minutes?"

"It won't take long, Rachel," the detective promised. "You can get back to sleep soon, okay?"

Rachel scrutinized the detective in his suit, unsure of him. He appeared uneasy. Could she trust him? After all, he was a man, and men were the people she feared now that she knew what they were capable of. But he was short like the jockeys at the track, a bit pudgy, and his warm brown eyes were concerned and pleading. He appeared innocent enough. "Okay."

"I need you to tell me what happened, with as many details as possible," he said, sitting down and opening his notebook, as if it were easy to spout off the whole story. He had no idea how horrifying this was. Rachel had trouble thinking about it, let alone talking about it.

"I can't. I can't talk about it. It will scare me to death. I can't. Don't you already know enough?" She did not even want to think about thinking about it.

"Well, hon, we know the basics, but I need details, such as what your kidnapper looked like, what kind of van it was, if you knew him, things like that. Is there anything else you can tell us that might help us find that man? The more you can tell us, the faster we can find him."

She thought for a minute, silently spinning inside her mind. Back and forth, she argued with herself. *Tell him and they can find him faster. It's too scary. I can't face it. The nightmares. Will they stop if they find him? It's too scary to think about. You have to tell him.* Before losing any further arguments with herself, she blurted out, "Middle-aged, dirty, smelly, overweight man in a black van. I didn't know him."

"Can you describe his face? What he was wearing?"

Rachel whimpered, fighting back tears as she pictured the repulsive monster who had attacked her. She was unconscious for most of it, but she remembered what he looked like, and she had to say it quick. She spat out, "He had greasy dark hair. Brown. Flat nose. Short. Out of shape. Smoked. Smelly, disgusting, dirty, black clothes, black boots, like army boots. The house reeked of mold and cigarettes. The van smelled like oil. It was black and had no seats in the back. Just...a hard...floor."

Rachel was breathing fast now as she covered her face with her hands and shook her head, trying to rid herself of the awful pictures in her mind. "No, no, no!" she repeated as she tried to deny the flashing images of violence inside her head. Julia sat on the bed next to her and put her hand on Rachel's arm. Rachel buried her face in her mother's side.

Detective Ritter frantically wrote down everything Rachel had spouted out. "I'm sorry. I think you've had enough for one day. I need to come back tomorrow and find out more. Unless you think you can tell me more today?"

"No. I don't want to talk about it. I don't want to think about it. I want to go to sleep. And not have nightmares about it." Rachel was in tears, nearly screaming with frustration. "I just want it to go away!"

Julia shook her head at Ritter, signaling that it would be best if he left and came back another time. He nodded and bowed in her direction, fumbling with his hat. "I will be back tomorrow. I'm sorry this has upset you so much, Rachel. We will find him, okay? I pr...well, we will do our best." He spun on his heels and hurriedly left the room.

Lunch was a chewy hamburger that looked more like what came out of the backside of a horse, runny mashed potatoes, a small carton of milk, and a plastic bowl of Jell-O. She made a face at the food, but tried to eat as much as possible. "When can I go home, Mom? The food here is terrible, and all I do is sleep. I could be doing that at home."

"I'm not sure. I'll ask the doctor when he comes around today to check on you. Last he mentioned it, they were waiting for you to gain some more weight and make sure your other injuries are healing. I think once you look a little healthier, they'll let you go home."

"God, I hope so," she said, poking a plastic fork into the Jell-O. *You can't screw up Jell-O, can you?* She tried to pull the fork out, but it was stuck. *Yeah, they can.* "I can't gain weight if I can't eat the food. Can you bring me something from home?"

Her mother nodded. "I'll see what I can get Grandma to whip up for you."

"Oh, thank you." Rachel sighed with relief as she pushed away her tray. "Mom, how long have I been here?"

"You don't know?"

"No."

"You've been in the hospital for a little over a week now. Do you remember coming to the hospital?"

"No, but I remember waking up after surgery. I was having trouble breathing, and I was trying to cough, but it was hurting my stomach. Then, there was this other police officer, not the one who was just here, and I think I told him a few things about it, but I don't remember what I said or how much. Then, I don't know. I've been sleeping so much, I can't tell day from night anymore. Other than you not being here at night, I guess. How long was I...gone?"

"You were missing for two weeks," Julia told her, then sat down at the foot of Rachel's hospital bed.

Rachel was surprised it had been that long. But she knew it was long enough to lose plenty of muscle and body weight. A memory of catching sight of her skeletal body in a mirror in the bathroom at the monster's house hit her. Bruises and dark circles under her eyes made her face look as though it had been run over by a truck. It surprised her that the bruises were still there from where he had hit her so many times. Then again, it had only been a week. Cuts and scrapes littered her body from what she thought was her fall from the second story window when she escaped, wearing nothing. Rachel ran her fingers over scabs on her legs as she remembered slipping from the make-shift rope made of button down shirts. She had been too weak to hold on long enough for the two passing garbage men to catch her. At least she made it out alive. Then again, was this sort of life worth living? Her clouded memory and her broken body made being awake unbearable, but when she slept, the nightmares were waiting to torment her.

Her mother had protected her so far from having to talk about it too much. Several of her friends had tried to call or visit, but Julia always turned them away, trying to protect Rachel.

For the first week, Rachel had been unable to talk, but now that she was more alert, she wondered where her friends were. They sent flowers and get-well wishes, but Julia had told the hospital to turn away all visitors, except the police, of course. Rachel didn't want her friends to see her like this anyway, and she didn't want to have to answer all of their questions. She was going to have to make up something to tell them at some point because the truth was too horrifying. Right now, though, she just wanted to avoid it.

The detective came back the next day for more details, which Rachel reluctantly gave. While fighting the horrific images in her mind, she tried to tell the detective everything she remembered so far. She also told him about a memory of two men collecting trash in the alleyway behind the row home. They had run over to her when they found her dangling from the window, but it was too late. She had fallen, broken her ankle, hit her head, and was knocked out cold. They had taken her to the hospital and saved her life. She wished for an opportunity to thank them and asked the detective to get in contact with them, but he told her they had refused to give their names. They had deposited her body, wrapped in a large coat, in the ER and left.

The detective suggested calling the company that owned the truck but she had no idea what it was called. She didn't even know where exactly she had been held, so there was no way to call and ask which truck it was, or who was there. It would have been healing for her to thank them, and she hoped for an opportunity to do so someday.

***

To Detective Ritter, it was obvious the person who had done this was either a track veterinarian or a private veterinarian called in by a trainer.

"Sir, I'd like to ask you a few questions. My name is Detective Ritter from the police department." Ritter invited himself to sit in a comfortable chair in the track veterinarian's office.

The vet raised one eyebrow as he stood next to the chair, then moved behind his desk and sat. "Yes?"

"You're familiar with Rachel McMahon's disappearance?"

"Yes."

"Doctors say she was drugged with significant amounts of Ketamine while in the kidnapper's home." Ritter took note of the hint of anger on the vet's face. "Do you keep a close watch on your Ketamine?"

"Of course."

"May I see where it is kept?"

With a sigh, Doctor Senjin stood from his desk and then led Detective Ritter to the supply cabinet. One door was ajar and a key swung back and forth from its resting place in the keyhole.

"This is where you keep the key?"

Dr. Senjin yanked the key from the lock and shoved it in his pocket. "Not normally, sir. I'm not sure why it was here. Somebody must have accidentally left it."

"Who has access to that key?"

"Every vet and assistant. Occasionally, private vets borrow drugs for the horses."

"You have a ledger, I assume?"

"Yes, sir."

Detective Ritter flipped through the pages of a brown book filled with records of medicines and dosages given to horses over the past six months. Doctor Senjin stood nearby with his hands on his hips and the same indignant look in his eye. "I suppose you know what I'm going to ask."

"I have not noticed any of the Ketamine missing, if that's what you were going to ask."

Ritter nodded as he thumbed through a few more of the pages.

"It's obvious we keep good records. Every ounce is accounted for."

"I'll need this book, and time cards and schedules for each vet and assistant for the entire month of February."

“Sir, you know that will be extremely difficult information to gather.”

“I can obtain a warrant, if you like.”

“I’ll be right back.”

Detective Ritter finally left the office with books and ledgers in his arms and a frown on his face. What a case to be given for his first assignment. It was going to take a month to go through all of this information. Also, and soon, he would have to interview each and every veterinarian employee. He let out a whoosh of air as he let the books fall into the back seat of his black car, then groaned as he flopped into the driver’s seat.

CHAPTER THREE

Using crutches, and with her mother's help, Rachel made her way up the three steps to her porch and into her house. Home. Finally. It had been a month since she had set foot in her house and she was so relieved to be back that she wept with joy. Her grandmother greeted her with open arms and placed her aging hands on Rachel's face, and then wiped away a tear with her thumb.

"Oh," Grandma whispered. "My poor baby," she added as she ever so slightly touched a fading bruise on her cheek. Then, she felt a sharp cheekbone, "You need to eat. You're so skinny."

"Yeah. That hospital food was disgusting. Good thing you sent that roast beef with mom, or I would have starved to death," Rachel answered as she headed into the kitchen. Mom was right behind her with her hand on Rachel's back. Rachel needed that touch. It was her lifeline. Whenever Mom let go, she felt alone and exposed, as if anybody might snatch her up and take her again.

"How's your leg?" a squeaky voice said. Rachel smiled at her brother waiting for them in the kitchen. Rachel's brother,

Billy, was a perfect mixture of Mom and Dad, though she only knew what Dad looked like because of the few pictures they had. He had been a jockey and died in a racing accident when she was three and Billy was a baby, leaving their mom to raise two children without him. Rachel was a miniature version of him with curly brown hair and big green eyes. Billy had the green eyes, too, but had gotten his hair from their mother. Billy's straight, chocolate brown hair wisped over his forehead and he occasionally shook it to one side.

"Okay, I guess. Doesn't hurt unless I put weight on it," Rachel answered as she slowly lowered herself onto a yellow plastic covered kitchen chair. Normally, she might have plopped down, but now she had to be careful, as her hysterectomy scar was only recently free from staples, and her insides felt as if they would fall out any minute.

She felt anger stirring inside at that awful man. He had taken the worst thing he could have taken from her. It wasn't just her virginity. He had taken her ability to get pregnant. He was a monster if she ever saw one, with no regard for anything but his own sick and twisted pleasure.

Fortunately, her brother spoke again, bringing her mind back to reality. "Can I sign your cast?" His voice cracked. He cleared his throat and repeated his question, this time forcing his voice to sound lower.

Rachel almost laughed at the misfortune of his puberty-induced voice changing. "Of course," she answered. It felt good to be home.

Billy grabbed a black marker and eagerly became the first person to sign the thick white cast that covered her right foot and leg up to her knee.

Her mom let go with a slight pat on the back, and stood. Rachel felt scared and alone as her mother walked away. She fought the urge to run to her mother's side and grab onto her like a toddler. It was impossible; she was on crutches with a broken ankle and knees that barely bent. Instead, she watched her mother make her way to the green refrigerator, open it, and stare.

Her grandmother followed Julia, then took her hand from the refrigerator door handle and said, "I'll take care of it, Jules."

"Thanks, Mom," Julia answered. There was great relief in her voice as she patted her mother's shoulder, clad in one of her ever-present flowered dresses, and then made her way back to the table to sit with Rachel and Billy. When she sat and took Rachel's hand, Rachel's shoulders dropped with relief at being connected to safety.

Glancing through the kitchen window, Rachel saw their neighbors on their back porch, smoking. Sudden terror rose within her, threatening to stop her heart and steal air from her lungs. Then, for a few seconds, her chest froze and she grabbed her chest in panic, hoping to suck in as much air as possible. But her lungs refused to cooperate. She wasn't sure how, but she saw the evil man smoking a cigarette and sitting on a metal folding chair right there in her kitchen. It was impossible to look away from him no matter how hard she tried. Was he really here in front of her again? It couldn't be.

"Rachel?" her mother asked as she leaned toward her daughter. Just as her mother stood up in alarm, Rachel sucked in a lung full of air with her mouth open wide. Gasping, she kept her eyes on her mother and tried to focus on breathing. Billy, still holding his marker, peered up, wide-eyed, at his sister.

Julia could not let go of her daughter's hand, though she was relieved to see her breathing again. "What happened?"

Rachel definitely didn't want to answer that question.

Everyone was looking at her and she felt exposed. She felt as if they knew what she had been through. Did they know what he had done to her? That he had ruined her chance at having children of her own? It didn't matter. *Making babies? Sex?* Rachel wanted nothing to do with that. She was never again going to have sex. It was way too painful. Instead, she had decided she was going to stay away from men from now on. She wasn't able to get pregnant anyway, so what good would she be? Who would even want her?

"Rachel?" Julia asked, lightly tugging on her hand. The tugging forced her to focus again on her mom, and she was grateful for the chance to come back to reality.

"Yeah," Rachel answered simply, her voice void of emotion. It was either that or start screaming.

Somehow, as Grandma made them dinner, Julia, Billy, and Rachel were able to sit at the table and talk, but never about what had happened to her. Those things were unmentionable, especially in front of her little brother. It was not only embarrassing, it was disturbing, and she promised herself never to scare her family by telling them everything she had been through. She was glad when they talked about other things.

"They should be sending Chivalry down soon," Julia announced with genuine excitement. Rachel knew her mom was glad to talk about something happy for a change, too, especially when it was about horses. This one in particular.

"When?" Rachel asked, sitting up straight in her chair. She remembered her mother mentioning this horse before, after receiving an excited phone call from Hanover Farm.

"Soon." Her mother wore a devious grin and a gleam in her eye.

"Mo-om," Billy whined, also anxious to know.

Rachel laughed at his reaction, surprising herself. She hadn't laughed at anything for a full month. Julia touched Rachel's hand and her face lit with sheer joy at hearing her daughter's laughter again.

Determined not to allow any thoughts that had to do with the kidnapping near her family, Julia kept the conversation going. "I don't know. Mister Hanover didn't tell me the exact date. He only said, 'soon.' But you know how it works. He usually sends the two-year-olds in late March. We'll work him for a month or two, and then try him out in a maiden race."

"Have they already worked him up at the farm?" Billy asked.

"Yes. They really think he could be the one."

"The one?" Rachel and Billy asked at the same time.

"Yes. The one."

To Rachel, that meant this horse might be the one to propel their stable to new heights. She grinned at her brother as she wondered about their chances to win the Kentucky Derby. Maybe even the Preakness and Belmont, too. The Triple Crown was the ultimate prize in horse racing. Maybe this horse could win it. They needed this win. After all, it had been twenty-one years since Citation won it in 1948. It was time.

Rachel cursed her cast, as it would keep her from riding for the next few months. Also, her knees were killing her, making it next to impossible to put weight even on her good leg. They had to heal, her ankle had to heal, her hysterectomy scar had to heal, and her mind had to heal. She had to build back her riding muscles, as well. *All in a month? Impossible*. Her heart broke as it dawned on her that she might not be the one to work him in the mornings.

Touching her cast, she felt tears coming, but she fought them. Rachel felt the others watching her and lifted her head. The expression on her mother's face was one of pity. It read *I'm sorry* all over it. But she didn't want pity. She just wanted to ride that horse.

CHAPTER FOUR

Rachel's eyes were closed, as she was too tired to open them. But she smelled him, which sent a wave of nausea through her belly, just like every other time he showed up in the room. Rachel tried to pretend she was still asleep, but he was watching her so closely that he knew from her breathing that she was awake. "Hello, precious," he crooned. He placed his hand on her stomach. She recoiled and squirmed to escape his hand, but it stayed with her. She had no clothes on but was grateful to have a blanket this time. As she tried to move her legs and arms, she realized she was tied to the bed again. She felt sudden searing pain inside her and tried to bring her knees in to curl up in a ball, but the ropes prevented her from doing so. Whimpering from the pain, she temporarily forgot where she was and struggled again against the ropes, marking her wrists and ankles. But it was no use. She was stuck. "There, there, my beautiful wife. What's wrong?"

"It hurts. It hurts. Help m–," As she wiggled, writhing from pain, she felt sticky, wet blood under her.

"You'll be okay in a few minutes. Here, let me get you some medicine."

Her heart thumped as she remembered that he had been shooting her with some sort of drug. It made her forget what was happening to her so none of it mattered. Now, though, she was petrified. What was this drug doing to her? How far was this monster going to go with this? How long was he going to keep her? Was he trying to brainwash her?

He left the room and came back with a long needle and syringe. She screamed when he stabbed the needle into her hip. The drug burned as it entered her bloodstream, but then she soon felt better. She was free! Rachel was floating above her partially covered and bloody body, peering down at the disgusting man who had been holding her captive. She wanted desperately to float away and go back home but she had no idea where home was. All of a sudden, she felt dizzy and then felt as though she were falling from the ceiling. She yelled out in pain as she hit the floor, but then somehow she was on the bed again, and drifting into oblivion.

"That's my girl," he said as she quieted and fell asleep.

Immediately, her mother was there, trying to wake her.

"Rachel? You okay?"

"Huh?" She reached up to her thick, tangled hair, pushing it out of her face as she tried to sit up. A sudden tearing sensation burned her abdomen from inside, and she cried out in pain. Julia helped her sit up, and then pushed Rachel's curls behind her ears.

"Be careful not to use those muscles yet, okay?" her mother warned.

"Yeah," Rachel answered, then chuckled knowingly and shook her head. "What happened?"

"You were screaming."

Rachel was glad that it wasn't real. Or was it? Yes, it was real. It had already happened. So, why was she forced to relive it again? Wasn't the first time bad enough? Letting out a loud and frustrated sigh, she looked up at her mom. "Sorry, mom."

"It's okay, Rachel," she answered, her hand resting on her daughter's shoulder.

"I'm trying." She hoped her mother knew what she meant. It was too hard to speak any more, as she choked on tears.

"I know, Rachel. It'll take time."

Rachel reminded herself continually that she was safe at home, and soon her tears stopped.

Once Rachel felt better again, her mother left the room, leaving her sitting up against her headboard. In her dark room, she noticed that the closet and window were in the exact same location as the room where she had been held. The moon lit up a few shirts in her closet, reminding her of how it had lit up the closet in that man's house, showing her several shirts. The shirts in that moonbeam had given her an idea. *Make a rope and climb out!*

She scooted toward the edge of the bed and sat with her legs hanging over the side. The window beckoned her. It was her way out. Escape. Now was the time.

Gradually, and using her hands to steady herself, she stood and leaned toward the window and looked out.

Rachel spotted a trash pile two stories down. She opened the window, lifted the screen, and then leaned out into the bitter cold night. Air rushed in, blowing papers from Rachel's desk. *Peering from her window, she searched for the garbage truck she had heard and hoped that the men inside the truck could save her. Next, sitting on the window sill, she picked up one leg and hung it off the other side. Just as she was about to swing her other leg over, she heard the door open behind her and her mother shouting.*

"Rachel! No!"

Mom? What is she doing here?

"Rachel!" she cried, running toward her.

The leg with the cast hung heavily out the window and Julia caught her and lifted her leg back into the house. With her arm around Rachel's waist, she helped get her back to the bed. Once she was in bed, Julia lifted Rachel's shirt and checked her scar, but thankfully, it wasn't bleeding.

Meanwhile, Rachel's face was blank. She felt nothing.

She knew what was happening. She knew her mother was there, but also wondered why her mother stopped her from escaping. But, why would she need to escape from her own bedroom? Was she...? *Oh.*

"I'm home," Rachel mused quietly as she took in her surroundings. Her dresser, her mirror, her clothes...

Her mother began to cry, nearly sobbing, and nodded. "Yes, honey. You're home."

Rachel stared at the open window, questioning her need to jump. She feared hurting herself in her sleep. "Mom, you have to stay with me. Please? Or can I sleep with you? Please, Mom?"

"Okay," Julia whispered as she wiped her tears. Then she closed the window, crawled under the covers, and held her little girl for the rest of the night.

***

Rachel awoke the next morning to find Grandma sitting on the foot of her bed, watching her. Mom must have gone to work and left Grandma to babysit. It made her feel like a child.

"Where's Mom?" Rachel asked needlessly as she sat up. The sun was coming up, and Rachel knew her mother had been at the track for at least an hour already.

"She's at work, baby."

Rachel nodded, and then without warning, tears fell. Covering her face, she tried to hide her tears. But Grandma saw, and moved to sit next to her, placing a protective arm around her.

"You want to go to the track, don't you?" Grandma asked.

Rachel nodded in reply, as tears choked words from her throat. She desperately missed the horses. It would have been so healing to be with them, but there would be no way she would be able to get there any time soon. The cast was due to be taken off in another four weeks and after that, she hoped to make her way there to visit. *Four weeks*. The thought was unbearable.

Normally, they would walk to the track since they lived across the street from Belmont Park, but Rachel hoped her mother would drive her in some morning, or maybe in the evening, to visit her beloved horses. They weren't hers; she just worked them in the mornings, but they were her best friends in the whole world and she needed them now more than ever.

Her human best friend, though, was Candy, whose house she had left before the monster had swooped in and stolen her. Rachel's mom had told her that Candy had called a couple of times while she was missing, but then she stopped hearing from her. Since Candy's home had no phone, there was no way to call her, either. Rachel knew Candy must still think she was missing, and it pained her terribly that her friend was hurting.

While Rachel was missing, Candy had left her grooming job in their stable without warning, and never went back. She had disappeared, as if possibly punishing herself for allowing Rachel to walk to the train alone that night. Unfortunately, Rachel and her mother were only able to speculate, as they had no real answers about Candy's whereabouts. Rachel hoped and prayed Candy would call again soon.

After cleaning up with Grandma's help, Rachel ate breakfast and sat on the couch in front of the television. Morning television was insanely boring – news for hours, then finally, game shows. At least the game shows were entertaining. Grandma sat with her, knitting or crocheting something; Rachel didn't know the difference.

When the noon news came on, they talked about civil rights issues, as they did most of the time. Rachel listened, knowing it was important to learn about the latest in the fight for rights. This is also how she had learned about the Civil Rights Act of 1964. That year, the government had made it so jobs were no longer gender-specific, and women could fill any role they wanted. Most importantly to Rachel, females could now be jockeys. Legally, Rachel had every right to get her jockey's license, though she knew she might still have to fight the New York Racing Association to get it. For now, she was glad the Belmont stewards had allowed her to exercise the horses, because at many tracks, women were not even allowed to perform that duty, despite their protection under the new law. Many women did not know how to fight the discrimination or prove that it was even occurring.

One brave horsewoman did, though. Just a little over a year ago, Kathy Kusner, whose picture she had hanging on her bedroom wall, successfully sued the Maryland Racing Commission and forced them to allow her to ride. The Hall of Fame Olympian's fight in court helped open up opportunities for women, and Rachel was determined to take advantage of this court decision despite the extreme resistance she would receive from the men at the track.

Julia had bravely fought discrimination for many years on the backside; they kept telling her she should be at home in the kitchen, especially since she always had her two kids with her. But the owner and head trainer of Hanover Farms thought Julia was the brightest and most competent horse person they had ever seen. In order to get her the assistant trainer's job, the head trainer gave her a man's name and filled out the form for her. Stewards approved the license right away. Over time, they were impressed with the new assistant in the Hanover Farms barn, but did not find out she was a woman for several months. By then, they were convinced she was capable and allowed her to continue. Julia became the first female assistant trainer at Belmont Park. Then, when the old head trainer died several years ago, Mr. Hanover made sure Julia was appointed as the head trainer for his horses at Belmont Park.

However, despite wanting women to advance in racing, Julia did not want Rachel to become a jockey. It was too dangerous. Julia had seen too many accidents in her lifetime, including the one that took her husband's life fourteen years ago.

Rachel had seen the accidents too, but despite that, she loved horses, loved riding, loved the life at the track, and knew she was a good rider. She never had formal lessons, but her friends had taught her plenty. She had also learned by watching intently or by talking to other riders and getting tips from them. Over the years, with much practice, she had become so comfortable on horseback that it was as if the horse were an extension of her own body. It was natural. She didn't even have to think about it. Oh, but now she would. She was going to have to work her way back to that level, and beyond.

Rachel was bound and determined to become one of the women pushing for equal rights in horseracing. As she watched news story after news story covering the female jockeys' successes and failures, she knew it was for her. A jockey is what she was supposed to be, and she was never more certain of anything in her entire life.

CHAPTER FIVE

Erick read his schedule, noting where to go for his first class. *Algebra. The worst.* The hallways were empty, since the other kids were all in class by now, as he had spent a good half hour talking to the counselor that morning. She had given him a map; he took it out of his pocket and opened it.

Thankfully, there were also signs pointing him in the right direction, and he found his classroom. After pausing, he twisted the silver knob and opened the door, which obviously interrupted the teacher. She stopped abruptly mid-sentence and glared at him. As did the rest of the class.

"Hi," he said with his head slightly downturned as he walked toward the teacher, then handed her a pass.

She glanced at it, and then waved her hand toward the classroom full of kids. There were girls chewing gum, whispering, big jocks in letterman jackets flirting with girls, and one square in glasses trying to hide in a back corner of the room. "Take a seat anywhere you'd like for now, Erick."

With a nod, he set off searching for a place to sit. He found only one open desk, so he went right to it and sat down. The teacher began talking again, but the students were all staring at him. He hoped they weren't going to tease him. It was something that happened way too often because of his size.

At only five feet tall, he was usually the shortest kid in school, male or female. He hated it, but he also knew it would be a blessing in disguise once he started his career as a jockey. His dream was to be famous one day, and prove the other kids wrong about him. He could be worth something at this size after all.

The girl next to him, a blonde with her hair poofed up behind a headband, was watching him settle in as she rested her chin on the heel of her hand. He turned his head, ready to shoot a glare her way for being rude. But she was so cute that it came out a grin instead. The girl's face tinted pink as she shied away and peeked up at him through mascara-caked eyelashes.

Class ended soon after Erick arrived, and he stood and pulled out his schedule and map again.

"Hi. I'm Peggy," he heard. She was standing next to him now. Of course, she was taller than he was, but not by much. Only a few inches. *One point in her favor.*

"Erick," he answered, holding out his hand. She shook his hand with a weak and almost limp grip, but kept her gaze on his. Girls had told him in the past that he had the most gorgeous eyes ever. They were blue, and a bit darker than other blue eyes. Girls always loved how they stood out against his thick, auburn hair, and it was obvious Peggy was impressed as well.

"Need help finding your next class?" she asked as she let go of his hand. Erick noticed that she blushed before pointing at his schedule.

"Huh? Oh," he answered, reading his schedule. "Yeah. Um, Biology. Room two forty."

"Oh. That's where I'm going. Just come with me," she answered as she skipped up her aisle to the front of the room where she stopped and waited for him. Her excitement swirled him in like a tornado, and he eagerly followed her to the next class.

Later, they met again to eat lunch together, and she introduced him to her friends. Most were girls, but there were some guys too, and he hoped and prayed they were not going to pick on him. Girls were safer, though, so he stayed closer to the girls. Besides girls always appeared to like him. That was much more fun than dealing with a bunch of guys, all posturing, and trying to prove something.

"Wow. Those eyes," one girl sighed. The girls at the table focused their attention on Erick and tittered as he shook his head, grinned, and lowered his head.

"Aw, come on, let me see," another girl whined, eager for his attention.

Reluctantly, but still smiling, he finally lifted his head. "Wow," she said in awe. Peggy was next to him and grabbed his arm in an obvious display of claimed territory. He didn't mind this at all. This school wasn't so bad.

***

A few days later, Erick went to his regular table at lunch and sat next to Peggy. She was talking excitedly to a girl across the table.

"I heard Rachel was out of the hospital and finally back home," Peggy said.

"Who's Rachel?" Erick interrupted as he pulled his sandwich from his brown paper bag.

"Oh, she's our friend, and she was kidnapped about a month ago. I heard she almost died. It was on the news and everything."

"Wow, that's crazy," Erick answered. "How did she get away?"

"Jumped out a window," Karen, the girl across the table answered. "Broke her leg, too." Peggy nodded in agreement as she took a bite of her sandwich.

"I should call her," Peggy said with a mouthful of bologna and white bread.

"I tried. They always say she's asleep," Karen answered, then flipped her long brown hair from her shoulder and leaned forward to scoop some pudding into her mouth. Karen was quite a bit taller than anyone at the table. And thin. Erick thought she was tall enough to be a model. Almost pretty enough too. But, definitely, no one he would ever ask out on a date. He didn't want to look like another Sonny and Cher.

Peggy was much closer to him in height, and besides, she had made it obvious she was interested. He knew if he asked her out she would say yes.

After school, he waited by the door and caught her on the way out.

"Geez, it's cold up here," Erick said with a distinct shiver to his voice. He wrapped his new coat tighter around himself. He had never worn a coat so thick before. Dallas weather was much warmer. "I should have bought a parka."

Peggy laughed loudly as she touched his arm. He knew the joke wasn't that funny, and she was obviously laughing at his jokes to flatter him. He knew she wanted him to ask her out on a date. *Here goes.*

"Hey, want to go to the movies with me tomorrow night?" he asked casually. They had begun walking away from the school, and he was watching the ground for ice patches so he didn't look like a dork and slip on one. The other kids walked over them as if they were nothing. He figured they all had to have spikes on their shoes or something.

"Of course," she answered, grabbing his hand and holding it. She weaved her fingers with his, and he almost laughed at her eagerness. He glanced up and flashed his perfect teeth, newly freed from braces, then faced the ground again to avoid falling – and embarrassment.

***

On Saturday, the day after his date with Peggy, Erick looked through the *Daily Racing Form* for job openings at Belmont Park. His date had gone well last night, and he had kissed Peggy in the back of the theater. Aside from the weather, he was happy about things here in New York so far. Everything was going his way. He hoped that his luck would continue while he searched for a good job at Belmont. Peggy had mentioned the fact that Rachel was not working now and that her mother might be hiring someone to replace her. He looked for an ad with the name that Peggy had given him, Julia McMahon. Fortunately, he found an ad, along with her phone number, and called.

"Hi. Are you, uh, Rachel's mom?"

"Yes."

"I'm Erick Bennett. I just moved here, and my new friends at school know Rachel. They told me you might be hiring and I found your name in the *Daily Racing Form*."

"Yes, I am. This position would most likely be temporary, ending when Rachel recovers and is able to work again. In the meantime, I need someone to fill her shoes. She does everything, but mostly exercises the horses in the mornings."

"I'm licensed in Texas and have ridden a few races there at the Dallas Fairgrounds. I was an exercise boy, too, and have done that for several years now."

"How old were you when you started riding?"

"Oh, I guess I was about six. Just quarters horses at my grandfather's ranch. But I always had this dream of becoming a jockey. So, I got myself a job at the track when I was fourteen."

"Walking horses?"

"Yes, ma'am. Didn't take long to started working horses, though. They say I'm pretty good with the fractious ones."

"Can you meet me at six tomorrow morning at the gate? We'll get you in so I can watch you ride."

"Sure, I can do that. Thanks." Erick did his best not to sound overexcited, though he was.

"I pay three dollars a ride. That's the going rate here."

"Oh. Yeah, money doesn't matter to me. I mean, three dollars is fair. I mean, yeah, I would do that. You know. Ride. Mornings," he stammered, and then took a breath to calm himself. *Riding already*? He was so excited to ride a horse again that he was about to jump out of his skin.

***

The next morning, as the sun peeked over the horizon, Erick was lifted onto the back of a tall thoroughbred. He hadn't ridden for a few weeks now and it felt good to be back up on a horse again. Sitting up straight, he adjusted his stirrups while a young boy on the lead pony led him to the track. Erick questioned the boy's ability to do this at his age.

"Name's Billy," the boy said, glancing his way.

"Erick. Nice to meet you," he answered as he clipped his helmet strap.

"I'm the trainer's son, by the way."

"Oh. That's neat."

Billy let the horse go as they went through the gap in the fence, allowing Erick to take control.

The horse was strong and continually pulled on the bridle. He was on his toes to run this morning, and Erick knew it was going to be tough controlling him for a breeze and not a full out run. Erick was practically standing in the saddle as he gripped the reins and held the horse back for his warm up. Just as his fingers started to go numb, they reached the half-mile pole, and he turned the horse, brought him to the inside rail, then let him go.

They took off so fast, he almost lost his balance, but he managed to hold on tight. For a second, Erick rested his arms, but knew he had to slow the horse down or he would run too fast for his workout.

"Easy, boy," he murmured. He continued to talk to the horse, trying to get him to relax. All the while, he held the reins tightly, with the horse's head and neck arched as they ran. With the finish line fast approaching, it struck him that he had forgotten to count the time, and he mentally slapped himself for his carelessness. It felt fast to him, and may have been too fast. He hoped Mrs. McMahon wouldn't be too upset with him. She had to have known how strong this horse was.

When they passed the finish line, he stood and pulled on him harder, still trying to talk softly and calm him. *One tough horse*, he thought. Finally, after another quarter of a mile of cantering, he got the horse to slow to a walk. Then Billy was there, grabbing the bridle and giving Erick a chance to rest his arms and legs.

"Whew," Erick gasped as he tried to catch his breath. He desperately wanted to shake out his arms, but resisted so he didn't appear weak.

Billy laughed. "I can't believe she put you on this one already."

Erick turned to Billy and dropped his jaw. "Huh?"

As Billy shook his head, he laughed again. "Yeah, he's a toughie. You did well with him, though. Rachel usually rides him, and she can handle him. She can handle anything. But sometimes he gets away from other riders. You did well."

Erick relaxed at hearing his compliment. Billy's mom was at the gap waiting for them as they approached the backside area. She was smiling, and he hoped that meant good news for him.

"Mom, why'd you put him up on Guru already?" Billy asked with a grin.

She winked at her son, and then patted the sweaty horse. Focusing her attention on Erick, she asked, "What did you get?"

Oh no. "Um, I sort of forgot to count since I was trying so hard to talk to him and keep him calm. Sorry," he added with his head lowered.

She patted the horse again and took the bridle. "Go get Summer Rain, Billy," she instructed her son. Billy nodded and trotted back to the track. Then Mrs. McMahon headed for the barn, leading the horse with Erick still on his back. "This is Groovy Guru. He's a pistol sometimes. He's due for a race soon and he's strung tighter than a drum right now. You did well with him, Erick."

"Thanks," he answered, still worried he had lost his chance at the job because he forgot to time it.

When they reached the barn, he hopped down and unbuckled the saddle, then slid it from the horse's sweaty back. Mrs. McMahon handed off the horse to a groom, who began walking the horse to cool him. Julia held out her right hand and Erick lit up with joy. As he took her hand and shook it, he nearly laughed with joy.

"Come back at six tomorrow, Erick. You're hired."

"Thank you," he answered, and then remembered to hand the saddle back to her.

CHAPTER SIX

"Mom, I don't want to go back to school."

Julia kept her voice low, trying to stay patient. "Why not?"

"You really don't know? There's no way I'd be able to handle being around all those people. Friends or not. I can't even talk to them on the phone. How am I supposed to be with them in person?" Her heart was racing just thinking about it. Going to school would make her heart explode out of fear. She wanted nothing to do with being in public, or even leaving the house. The track, she knew, she could probably handle. But school, no way. There would just be too many people staring at her, treating her like she was fragile and damaged. People would be everywhere – behind her, in front of her, all asking questions, touching her, wanting to hug her – all things that might set her off.

Julia pointed to the phone on the kitchen wall. "We could call the school. They offered home tutoring for you but I wanted to check with you first. Could you handle someone coming into the house?"

"I guess."

"I want you to graduate on time and with your friends."

Rachel eyed the floor as she thought about having to be at a graduation ceremony. So many people there, all around her. Anything could happen. What if someone in the crowd rushed up and took her again? What if her friends were mad at her for not calling? "My friends probably hate me by now."

"No, they don't, Rach. They understand."

"I haven't talked to them at all since..." Her voice trailed off.

"Then call them."

"I can't. They'll just ask me what happened."

"Tell them you can't talk about it. Or say you don't want to answer that question. It's okay. They'll understand."

Rachel shook her head. "I don't know, Mom."

Her mom pulled out a pot and began filling it with water. "Call Peggy, at least. The new exercise boy I hired is going out with her, and he told me she's been eager to talk to you."

So, she'd been replaced. With pursed lips, she glared at the green shag carpet beneath her sock-clad feet. When was the last time she had worn shoes?

"Honey, you know I had to hire somebody. I need someone to ride your horses until you get back."

"Will you fire him when I get back?"

"Maybe. He's new in town. I hate to give him an exercising job, and then take it from him after a few weeks. He came right in working horses; didn't have to walk hots or anything."

"Maybe he could walk the horses I work then."

Julia laughed almost silently. "We'll see. He's a good rider, Rachel. He's doing as well as you do in the mornings."

"Oh, that's great," Rachel answered as she rolled her eyes. Positioning herself on her crutches, she hobbled her way to the couch and gingerly sank into the cushions. The couch had become her safe haven, the place she went to for comfort. Many nights, she slept on the couch to make sure she didn't try to jump out the window again in her sleep. She'd had her mother and brother move her bed to another wall to make it different from the room where she was held prisoner for two weeks, but it wasn't enough. The nightmares kept coming and her room scared her to death. She hated going in there. She knew it was ridiculous, that it wasn't the same room. It was her room and it was safe. There were plastic horses everywhere, pictures of her in the winner's circle with her mom's horses, and a couple of posters featuring the Beach Boys and Bobby Sherman. Despite that fact, it still sparked fear inside her. Lately, she would start out in her room, only to move to the couch later in an attempt to relax.

"We should put your room in the basement," her mother had suggested. Rachel didn't like that idea, either. Sure, it was safe, and impossible to jump from a window by the ceiling, but the basement was dark, musty, and cold. She didn't want that either. In fact, she wished she could sleep in a stall at the barn.

She missed her horses more than anything. But just as much as she missed them, she feared leaving the house. She was even afraid to ask someone to drive her to the track. As tears silently rolled down her cheeks, she tried to hide her face from her mother, but she knew something was up, and came over to sit next to her. When she put her arm around Rachel's shoulders, Rachel sobbed and buried her face in her mother's shoulder.

"Honey, you'll be back there before you know it."

All Rachel wanted was to touch the horses' soft muzzles, rub their ears, and let the horses rub their noses on her back pocket as they searched for mints. She missed their eyes, too. Their kind, dark eyes always understood her and made her feel better. The horses had always been able to carry her away from her troubles, easily sweeping everything away with the wind as it rolled off her back. It was killing her to have to wait for her legs to heal.

***

"Hello?" Rachel answered after picking up the yellow phone hanging on the wall in the kitchen. It was the first time she was able to muster up the courage to answer the phone since coming home a month ago. Grandma was busy cleaning, her mom was at work, and Billy was at school, leaving her alone to answer the phone.

"Rachel!" She recognized Peggy's shrill voice on the other end. The sound scared her at first, and she pulled the phone away from her ear, but then brought it back.

"Hi, Peggy," she answered sheepishly. She knew she hadn't talked to any of her friends since the kidnapping. She had been too afraid they would ask about it, but now, she had a plan. Any time someone asked about it, she would simply answer, "I can't talk about it."

"Rach, it's so good to hear your voice!" Rachel heard Peggy's voice choking and she sounded as though she were on the verge of tears. "I'm so glad you're okay. I thought, well...are you coming back to school soon?"

"No. I don't want to."

"Well, none of us do, Rach, but we still go." Peggy laughed for a second, and then continued. "We all miss you so much. Why don't you want to come back?"

It wasn't going to be easy to explain it without bringing up details of the abduction. She tried to be vague. "I've been through a lot, Peggy. I'm not feeling well enough yet."

"But maybe later?"

"I don't know."

"There's a new guy. He's so cute, Rach. He's been hanging out with us."

"Is that Erick? My mom hired him to replace me."

"Yeah. That's him. He's so cute, and we're going out now."

"I heard. Mom told me."

Peggy laughed. "Funny that you find out the school gossip from your mom."

Rachel laughed in reply. "Yeah, I guess."

"Rach?"

"Yeah?"

"Can you tell me what happened?"

"No. I can't talk about it." *Whew.*

Peggy was silent for a moment and Rachel hoped the subject was over. Peggy could be annoying and pushy. Thankfully, though, this time she didn't push. Rachel was relieved that Peggy sensed Rachel's need for space. She was even more grateful when Peggy changed the subject.

Once they hung up, Rachel reviewed in her mind everything Peggy had told her about her friends at school. It was senior year. There was prom. They were about to graduate, and they wanted desperately for Rachel to walk across the stage with them. It was nice to be so loved, but was it enough to help her overcome her fear? She hoped so. She wanted to go back to school, and wanted to get over her fear of being away from home, though it seemed an impossible mountain to climb. Going to doctor appointments was hard enough. She made sure her mom had a hold of her all the time, even if she was only touching her shoulder or back. The knowledge that no one would take her from the doctor's office did nothing to assuage her fears.

The police hadn't yet caught the monster that had stolen her from the street in Queens that night. Being there was the dumbest decision of her life, she knew. She shouldn't have been walking alone at night in that neighborhood, but Candy's house wasn't far from the subway station. Only a block or so. That's all it took for someone to change her life forever.

The man in the black van had leaned out the window, whistled at her, tossed crude comments her way. She was used to hearing that from the guys at the track. Those types of things were easy to handle. *Just ignore them, that's all.* It hadn't worked with this guy, though. It had only made him try even harder to get her attention. So hard that he pulled the van to a stop and ran after her, trapped her, picked her up and carried her away.

No one was there to save her. No one knew where she was. No would ever find her again. She would never see her family again. She would never see her best friend again.

Her friend, Candy, worked at the track as a groom, and Rachel hadn't talked to her since that night. Candy had called Rachel's mom after she heard about the kidnapping on the news.

Because Candy's parents had both died a few years ago, she and her older brother had to fend for themselves. Since she had stopped working, Rachel assumed that they didn't have money for rent, and were most likely evicted from their house. However, no one knew for sure what had happened to her. Billy had talked to her a few days after Rachel's disappearance, but she hadn't called since. Candy probably didn't know Rachel was okay, but it was impossible to find her now. The thought of not being able to tell her friend she was all right made her sick to her stomach.

Fortunately, her grandmother came into the room, interrupting her thoughts. "What are you making for dinner?" she asked Rachel.

Rachel laughed silently, thankful for the chance to feel a hint of happiness again. "You don't want me to cook, Grandma. I would burn water if you let me."

Grandma laughed and patted Rachel on the back, then searched the kitchen for something suitable for dinner.

***

During dinner, she was reminded of all the times she had worked all day with her family and then come home to Grandma's cooking in the evening. Sitting here was like those times. Only she hadn't come home from having fun. Billy and her mom did, though and it almost made her jealous. Almost? No. She was definitely jealous.

What would it hurt to go visit? No one could get to her there. Her fellow stable workers and her family would be there to protect her.

Around here, it was the same old kitchen table and chairs, the same old couch, same old curtains, same old television, same old crocheted blanket. She had seen too much of this house lately. Nodding to herself, she decided it was time to take the next step.

"Mom, I think I want to go to the track. Can you drive me over?" Rachel asked casually as she mixed up her salad in a little wooden bowl.

Julia froze for a moment, her fork in mid-air on the way to her mouth. After a beat, she composed herself and replied, "Well, yeah, honey. Sure. When?"

"Tomorrow?"

"Definitely. Let's get you over there to visit the horses."

Rachel bounced with joy and shoved a fork full of lettuce into her mouth. She couldn't wait.

***

After sleeping on the couch again, she got up and went to her room to dress. *Only one more week and I'll be out of this cast*. Her knees were still sore, but healing slowly. She was finally able to use her abdominal muscles again without too much pain. Sneezing sometimes hurt and sent tearing pain shooting from her scar, but that was getting better as well. Most of all, she couldn't wait to get out of this cast so she could walk again and, more importantly, take a shower.

She went to the bathroom and washed herself with a washcloth, then using a ribbon, she tied her hair up in a high ponytail. She hoped she didn't smell too awful, but she knew manure would overpower any scent emanating from a human.

Once she was ready, she met her mother in the kitchen. This was it. She was going to leave the house. The thought petrified Rachel and she shivered with fear. She tried to hide it, but her mother knew.

"I'll be with you, okay? Or Billy; there's no school today so he's going with us. We won't leave you, okay?"

Rachel nodded but kept her jaw clamped, afraid to open her mouth for fear a scream would slip out. She watched her mom fixing her coffee, and after a moment, she finally found enough strength to say, "Mom..."

"Yes?"

"Tell me I'm being ridiculous."

"What?" Julia put down the carafe and looked at Rachel.

"I'm being ridiculous for being so afraid. I shouldn't be scared. No one's going to get me. Right?"

"Of course, dear. We're going to drive right up to the barn, too. Okay?"

Rachel nodded, glad for the direct route to the barn and ability to park next to it. Police hadn't caught her kidnapper, but it was safe at the track. There was tight security and no one was allowed on the backside without a pass.

Unless he worked there.

Her heart nearly stopped and her face blanched white as the blood rushed from her head. With a groan, she plunged her head between her knees as she attempted to stay conscious. Her mother ran over to her.

"Hey, Rach. It's okay. He can't get you there. And I promise we won't leave you. Okay? You trust me, right?"

Rachel nodded, and then sniffed. She was so tired of crying. In an effort to be stoic, she held her head and sat up. Her body shook as more sobs overtook her, but then she regained control by talking herself into believing that she was okay. She had to be. She didn't have any other choice. Living in fear was not living. She nodded again and decided this was it. From now on, she was determined to live.

Soon, Billy, Julia, and Rachel were in the car for the short trip from their house to the track. Rachel jumped at everything outside the confinement of the car during their short ride, but she forced herself to be brave. She forced herself to face the world. Living in fear was miserable and she wanted no part of it. Besides, if she were ever to become a jockey, learning to overcome fear was a necessity.

Riding a thoroughbred at nearly forty miles per hour around a track is dangerous work, especially during a race. The jockeys who rode there day after day continually faced fear and overcame it. They used that fear, or perhaps their nervousness, to be strong during the race. They turned it around for their advantage and Rachel knew she would have to do the same. If only Mom would let her get her license.

Within a few short minutes, they were through the gate at the track and headed down the pathway toward their barn. From the car, Rachel saw horses being ridden to the track, their riders perched upon their backs, whips sticking out of their back pockets. Already, some horses had finished their workouts and were being bathed between barns, steam rising from their heated bodies. Some were already attached to the hot walking machine and were obediently walking in circles as they bobbed their heads up and down. Then she recognized familiar faces. Some were famous faces that most people only saw on television, but she got to see every day; jockeys, trainers, and owners were there talking, working with horses, mingling, drinking coffee.

Rachel curled in her lips and bit down to avoid happy tears. She wasn't sure if she should laugh or cry. Maybe both. She wasn't afraid here. She was happy.

Finally, Mom parked the car and the three of them made their way into the barn.

The warmth from the heaters inside the stalls welcomed Rachel and soothed her. She breathed in the scents she had missed so terribly – the sweet smell of alfalfa, the warm, earthy smell of manure, sweaty horses, sweaty tack, the rank fumes of ammonia from the urine the grooms were cleaning out of the stalls. She smiled to think she even missed smelling the sweaty people who worked there every day. The minty smell of the liniment they rubbed into the muscular legs and shoulders of the horses invigorated her and helped wake her up, despite it still being dark outside.

Some of the employees came over to welcome her back. She was happy to see them, but scared at the same time. However, she didn't let that fear overwhelm her. These people were her friends. They would never hurt her, she reminded herself.

Occasionally, Rachel peeked over at her mother to make sure she was still there. She was, of course, but then so was everyone else. Rachel's heart grew cold as the crowd gathered around her. She didn't say much, as her throat was constricted. She tried to remind herself, *I know these people. They're nice. They're on my side*. Julia gave her an occasional reassuring pat on the shoulder as one by one, her fellow workers greeted her. After saying hello, they gradually left her and went back to work, leaving only one person standing there.

Frozen in place, she found herself staring into the most captivating blue eyes she had ever seen. It took her a moment or two to take in the rest of his body. He was the same height as she, wearing cowboy boots and a black cowboy hat with a stampede string. No one around here wore that stuff. He was different. And gorgeous. She was sure her eyes were as big as saucers now.

"Hi," he said simply. She was sure he could tell her insides were doing somersaults.

Rachel clamped her mouth shut, then found her voice. "Hi," she finally replied, then swallowed what felt like an entire frog.

"Rachel, this is Erick. Erick, this is Rachel, my daughter," Julia said, waving her hand back and forth between them.

Erick reached out his hand and Rachel took it. His hand was warm and gentle, yet strong at the same time. So she tried her toughest handshake, as she always did with men, to prove she was strong, too. Despite trying, her hand felt weak and shaky. *It has to be from walking with the crutches so much lately. That's it.*

His gaze made her feel like they were the only two people in the world. Everybody else had disappeared. The barn had vanished. Now, it was just the two of them in their own world, their own racetrack. A vision appeared before her of the two of them riding horses around the track together, side by side. It turned into a carousel as they continued around and around, just like at Coney Island. Did he know about Coney Island? Maybe she could show him... *But wait. He's taken.*

How long had she been holding his hand? Quickly, she let go and put her hand back on the handle of her crutches.

"Well, I should get to work," Erick finally said, breaking the silence and glancing at Julia. With a knowing smile, Julia nodded in reply. Erick glanced at Rachel one more time, flashed an unintentionally sexy smile, touched the brim of his hat, then spun on his boot heels and walked away.

"Still want me to fire him?" Julia joked quietly as she reached for her clipboard on the wall.

Rachel grinned. *That's Peggy's boyfriend*, she reminded herself. But he was such a hunk. Peggy was one lucky girl.

Rachel visited the horses, helping wherever she could. There wasn't much she could do in her condition, which drove her crazy.

Leaning against the wall, she watched as one of the assistants pushed a wheelbarrow from stall to stall and dumped feed into the horses' buckets. Mark was rambling on about the cold weather, and how it hurt his arthritis. Rachel tried to listen, but had no idea what to say in reply. She was not interested in making small talk.

She lifted her head to check for her mother. She wasn't there. Neither was Billy. How long had she been without them? Had she walked off? Or did they? Mom promised to stay with her. Where was she?

Mark was still talking and Rachel tried to focus on what he was saying "...and these vitamins, well, your mom's just spending too much money on unnecessary things again. Typical woman..."

To Rachel, his words made no sense. Also, he was a man. She was alone with a man. She knew him, knew he was a nice guy, but the thought still petrified her. What if he wasn't who they thought he was? What if he grabbed her? Shivering with fear, she had to get away from him. Now.

"What's the matter?" he asked.

"Mom?" she asked, her voice squelched by fear. "Mom?" she asked again, a little louder this time.

"She's right over there," Mark said, then touched her arm to help lead her in the right direction. But that touch sent her over the edge of the cliff and into a trench full of dirty and smelly men.

Each man had a cigarette hanging precariously from his lip, and each man chuckled deeply as they eyed her petite body.

"No!" she screamed, and then tried to escape the pit. But she had these crutches. They were in the way. So she threw them down and tried to run without them, but fell, and then tried to climb out. "No, no, no," she repeated, crying out desperately in hopes of escaping. "Please, please," she continued as she clawed her way up the dirt wall of the pit.

"Rachel," she heard and lifted her head. Her mom was waiting for her at the top of the hill. With a cry of relief, she reached out for her mother. Her mother took her hand and pulled her up, helping her stand.

She shook the fear from her head, then focused again on her mother. "Mom," she cried. Relieved, she wrapped her arms around her mother's waist. With her head buried in her mother's chest, she continued to sob. Julia held her daughter close and tight, and as the minutes crawled by, Rachel eventually felt safe again.

"It's okay, Rach," Julia kept saying. "I'm right here."

"Don't leave me, Mom," Rachel whimpered.

"I won't."

"She okay?" Mark asked. "Was it something I said?" His face filled with concern.

"No, Mark. She's okay. It's okay."

Hearing Mark's voice again, Rachel pulled away, though she kept a tight hold of her mother's coat. She found herself in the barn again, now with every eye on her. Every horse, as well as every worker was staring at her. She was mortified with embarrassment as she realized what had happened.

She wasn't in a pit. The monster wasn't there. There was no hill to climb. As she studied her hands, she found dirt under her short fingernails and smeared onto her palms. The knees of her sweatpants, the only thing that fit over her cast, were caked with dirt. Her crutches were on the ground, but Mark bent over and picked them up.

He stood there for a second, unsure whether to hand them to Rachel or her mom. He opted for her mom. As Julia took them, Rachel felt fear as one arm was no longer around her. She shook her head, frustrated with herself.

"I'm sorry, Mark," she said sheepishly as she faced him. "I'm...crazy. I guess."

"Hey, it's all right. You'll be okay."

Rachel wished she believed that. Would she ever be okay? She was almost eighteen years old and almost out of high school. She shouldn't be clinging to her mom like a fearful toddler.

***

"Do you want to go home?" Julia asked Rachel.

"Um...," But before she was able to answer, Peggy bounced up to her with excitement.

"Rachel!"

Rachel winced, knowing what was coming. Peggy grabbed her and tried to hug her, but Rachel pulled away. Peggy stopped, wide eyed, her arms outstretched.

"Oh, gosh, Peggy, I'm so sorry. I'm sorry. I don't know what's wrong with me." Rachel glanced around to make sure her mom was still there, and she was. Julia lightly rubbed Rachel's back, trying to calm her.

Then Erick was there, too, right next to Peggy. It was obvious from the look on his face that he felt sorry for her. *How embarrassing.*

"It's okay, Rach. I understand." Peggy's voice cracked and was a bit wobbly as she fought her own tears. When Rachel saw the emotion in Peggy's face, a tear slipped from her eye as well. Rachel reached out her hand, and Peggy took it.

"I'm a little nervous. Like a skittish horse, huh?" she asked, glancing at her mother. Julia nodded as she considered the claw marks still in the dirt beneath her feet.

"Want to go sit down at the table?" Peggy asked, motioning toward a small bistro table.

Rachel silently and hesitantly asked her mom, who nodded again.

"I'll be around, okay, Rach? I'll be in my office or outside here, okay?"

Petrified, Rachel nodded, but knew she had to let her mom work.

Peggy, Rachel, and Erick went to the table and sat down. Rachel was glad to be off her crutches. The cold metal chairs needed pads and were uncomfortable, but it was better than standing. Sitting on the chair sideways, she leaned her crutches on the table, rested her back against the wall of the barn, and tried her best to appear relaxed, despite feeling Erick's gorgeous blue eyes on her. She tried to drape her arm over the back of the chair, but it was hard and hurt her arm. She tucked it beside her instead.

"How much longer do you have to wear the cast?" Peggy asked. Rachel was glad for an excuse to have someone to look at besides Erick.

"Another week or so. I can't wait. It's so heavy."

"That leg will be strong, though," Erick answered. Rachel grinned and was only able to glance at him, and then back at Peggy.

"Have you thought about coming back to school? You gotta be back before prom, you know," Peggy chimed in.

That, she knew, was impossible. Dancing with a man? That involved not only being close to him, it meant touching, being held by him, and not panicking. Impossible. As she felt her throat tighten, she tried to come up with something to say. "I don't know," was all she was able to come up with.

Then it was quiet. No one knew what to say. She knew they were both uneasy around her, and it hurt that she had that effect on them. Not only was Erick making her nervous, their questions also sent her heart fluttering inside her chest. She felt like a fool as they both sat there watching her, trying to analyze her and figure out what had caused this change in her. Rachel's instinct was to run away, but she knew she had to learn to be strong again. It wasn't time to run from problems. It was time to face them, even if she had to fake it at first. *Fake it? Yes! Fake it!*

"So, Erick," she said, now looking confidently at him. She thought it surprised him, as she noticed his pupils grow slightly larger. "I hear you're from Texas."

"Yeah. Dallas area."

"How come you don't have an accent?"

"I don't know. Maybe because I'm from north of Dallas. I think up around our area, we don't have the southern twang. But I notice you guys have a serious Long Island accent. It's like being in a gangster movie or something," he added, laughing.

"Well, I didn't want to say nothin', but my family is very powerful around hee-a," Rachel said softly as she pretended to peek around for prying ears. Her exaggerated Long Island accent made her sound like the daughter of a mob boss. Rachel was horrible at keeping a straight face and her lips, pressed together tightly, were quivering as she tried not to laugh.

For a split second, Erick believed her, but then noticed her expression. Peggy was holding her mouth with both hands to keep from laughing. All three lost it at the same time and burst out in laughter.

***

It wasn't wise to be alone. But Julia swore she would be right back and had Rachel wait in her office. Billy was who-knows-where, but at least she had a few barn workers to rely on if she had to scream for some reason. Rachel thought better of sitting inside the office, though. No one would hear her calls for help, so she stood and hobbled to the doorway instead. She bit a fingernail as she watched one of the grooms slapping his white rag on his plaid pants as he walked by. He could definitely help her if someone barged in to attack her. Everything was fine until Erick walked up to her.

"Your mom in there?"

"No. She should be back in a minute. Why?"

"Oh. Um, I wanted to check the schedule for tomorrow." He stopped in front of her, so close that she felt that fear again. She fought the urge to back up a step by looking down instead of directly at him again. Nervously, she shifted her weight back and forth from her cast to her other foot, and searched for her mom. She refused to allow her mind to wander back into hell while around him and when Mom wasn't around, not that she had much control over it.

"I um, I don't want you to worry about your job. I mean, you should be back to riding again in a few weeks. So don't worry. I'll step out of the way. Okay?"

He was so close that she would have heard him even if he were only whispering. She knew he hadn't diverted his attention at all from the top of her head, even as she continued to study the ground beneath her feet, but she had to respond. So she nodded. Not wanting to appear too rude or shy, she glanced up at him for a second. Or at least that's how long she meant it to last. Instead, she was caught again by the kindness surrounding him. So much kindness that she wanted to jump in and drown.

A blush rose into her cheeks; she hoped he didn't notice, but knew he most likely did. For a fleeting second, she noticed him focus on her lips, and then on her eyes again. Was he thinking about kissing her? It scared her to death to think about kissing anyone. It always started with kissing, and then moved on to touching other body parts, and that was never going to happen again. It didn't matter that he was the best-looking guy she had ever seen. Ever. What mattered was that he was a man and she had to avoid men forever. She had to keep her distance. Besides, he was Peggy's boyfriend. He wasn't supposed to be this close. It would hurt Peggy. She found the strength finally to back up a step.

That's when he glanced at the rest of her, since that little distance made it easier for him to make out her entire body. Though she was wrapped inside a thick coat, she knew what he was thinking. It was what men always thought about – girls without clothes. Again, she felt the choking sensation and tried to swallow, but her throat immediately dried like a desert. She coughed and swayed slightly. The world closed in on her like a tunnel decreasing in size.

"You okay?" he asked, stepping closer again. He reached out one hand to steady her, then though better of it and dropped it again.

"No!" she shouted as she flinched away from his hand. "No. Just..." and she backed up again, this time into the wall, and wobbled as she almost lost her balance. A spinning sensation overtook her, and she grabbed onto the wall for dear life, but there was nothing to grasp. Whimpering, she tried to make her way into her mother's office to sit, but that only made her more dizzy, and as she gasped for air, her legs gave out on her and...

"Rachel?" It wasn't Mom this time. It was a man's voice. No. Impossible. It was gentler than the monster's voice, but she wasn't sure. Maybe he was tricking her. Then she felt a hand on her face, softly caressing, brushing hair from her face and pushing it back. "Wake up, Rachel," the man said. How did he know her name? He didn't. "Come on, please? Oh, God," she heard as he let go. She sensed him standing up and calling for help. It was quiet for a few seconds.

"Rachel," she heard. *Finally!* It was Mom. She was safe. Didn't matter who the man was. As long as Mom was here, everything was going to be okay. Mom took her hand. "Rachel, wake up." *Wake up? Maybe it's time for school.* She opened her eyes and tried to figure out why she was on the ground at the barn again.

"What happened?" Julia asked Erick. He was standing behind her as she knelt next to Rachel, his face full of fear.

"I don't know. She just passed out. I don't know why," he said softly. "I hope I didn't say something wrong."

"Well, I don't know." Julia took her hand and lifted Rachel to a sitting position. "What happened, Rach?"

"I got dizzy," she answered, making sure not to look at Erick. "I wanted to sit down. But I guess I didn't make it."

Julia glanced at Erick, who was obviously scared to death as he spoke next. "Did I say something wrong? Did I trigger something?"

"I don't know. I don't think so," Rachel finally answered.

"Are you hurt?" Julia asked. "Did you hurt yourself when you fell?"

"I don't think so."

"Her eyes rolled back and I caught her before she hit the ground," Erick answered. Julia and Rachel both peered up at him and frowned. "I couldn't let her fall," he insisted.

"Of course not, Erick. It's okay. I was just wondering why that happened," Julia finally said, checking her daughter one more time.

"Doesn't matter, Mom. Can you take me home now?" she asked, her voice shaky. One stray tear fell from her eye and she angrily swiped it away.

"Of course, Rach. Let's go home. Can you stand?" she asked as she tried to lift her. Rachel pulled on her mother's arm and they stood together. Erick handed her the crutches.

"Thanks," she told him, trying to avoid looking at him. *Those eyes. No. I can't have those thoughts anymore. Men are evil. But certainly not him. Or his eyes. They're so calming. Then again, that's what made me pass out. How in the world were gorgeous eyes able to make me lose consciousness? That's ridiculous.* Then she was stuck again, staring. But, so was he.

"I'll go get the car. Erick, can you stay here with her?"

"Sure," he answered, still watching Rachel.

As her mother walked away, her whole body shook with fear. Erick put his hand on her arm, wanting to lead her to the door to meet her mom, but he felt her shaking and pulled away. "You okay?" he asked.

She nodded, unable to speak.

"Let's go to the door, okay?"

Quickly nodding again, she repeatedly reminded herself that he was not going to hurt her. *He's not going to hurt me. He's not going to hurt me. He's not going to hurt me.* When he touched her arm again, she surprisingly felt at ease. Safe. She almost laughed with relief at how quickly the fear had dissipated.

Using her crutches, she made her way to the large doorway of the barn, all while distinctly aware of Erick's hand on her arm. At least this time it didn't make her faint. This time, it was comforting. When her mom pulled up her car, Erick opened the door and helped Rachel sit while holding her crutches, then placed them next to her on the seat.

"Thank you, Erick. I'm so glad you were here," Julia said, leaning down to see him through the passenger side door.

"Thank you. Erick," Rachel added with a glance. He was so patient, so kind. It melted her heart as he nodded and caught her gaze, and then hesitantly touched her shoulder before closing the door.

As they drove, Julia occasionally glanced at her daughter, making sure she was okay. "Do you know what caused you to pass out? Do you need something to eat or drink?"

"No. I, um, I don't know why, Mom. I was talking to Erick, and out of nowhere got dizzy. I don't know why."

"Okay. Well, maybe you need some water. Let's get you home and get you something to drink."

But she knew it wasn't thirst or hunger. It was Erick.

***

After countless nights comparing schedules of employees in the vet's office and the use of Ketamine, Detective Ritter found no patterns. He had hoped to find one employee using more than others, but, unfortunately, that piece of the puzzle was not in the books. Despite his neat charts and lists, he found nothing that might lead him in the direction of the perpetrator.

A good detective follows his instincts and hunches. His hunch now was that the vets at Belmont had nothing to do with this. Not only did they use normal amounts of Ketamine, the fact that they were working regularly led him to believe they could not have had time to follow through with this crime.

Despite his hunch, he interviewed each employee. Just as he had suspected, they each could explain where they were for the two weeks in question, and could explain their Ketamine use. Ritter went home frustrated, as he was eager to help Rachel and to solve this case. He worked on other cases as well, but this one affected him the most.

His colleagues had warned him not to bring emotion into it, which was good advice, but sometimes impossible to do. His daughter was also a teenager and went to the same school as Rachel. He couldn't help but wonder how he would feel if his own daughter had been assaulted in this way.

CHAPTER SEVEN

It had been over two months since her kidnapping, and despite being free from her cast, Rachel still did not want to go back to school. Several friends had begged and begged her to come back, but Rachel knew it was impossible. Her favorite place on earth was the track. If she had two incidents while at her favorite place, it would definitely happen at school. Besides, Mom wouldn't be there to save her. Her mother understood and didn't force the issue, and they continued with her tutor.

For Rachel, though, the most important thing was getting back on the track to ride again. She lifted weights at home, did squats and other leg exercises as she tried to get her old muscles back. She was determined to ride Chivalry, especially after listening to mom and Billy talk about him nearly every night over dinner. Her mother had never been so excited about a horse.

After a few weeks of sleeping on the couch, she eventually tried again to sleep in her room. Night after night, she had nightmares, and woke up screaming, but even though she was shaking and scared to death, she stayed in her room, forcing herself to get through it and take her life back from the monster who had stolen it from her.

Sometimes the nightmares were so realistic that she positively knew she was back in that room again. She even felt the knife slice through her skin, leaving behind long scars that made her look as though she had been attacked by a wild animal. Maybe she had. Her fear, the pain, and the tears sometimes woke her with her hand on her stomach. But when she would lift her hand, there was never any blood. The scars were still there though, and would be forever.

Who would ever want such an ugly woman with these scars? What man would want a woman who was afraid of sex? Who was barren? It wasn't fair. Burying her face in her pillow, she sobbed so hard she choked on her tears. Sometimes she hoped to suffocate herself in her pillow and not wake up the next morning. Life wasn't worth living if she would have to be alone the rest of her life. She would always be alone. No one would want her. And it hurt. It hurt worse than being raped by a huge and hairy monster, or being marked with a dull and rusty knife. It hurt more than breaking her leg as she fell from the second story window when she escaped that house. It was the most painful thing she had ever felt in her entire life.

When she woke up the next morning at five, she heard her mother and Billy getting ready to leave. She desperately wanted to go with them but she didn't want to be in the way or embarrass herself again. The tears began again, but this time out of frustration as she repeatedly slammed her fist into her pillow, hopelessly wishing to be normal again. It was futile, she knew.

"Rach?" her mother called softly through the door. Quickly, Rachel stopped her sobbing, sat up, and wrapped her arms around herself as she rocked forward and back.

"Yeah," she answered, trying to sound like she hadn't been crying.

"Can I come in?"

No. She didn't want Mom to come in and see her like this. But then again, she needed her. And when she didn't answer, her mother came in.

"What's wrong, honey?" she asked, sitting on the edge of the bed next to Rachel. She put her arm around Rachel's back, and Rachel relaxed.

"I want..." She felt herself wanting to cry again, but was determined to stay strong. "The horses. I want to ride."

"Okay. Your exercises are coming along well. You look great. I can tell you're getting strong."

"I feel okay. I just don't want to go back there and screw everything up like I did last time. I want to go, but I'm so afraid."

"You know what bravery is, right?"

"Yeah," she answered, as if it should have been obvious.

"Bravery is when you're afraid but you do it anyway. I know you're brave. You always have been. Since that time you fell off your pony and had to get stitches. Remember that?"

Rachel giggled through her tears and nodded.

"The doctor and I told you it would only hurt for a second while he numbed your forehead. He had to give you a shot. You were scared to death, of course. You were only five, and you'd never seen that before. You'd never experienced that. But you stayed still; you waited patiently while he stuck a giant needle into your forehead, and then sewed you back up. You were brave. You remained quiet and still while he did what he had to do. Not many kids would have done that. Any other kid would have been screaming and fighting the whole time.

"Then, when we got back to the track the next day, you went right back to Goldie and rode him. You were scared, too. You even said so. You were worried you would fall again, but you wanted so badly to ride him that it didn't matter anymore. You got right back up on him — at five years old, Rachel. Do you know how many others older than you would never have done that?" Julia pushed unruly curls from Rachel's face.

"I know this situation is different and more difficult, but I know you can handle it. You have always been brave, which is one of the things that makes you a great rider. I entrust you with million dollar horses, Rachel. You are brave enough to take on an animal that weighs ten, twelve times your weight. You're brave enough to let them run forty miles per hour underneath you. Is it scary? I'm sure it is. But you do it anyway. You are a brave and courageous person, Rach."

"I'm not the same person I was," she admitted as she flicked her fingernails together, making nervous noises.

"How so?"

"I don't know. I feel different. I don't feel brave anymore. I'm afraid of everything. Men, especially. When Mark touched my arm, I freaked out. I thought I was in this pit, stuck there with that man that kidnapped me. And Erick – well, he didn't touch me. He was too close and it scared me to death. Besides, he has these eyes..."

Julia smiled and nodded.

Rachel looked up at her mom, surprised. "You noticed, too?"

"I'm not blind, Rachel," she answered with a grin. "I guess that's enough to make any girl nervous even if she feels fine. Even if she didn't have to think about the things you have to deal with."

“That’s why you hired him, isn’t it?” Rachel joked, putting her hands on her hips.

Julia laughed, then lightly tapped Rachel’s arm. “No, Rachel. I’m old enough to be his mother. I hired him because I needed a regular rider, and he was a rider looking for a job. I watched him ride, and he was good with Guru. Held him back. And I noticed that he sort of sits like you in the saddle. He reminded me of you, and I thought maybe the horses might feel the same way and not miss you so much. Still, I know they miss you, Rach. I know they can’t wait until you ride them again.”

“I want to ride, mom.” Her mind was made up. “Today. Let’s go. I want to try it.”

“What? Are you sure?”

“Yes.”

“But, well, are you strong enough?”

“Maybe not for Guru. But I could ride a stable pony,” she answered with her face lighting up as she anticipated being up on horseback again.

“Well, get dressed, then. Let’s go,” Julia answered, rising from the bed. Rachel sprang up from under the covers and was already tearing off her nightgown before her mother had even closed the door behind her.

***

They decided that their old stable pony, who they lovingly called Old Guy, was the best candidate for the job, and they tacked him up. Julia held out her hand to boost Rachel into the saddle and it was a smooth and familiar mount as Rachel sprang up while Julia lifted her ankle.

Rachel’s legs felt weak against the strong horse’s body. She was glad it wasn’t a fractious colt because she didn’t think she'd be able to hold on if he took off running. She walked Old Guy to the grassy area between barns. Immediately, he stopped and put his head down, chomping on grass and refusing to walk. Rachel giggled uncontrollably. It felt so good to laugh. Julia laughed too as Rachel tried pulling his head up with the reins. She was laughing so hard that she was unable to lift her own arms, let alone his head.

Finally, she decided to give him a little kick as she clucked. He woke up and went right into a trot. *Bounce, bounce, ouch.* She remembered to post after the second bounce. There wasn't room to go any faster, and her legs were already getting tired from lifting herself off the saddle every other stride, so she backed him down to a walk. After about ten minutes of walking in circles, she was ready to get off the horse and rest. She slipped down the horse's side and landed on wobbly legs. Rachel didn't remember riding horses being this hard before. She used to be able to ride without thinking or getting tired at all. It had been second nature to her.

Then, seemingly out of nowhere, Erick appeared, walking a colt toward the grass. "Hi, Erick," she called.

"Hey there." He turned to look at her, his eyes crinkling under his dark hat. "You're riding."

Rachel's heart leapt for joy at his cheerful greeting. "Yeah. Finally. I feel weak, though. My muscles aren't what they used to be," she laughed, flexing one scrawny arm.

"Well, I guess not. It will come back to you, though. You'll see." His face lit up as he watched her with her horse. It was a switch from the last time she had seen him; she was a mess before. But today, she was brave.

"Yeah," she answered, finding her head completely void of thought. Then she broke eye contact, blushed, and said, "Well, I gotta run. I mean walk. You know. Getting tired. Grass is all yours," Rachel said, waving her hand over the open area.

"Why, thank you kindly, miss," he said with an exaggerated Texas drawl while nodding his head and touching his cowboy hat in her direction. *He's wearing those cowboy boots again, too. Nothing sexier than a cowboy and a horse. Even in New York*. Rachel forgot all about her mother standing behind her.

She blushed and said, "You're welcome, cowboy." Then, she glanced around for Peggy. Surprised that Peggy wasn't there, she asked Erick about her.

"She stayed home today. Not feeling well," he said. She saw relief all over him, which told her he was glad to be without the clingy blonde today.

"Oh, I'm sorry. Tell her I said I hope she's better soon."

"Will do," Erick said, mirroring her contented face and holding her gaze for a few seconds. Rachel's mind went blank, though she wanted to stay and talk to him. Then, she watched as Erick slid down against a tree, took off his hat, shook out his thick hair, then rested his head against the tree while the colt he had led into the area browsed the fresh spring grass.

Rachel allowed herself to stare at him. *Just a quick glance. He is so cute*. Hair just messy enough to be sexy, he had a mop top – the latest style, a shell necklace that didn't seem to fit with his style at all, muscular arms, t-shirt just tight enough to display the muscles under it, well-fitting jeans, sexy cowboy boots...

She broke her gaze and shot a surprised glance at her mom, having forgotten she was even there. Her mother had a huge grin on her face, and Rachel shook her head and tapped her mom's arm. That was Peggy's boyfriend, not hers. Besides, men were off limits. It wasn't the time to think about men. The important thing now was getting her riding legs back.

It was an exciting day, her first time riding again. Back at home, too tired to eat much, she left the table after only a few bites, and went right to bed in her room. Tonight, she was so happy that she knew she could avoid the nightmares. Holding her pillow in her arms, she fell asleep feeling happy and safe.

***

Rachel tried to scream, but then was hit in the face. Every time she so much as looked at him the wrong way, he hit her. Her facial bones protruded sharply, and every ridge was red or purple from each time he had hit her there. She was afraid to even open her eyes for fear of being hit again.

Her whole body shook from the cold and the fear. The awful man disappeared, then reappeared with a syringe and shot her in the hip. In a moment, she felt better, hardly noticing the disgusting man standing over her.

But, coming through the door was a giant spider, as big as a German Shepherd. She screamed, and the man laughed wildly. He faced the doorway and asked, "What is it, my dear? What do you see?"

Words failed her. Nothing could express the horror of this creature. Spiders didn't come that big, not even tarantulas. How is this happening? What is that thing? "One, two, three, four, five, six, seven, eight," she whispered quietly to herself. There were eight legs. It had to be a spider. But now it wasn't moving. It stood there staring at her with four beady black eyes. The man laughed again as she whimpered.

"Rachel? Wake up. Rach. Wake up."

Mom? Finally!

"Rachel, come on." Julia was pushing Rachel's arm, jostling her back and forth in her bed.

"Oh," Rachel glanced at the door, searching for the spider. Thankfully, it was gone and so was the man. Grabbing her mother's arm, she sat up, breathing hard. "Sorry, Mom."

"It's okay."

"I think I should sleep on the couch."

"Whatever you think is best, honey."

Rachel nodded, and her mother helped her stand, pulled the quilt from her bed, and followed her to the living room.

"Goodnight," her mother said softly, patting Rachel's head.

"Goodnight, Mom."

***

When the sun came up the next morning, Rachel was still in a deep sleep on the couch. She hadn't heard anyone in the kitchen grabbing their breakfast before work, and was surprised that she had slept through her family getting ready for the day. *I must be worn out from riding yesterday. For ten minutes. Ha. But I'm going back today.*

After dressing, she called over to the barn and asked her mom to send Billy back to walk with her.

"Well? You ready to go?" Billy asked with his newly refined deep voice as he barreled through the front door. He had obviously run all the way. The sudden noise startled Rachel, and her heart pounded as she sucked in a room full of air. Billy stopped dead in his tracks, knowing he had scared her.

Rachel had a death grip on her grey pea coat with one hand and the back of the couch with the other hand.

"Oh. Sorry, Rach," Billy said in a low and soft voice as he approached her.

"It's okay. It's okay," she repeated as she grabbed her chest. "Ha. I should have watched out the window for you, I guess."

"No, I was in a hurry to get here and, well, let's get going." Billy motioned for her to follow, so she tossed her coat on and followed him outside. "So you're ready to walk over today?"

"I guess. I figure I need the exercise. Plus, I know if anything happens, my enormous little brother will protect me," she said as she jabbed his side with her elbow.

"How did this happen?" he answered, towering above her.

"I guess you take more after Mom. But I bet you'll wind up taller than her."

"Probably. You know, this time last year, I was shorter than you."

Rachel laughed as she peered up at his boyish and freckled Irish face, marveling at his height that had changed so much in only a year.

As they walked along the open street, she was scared to death, but did her best to hide it. Since it was so early, and the weekend, hardly anyone was out, for which she was extremely grateful. All the way, even as she talked to her brother, she repeatedly told herself no one would hurt her. She took it step by step, and soon they were at the Belmont gate.

Erick was already there and on horseback when they arrived, safe and sound. Out of the corner of her eye, she sensed his eyes on her, so she waved. She loved the way his whole face smiled, and now, she noticed a dimple on one cheek.

"Rach?" Billy said as he poked her shoulder.

With a jump, she jerked her head toward him. "Geez. You need to stop scaring me like that." Nervous laughter escaped her as she grabbed the coat over her chest.

He drew closer to her. "Maybe if you realized other people were around you besides Erick," he started. But she slapped his arm, making him laugh hysterically. She shook her head and pretended to be annoyed as she sighed a loud and frustrated sigh.

***

During their break, Peggy showed up again, bouncing down the path and practically running as she spotted Rachel. Rachel watched her and laughed. But where was Erick?

"Hey!" Peggy squealed. She almost hugged Rachel, but stopped herself. Rachel forced a weak grin, ashamed she was too afraid of her friend to hug her.

"Hey, Peg. Sorry."

"It's okay. Don't worry. Hey, let's wait here for Erick. He told me to meet you guys here."

You guys? A slight sense of pride washed over her, as if he were a movie star or someone famous. Everything about him was movie star gorgeous and perfect. It made her heart flutter that she was privileged enough to be in his presence.

They sat at the tiny bistro table again to wait.

"Rach, he's so gorgeous. Every girl in the school wants him, but he's mine. He's such a hunk," she whispered loudly after leaning toward Rachel.

She only nodded and grinned. Peggy was lucky, though. No doubt about it.

"Don't you think?"

That was a trick question if she ever heard one. "Yeah," she said simply, afraid to say anything else.

Peggy was silent for a second, and Rachel hoped she had passed the test. And now, she had to change the subject. "What's going on in s–?"

"Erick!" Peggy squealed as she hopped up from her chair. She ran over to him and flung her arms around him. He shuffled his feet and lightly put his arms around her, his eyes darting from Rachel to the ground and back.

Peggy led him back to their table and he sat down while still focused on Rachel. Rachel tried desperately not to stare back. Still, she had to say hello, right?

"Hi," she said and glanced at him for only a second.

"Hey, Rachel," he answered with his movie star mouth that she only sensed peripherally, since she was avoiding looking his way. She wondered if he had ever been a model, even at his height.

Despite her thoughts, she only looked at Peggy. Peggy was watching Rachel like a hawk, and she knew why. She probably watched the girls at school as well.

As they talked about things at school, Rachel accidentally bumped into Erick's foot under the table as she was adjusting herself in the uncomfortable metal chair. Peggy was in one of her "stream of consciousness" speeches about how unfair a teacher had been to her, and Rachel was unable to fit in an apology to Erick. When she glanced up at him, he wore a smirk, almost laughing, and she grinned back and mouthed, "Sorry."

He mouthed back, "It's okay," and blinked.

Long eyelashes, she noticed. She nearly swooned.

"What?" Peggy asked, stopping her rant.

Both Rachel and Erick jumped. "Huh?" Rachel finally said.

"Were you guys listening to me?"

"Of course, Peggy," Rachel answered. Erick pressed his lips together, and it was written all over his face that he hadn't heard a word she had said. He desperately needed Rachel to save him. So she tried to remember what Peggy had said. *Here it comes.*

"Okay. What did I say, then?" Peggy asked, slamming her hands onto her hips.

"You said, um, Mr. Alessi wouldn't let you, um, turn in that assignment. Because it was late."

Peggy raised an eyebrow at her, then at Erick. He looked scared. So scared, Rachel laughed, but then slapped her hand over her mouth. Peggy shot Rachel a quick evil eye, and then went back to Erick.

"Were you listening?" she asked him.

"Of course," he answered with a devilish grin. Then, he leaned forward, staring at her intently, as if to hypnotize her into calming down and not questioning him any further. Rachel studied the interaction closely. "You look hungry," he finally said.

"Yeah," Peggy answered, stunned.

"Let's get some lunch," he suggested as he stood and held out his hand for her. When Peggy and Rachel stood, Erick sneaked a peek behind Peggy to Rachel and winked. Rachel covered a grin with her hand.

Seated at the table in the track kitchen, Rachel sat across from Erick and Peggy. Peggy talked again with her usual non-stop rambling, leaving Erick and Rachel bored. He kicked Rachel's foot.

For a second, she was surprised, but tried her hardest to hide it so Peggy wouldn't get mad again. She kicked him back. Another few times back and forth, and they were both biting their lips, trying to keep from laughing. As their attention was only on each other, they weren't watching Peggy, and didn't notice that she had figured out what was going on. She had even stopped talking, but Rachel and Erick didn't notice for several seconds.

Rachel glanced at Peggy, who had steam coming from her ears. Rachel leaned back in her chair, lowered her face, and glanced at her again. Erick had resigned himself in much the same way, leaning back and giving in.

"How old are you guys?" Peggy asked, sounding like a mother. They laughed, but then stopped abruptly as they glanced at each other. Peggy shook her head and groaned. "Let's go," she said as she stood and grabbed Erick's hand. She yanked him up from his chair and pulled him toward the door.

He peeked back at Rachel again, as Peggy was in front of him, still pulling, and he mouthed, "Help!"

Rachel laughed into her hand and hunched her shoulders, but stayed quiet.

***

The next day, Julia took Rachel to the grandstand to watch workouts. Rachel helped her mother keep track of where each horse was and what their times were.

Rachel watched as Erick rode Groovy Guru onto the track, with Billy, who was atop Old Guy, gripping the horse's bridle. Even though Guru was much younger and more headstrong, Old Guy remained strong against the younger horse's bumps. Guru occasionally shook his head in defiance, but Erick and Billy held on throughout their long warm up. Julia had her binoculars set on Guru, silently watching.

"He seems antsy today," Rachel noticed.

"Guru? Yeah. I always put Erick up on him these days. After his race last week, it seems like he has become even more eager to run. He's been tougher to handle."

"You're kidding. Man, he was already a handful. Make that two hands full."

Julia nodded, then held her breath as Billy helped turn Guru. She dreaded this work for Erick, knowing he would be exhausted after this ride. Erick's instructions were to hold him back for a slow and easy gallop.

Erick and Billy stopped Guru dead in the center of the track as horses passed by on either side of them. Guru snorted as his body quivered with anticipation. Old Guy eyed a warning at the colt while standing patiently at Guru's side. They stood still for several seconds, waiting for a good opening to get to the rail, until Guru began impatiently pawing at the ground.

Erick glanced at Billy. "You ready?" Billy asked.

Erick took a breath, gathered the reins tightly, then nodded. Billy let go of Guru's bridle.

As soon as he let go, Guru saw his chance. He shook his head repeatedly, then arched his back and bucked like a bronco. Erick held on tightly and Billy came closer, hoping to grab Guru's bridle again. Instead, just after tossing Erick around, throwing him off balance, Guru grabbed the bit and shot forward as if slung from a slingshot.

Billy pushed his horse, but could not keep up. Guru was running his fastest down the middle of the track. Billy signaled for an outrider's help.

Erick tried yelling warnings at other horses and riders, but they hardly had time to react before nearly being run over by the speeding bullet. Erick stopped yelling, knowing it was exciting his horse further.

Erick took up the reins sharply and then wiggled the bit from Guru's teeth. Guru still refused to slow down. Erick talked to the horse in a calm voice, a constant stream of low murmurs and sounds. They had rounded the turn and thundered into the homestretch when finally Guru began slowing. It was gradual, but at least he was slowing. By now, Erick had regained enough control to get him to the inner rail, which was reserved for faster runners.

Then, he saw an outrider heading straight for them from the side. The outrider's horse knew his job; he had to keep up with Erick, draw up next to him so that his rider could grab Guru and help Erick slow him. But as they drew closer, Erick waved them away.

Allowing the outrider's horse to run next to Guru would have been just the thing to reignite Guru's speed, and he couldn't have that. Fortunately, the outrider understood and slowed his horse.

Gradually, steadily, Erick managed to slow Guru by the time they reached the clubhouse turn. He was still talking to the horse, calming him, but inside, he wanted to shout at the pain in his fingers, arms, and back. Halfway around the clubhouse turn, Guru finally stopped. However, Erick did not allow himself to rest. He turned Guru toward the outer rail, facing it in hopes he would not bolt again. Erick turned his head to find Billy running up behind him, but slowing well before reaching Guru. Both horses were foaming and sweating heavily.

Poor Old Guy hadn't run this hard and this fast since his racing days. He was exhausted, and gratefully slowed when Billy gave him the signal.

Erick groaned with relief at finally having help. Billy came up alongside them and then reached for Guru's bridle, snatching it at the last second. Guru shook his head one more time, but Erick scolded him, though quietly. They headed for the gap in the rail.

Julia met them at the gap with Rachel at her side. Both of them were concerned, but knew Erick had managed the horse well by guiding him to the right path, and then slowing him down.

Once they were off the track, Erick rested his arms. He leaned over and groaned, this time not caring what anyone thought. He didn't care if he looked tired. He *was* tired. His arms shook with exhaustion. Julia and Rachel walked with them back to the barn.

"Nice job, Erick."

Erick glanced at Julia, wondering if she had meant that sarcastically. He certainly didn't think it was a "nice job" since his horse had run away on him. Nevertheless, she and Rachel were smiling and at ease. Julia patted Erick's leg in support and silently walked with them.

***

Later, in the barn, Erick apologized. "Sorry about that. He was really wound up today. There was no way he was going to go slow and easy today."

"It's okay, Erick. It happens sometimes."

"Never happened to me," Rachel murmured. She tried desperately to suppress her devious smirk, but it would not be denied.

"Rachel!" Julia scolded.

Through her eyelashes, Rachel glanced at Erick, who was shaking his head. Thankfully, he lit up despite her words. "Sorry," Rachel said softly.

"First time for everything." Erick winked. "That was the first time he'd ever run off with me."

Rachel covered her mouth to suppress a giggle, but it happened despite her efforts. She was glad her words hadn't angered Erick. In fact, they seemed to help him feel better about it somehow. Rachel wondered if his competitive side was coming up with a plan for some way to get her back. She certainly hoped so.

***

It took another week for her to feel strong enough to help lead horses to the track for workouts. When she announced to her mother that she was ready, she was so excited, she didn't even wait for a response and ran to get her saddle, leaving Julia to shake her head and grin.

As Rachel led Erick's horse to the track that foggy morning, she desperately tried not to flirt. It was so hard not to, though. With other hunks, it had been an automatic response to smile, bat her long eyelashes, and say something cute. It was something she had done all the time before. But not now. She had to learn not to do that anymore. There had to be no more men in her life. Besides, he was Peggy's.

"So, you guys are going to the prom?" Rachel asked, trying to sound casual.

"Yeah. I guess."

"You don't seem too happy about it."

"Not really. I just don't want to go with her. In fact, I've been trying to break up with her."

What? Oh no. "Trying? What, is she talking you into staying with her or something?" *If he becomes available, what then? Will he ask me out? It will be next to impossible to say no to him. Peggy would kill me.*

"Yeah, kinda. Every time I start to sound like I'm going to break it off, she distracts me with something. Gives me a peek of something I don't want to see, or she rubs my shoulders, or stuff like that. I think she's an expert in mind control. Somehow, she always keeps me from saying it."

"She never said anything to me about it. I talk to her on the phone almost every day."

Erick glanced at her, and then shook his head. "Of course not. She would never admit that a guy wanted to break up with her."

Rachel knew he was right. Peggy would never admit she lost a guy. And if she knew Peggy, she knew that if Erick broke up with her right before prom and left her without a date – well, it wouldn't happen. But if it did, she would never tell anyone the truth. She would tell everyone *she* had broken up with *him*. She was too perfect.

"Are you going?" he asked quietly, as if he almost wasn't going to ask, but it slipped out anyway.

"No," she answered as she laughed. "I'm not, I mean, there's no way."

"Why not?"

Rachel didn't want to think about it. It was too dangerous to deal with a flashback or some sort of strange blackout while on horseback. So she did the only thing she knew to do. She shut down her mind and focused only on the horse she was holding. The skittish three-year-old was a handful, and she concentrated on keeping the colt's head at her side. She pulled his head closer to her leg and didn't say another word.

For the rest of the workouts, whenever she was with Erick, they only talked about the horses, and nothing else. Not Peggy, not school, not the prom. Just horses. It was safe.

"I think Mom's going to put you on Chivalry in a few days."

Erick perked up. "Really? What about Billy?"

"I think you impressed my mom with Guru last week. She thinks you'd be good with him. He's not as ornery as Guru, but he is still only two. She thinks you'll be able to handle him well."

"I don't understand. Guru ran off with me."

"She liked that you got him calm, regained control, and eventually got him to stop. And especially that you didn't fall off when he bolted. Last time he did that, the outrider had to get him."

"Were you riding him?" Erick couldn't help the grin on his face.

"No," Rachel stated firmly with a false frown. It dissipated almost as quickly as it appeared. "Actually, it was Billy. It was while I was, um, not here. Mom just told me about it the other day. That's when she said she thought you were good at keeping the horses calm and in control, and she didn't just mean Guru."

"You're kidding," Erick mused as he stared ahead of him. Maybe he wouldn't be fired once Rachel was back after all.

As the morning progressed, the fog lifted, and the dew evaporated as the sun warmed the air. The weather was getting warmer now, and Belmont was now open for the spring meet, which included the Belmont Stakes in about six weeks. This year, Julia didn't have any horses running in the Triple Crown races. However, their team hoped to have Chivalry there next year. This time next year, hopefully they would be running in the Kentucky Derby.

CHAPTER EIGHT

Rachel wished she were riding Chivalry for his first fast workout, but she was excited for Erick. Keeping her mother in sight, she headed up to the tiered grandstand seats, where she would see every stride the young horse made. She gave herself an assignment – to count the time and practice for when she started exercising the horses again.

As Chivalry stepped onto the track, Rachel saw that everything else came to a standstill. The normally busy track workers stopped what they were doing and turned to watch. They knew that Chivalry would be asked to give it his all this morning and Rachel could feel the hum of excitement in the air. The regal chestnut was sidestepping and prancing as Billy led him in a slow warm up. Erick held on, even when the eager colt bucked a few times. Rachel admired the way he moved with the horse.

By the time Erick let the horse go at the half pole, the other trainers and track handicappers were watching, stopwatches in hand. Rachel knew they had heard the rumors about how good he was, though not one person at the track had ever seen him work fast before.

Chivalry pushed himself without urging from his rider, and as they rounded the wide turn for home, Rachel's heart beat faster and faster. She had counted the first eighth in eleven. In the second eighth, she counted eleven again. Third, eleven. Fourth, eleven. *Keeping the same time throughout? How? He's only two.*

Erick heard applause from the stands. He pulled up the colt and glanced up into the stands. Everyone was staring, open mouthed. Every trainer, every handicapper, every jockey, everyone. Billy caught up to him.

"What was your time? Do you know?"

"I must have been too excited. I counted forty-four." Erick was winded from the work, but eager to get to Julia and find out the time she had clocked. Billy led Chivalry toward the gap, where Julia was laughing with two other trainers.

"Jules, you gonna put that one in a thousand dollar claiming race? I'll take him off your hands."

"No way, boys. I'm not losing this one."

They chuckled, shook their heads, and walked away.

"Mrs. McMahon, what was his time?" Erick asked her.

"I thought you were a better clocker than that, young man. What did you get?"

"Forty-four," Erick laughed and shrugged.

Julia nodded with an almost wicked grin, eagerly anticipating beating the boys at their own game.

Rachel jogged up to them. "Forty-four?"

The others nodded with eager faces. They knew they had something in their barn now that was more valuable than anything in the world. Not all the precious metals in the world could compare to how they felt about Chivalry. But would he stay sound? Would he be able to stay as fast as he was this morning? Was he already at peak form? Or would he continue to improve?

***

One of the more successful trainers at Belmont, peered at Rachel from under his plaid fedora. Rachel shuddered as she ducked into the office at the end of the shedrow and hid behind the wall.

Julia slipped into the office behind her. "What's he so upset about?"

"Yeah, I was wondering the same thing. What's his problem?"

"I guess he's worried about someone beating him for a change. Especially a woman." Her mother shook her head and sat down at her desk to call Mr. Hanover, the owner. Picking up the phone, she scooted her squeaky old chair closer to the desk and dialed her boss. Mr. Hanover had hired Julia and her husband many years ago and the two had a friendship set in stone. Therefore, she was especially excited to tell him about Chivalry's work that morning.

Rachel sat next to the desk as Julia talked. He was apparently floored at the time, judging by her mother's response.

"Yes, I think he can keep it up. He's been consistent in his workouts so far. Yes, we will be especially careful with this one, Mr. Hanover. We will treat him like gold. He will be the most coddled horse in the barn, trust me."

Rachel beamed. Dare she get her hopes up for the Kentucky Derby? *Maybe Preakness and Belmont, too. Just imagine – the Triple Crown!* No one had won it in twenty-one years, not since Citation. Could Chivalry be the one to break the dry spell?

Regardless, their family was on their way to the big time now and she was enjoying the ride.

***

Rachel was overjoyed a week later when she found her name next to Chivalry's as his exercise rider. Erick and her mom stood back as she checked the board, and waited for her reaction. Rachel stood there for several long seconds before the realization hit her. She was going to ride Chivalry. Today!

She spun around to find her mom standing behind her with Erick, their backs against the outer wall. Rachel's face lit up like the sunrise, and to her, it felt like the sunrise. Not only was she going to finally be able to gallop a horse in the morning again, she was going to be on Chivalry. She ran right to her mom, flung her arms around her, and squeezed until her mom begged for mercy.

Erick laughed.

"Oh! Erick, I'm sorry..." she started, but covered her mouth, hoping to hide her joy.

"No, you're not," he teased with his hands on his hips.

She let go of her mother and doubled over with laughter. That was the last thing she expected him to say. She stood and poked him, and he poked her back.

"Let's get to work," Julia ordered as she patted Rachel's shoulder.

"Are you ponying Chiv for me today?" Rachel asked Erick with a wink.

"Ha. No way, chick. You're on your own," he answered with his own wink.

It didn't take long before they were tacked up. Rachel stood next to Chivalry as he stood patiently with Willy, his groom, at his head. Rachel patted her horse's muzzle and shared breaths with him. "I'm going to ride you today, Chiv. You gonna be nice?"

In reply, he nosed her pockets. With a devious snicker, she gave him a mint.

"I saw that. You're bribing him," Erick shouted from atop his filly.

"Shh," she scolded. Julia had always been taught that it was bad to feed them from your hand. However, she was the only person in the entire barn that followed that rule. No one else was able to resist sneaking in mints and carrots here and there. Julia was tacking up her horse and saw the sneaky bribe Rachel had offered the prized horse, but she only chuckled and shook her head.

A dark bay filly, Summer Rain, and Chivalry worked in company, warming up together and galloping an easy three-quarters of a mile.

"You like him?" Erick asked afterward. They were preparing the next pair of horses for their morning workout.

"Love him. Felt like I was riding Kelso or something," she answered, glancing over at him. He was genuinely happy and it showed in his face. She was also happier than she had been in many months.

"I wish I could let him go all out."

"You'll get your chance. He'll fool you, too. His strides are so long that it gives the impression that you're going slower than you really are. You'll have to be careful how you count the time."

"I'm pretty good at counting. I'm usually right on."

"Okay, if you say so." Erick had a teasing grin on his face and Rachel smirked at him.

A couple of hours later, they were done with workouts. As they were cleaning up and putting things away, Rachel and Erick joked back and forth, laughing. But the laughter stopped abruptly when they spotted Peggy standing by the door with her arms crossed. Peggy's angry scowl shot a lightning bolt of fear into Rachel's heart.

"Hey, Peggy," Erick forced himself to say. He walked over to her and kissed her on the cheek. Rachel made sure to look at something else for a second. When she focused on them again, Peggy had her arms wrapped around one of Erick's arms, and was still giving Rachel the evil eye.

"We should get going," Peggy said, facing Erick, finally. Rachel was relieved.

"Oh. Okay. Are we going somewhere?" Erick asked.

"Yeah. You're taking me to lunch," she said with spurious joy.

"Um, okay." And with that, she led him away, still hanging onto his arm. Rachel frowned as they left. Something hurt deep down inside her as she watched him walk away with Peggy. She knew she just had to stop feeling this way. He was Peggy's, and besides, she intended to avoid men for the rest of her life. Sometimes it was hard to remember that, especially around Erick, and even though she loved spending time with him.

***

When the phone rang after dinner that evening, Rachel knew it would be Peggy, since they talked most nights. She hoped she could clear things up with her and make sure Peggy didn't feel threatened. But despite her eagerness to talk to her friend, her heart nearly stopped when she heard Peggy's voice.

"Rach," Peggy said abruptly. Her voice shook with anger.

"Yeah?" she answered weakly.

"You certainly have a lot in common with Erick, don't you?" Peggy tossed out casually.

"Yeah, I guess. But don't worry. I'm not trying to steal your boyfriend."

"Oh, I know. You wouldn't do that."

Rachel sensed that she had rolled her eyes from the tone of her voice. "Of course not, Peggy. Besides I don't ever want to date anyone anyway."

Peggy's tone changed. "What? How can you say that?"

Rachel was shaking now, as she was petrified of broaching this subject with someone. She tried not to sound as scared as she felt. "Um," *What were we talking about again?* "Um," *Men. Disgusting. Pigs.* "Men are disgusting pigs."

"What? Not all of them. Erick's not."

Rachel took in a lung full of air and blew it out again, careful not to blow into the phone. This conversation was not going the way she had planned. "Of course, not Erick. I meant every other man in the entire world. The things they do, the things they want from women, I never want to – never mind."

It was quiet for a few seconds. Finally, Peggy answered, sounding again like the friend she had always been, "Rach, you just have to meet the right guy, that's all. You'll see. They're not all disgusting. There are men with manners and stuff."

Yeah, but sex hurts. Men hurt. Men smell. Men reminded her... She shook her head. "No. I can't do it. You have no idea how awful –" *STOP! Don't talk about it. You've already said too much.* "I don't ever want... Never mind. The point is that you don't have to worry about me stealing your boyfriend. Period. End of story."

They immediately changed the subject and talked only about things happening with their friends at school. After hanging up the phone, she was so confused. On one hand, she wanted to avoid guys because she didn't think she would ever be able to get married. She was worthless if she wasn't able to have babies. And there was no way she was ever going to actually want to have sex. Again. The thought made her shudder. The disgusting things men were capable of made her stomach churn.

On the other hand, she couldn't deny she was attracted to Erick. Could there be hope for her one day? No, not yet. It was too soon for her to even consider it.

CHAPTER NINE

Rachel knew Peggy was still jealous when she tried to set her up with boys from school. Besides, it was almost time for prom and Rachel knew Peggy desperately wanted her to go. However, to go, one has to have a date, and that, she most definitely did not want. Rachel repeatedly told Peggy of her reluctance to go, but Peggy never seemed to hear her.

Finally, just to get Peggy to leave her alone, Rachel agreed to go on one date. Peggy had arranged for a tall and lanky choirboy to meet her at the diner after school. Rachel hadn't been there since before her kidnapping, and was so scared to walk there by herself that she refused to go unless Peggy and Erick came to get her first. The three of them walked together from the track to the diner, which was across the street from Belmont Park.

"I told you I don't want to go out with anybody, Peggy," Rachel told her quietly, hoping to hide her words from Erick as they walked. However, he heard, and peeked at her oddly from the other side of Peggy. She glanced up at him, clearly ashamed, and then glanced away.

Peggy seemed not to notice. "Nonsense, girl. You'll see. Once you meet the right guy, you won't feel that way."

"What way?" Erick asked.

Rachel stopped dead in her tracks. She was unable to look in Erick's direction, and fortunately, Peggy was blocking her view of him. "I can't do this," Rachel whispered. "Please, Peggy. I can't." Tears blocked her vision as she pleaded with her friend. Peggy placed her hand on Rachel's arm.

"Just talk. That's it. We're going to sit at the same table and talk. That's all. We're not going anywhere. Okay? We'll be right there with you," Peggy answered quietly. Erick appeared to understand Rachel's need for space, and didn't say another word.

Even when they entered the diner and sat down, he still said nothing. Rachel knew he was watching her, though, and it made her so nervous that she could hardly think. Fortunately, when Lou came in and sat next to Erick, Peggy tried her best to get a conversation started. As it turned out, she ended up dominating the conversation while Rachel and Erick watched and listened.

Rachel relaxed a little because the pressure was off now, and she wasn't being forced to talk to him. Peggy was taking care of that part. She was definitely good at talking.

When Erick tossed his beautiful and perfect smile her way, Rachel unconsciously mirrored his expression, but then she wondered what he was thinking. Why was he paying so much attention to her? What about Peggy? Shouldn't he be eyeing her this way? But those thoughts flew from her mind as Erick tapped her foot and nodded at Lou. Rachel knit her eyebrows, glanced at Lou, then back to Erick.

"...set design was beautiful. I loved the colors and the detail." Peggy was thoroughly engrossed in conversation with Lou.

"We worked pretty hard on it. I painted the flowers."

"Oh, I loved those flowers. You did such a good job, Lou."

Erick began glancing from Peggy to Lou, then to Rachel, forcing her to hide her giggles behind her hand. He leaned in and nodded as if completely and totally interested in the conversation, but he never said a word. This made Rachel laugh silently too, and it was becoming increasingly harder and harder for her to keep herself from laughing out loud. A few times, she almost let out a loud laugh, but pretended she was coughing, and took a sip of her water instead.

"Next year, I'll go for the part of Hamlet. I would make a good Hamlet, don't you think?"

"Oh, yes, definitely, Lou. You are such a good actor. Will you be singing, too?"

"Of course. We'll do the musical version..."

Rachel coughed loudly and Peggy patted her back.

An hour later, Erick finally broke into the conversation and let them know he and Rachel had to get to work. Rachel felt an overwhelming sense of relief.

"It was nice talking to you," Rachel said to Lou as she left with Erick. Erick nearly laughed, but caught it before it escaped. Peggy stood up, her face full of surprise, said a quick good-bye to Lou, and followed them outside. When they were a safe distance from the diner, Rachel finally let her laughter go, and so did Erick. They were doubled over with their hands on their thighs, having trouble breathing, and holding onto street signs for support when Peggy finally caught up to them.

"Well, I'm glad you two are amused. I'm sorry I even tried. It won't happen again, Rach," Peggy announced as she crossed her arms and turned away. Rachel wiped her face with her sleeve to dry her tears.

"Aw, I'm sorry, Peggy. I appreciate your effort. But think about this. Have you ever seen me go out with a musician or someone so...feminine? He might...like guys instead," she said whispering her last few words. Erick doubled over again with laughter. Peggy glared at him and he sucked both lips in to stifle the laugh. Rachel tossed her hands in the air in defeat. "I told you I'm not ready to date yet, anyway." She was instantly solemn, reminding herself of her reasons.

"Well, I won't do that again. I'm through playing matchmaker. Erick seems to know what you like. Maybe he should find someone for you," she said giving him an urging glare.

Erick stepped back with his hands up. "What? Me? No, I'm no matchmaker."

Just find me a clone of you, Rachel thought as she glanced at him. For a fraction of a second, there was a longing in her eyes, and she thought she found the same in his. Or was that only what she wanted to see?

"Maybe one of your friends, Erick? Can you think of anyone?" Peggy asked.

"Not off the top of my head. I'll think about it, okay?"

"Okay."

No one asked me, Rachel thought. *Does no one care that I just said I'm not ready to date yet*?

***

Later, after Peggy had gone home, Rachel was wrapping one of her horse's legs with an Ace bandage when Erick walked by and saw her in the stall. He leaned on the stall door silently and waited for her to notice him. She didn't see him after several seconds, so he thumped his elbow onto the ledge and leaned his head on his hand. When she heard him, she snapped upright to face him and his cheesy grin.

She realized she had been bending over and he was behind her. For how long? *Oh no*. "Erick. How long have you been standing there?"

"Oh, long enough," he grinned.

"Long enough for what?" she asked, laughing.

"Um, nothing?" he cracked.

She knocked his arm off the stall door. "You little imp. You were checkin' me out, weren't you?" Her cheeks flushed as she shied away.

"So what if I was? Anything wrong with that?" he asked, moving closer.

"Yeah. I'll tell Peggy on you," she quietly joked and glanced around for Peggy.

Erick grinned an evil grin, but said nothing. Rachel picked up another roll of purple wrap and tossed it at him. "Well, since you're not doing anything *important*, why don't you wrap the other side while I get this side?" She stuck her tongue out at him.

His pupils dilated as he focused on her tongue. "Okay. Just a second." He laughed nervously and shifted his feet.

She knit her eyebrows at him. "What? Why?"

"Oh, um," He paused for a few seconds, hoping to make the reaction in his jeans less obvious, and then opened the door, blocking the way to keep the horse from bolting.

"You're an imp, all right," she poked him on the arm as he passed her by. He poked her back, and together they wrapped the horse's legs.

***

When it began to get dark and it was time to go home Rachel searched for her mother or brother. She could not walk home alone. She needed them. Neither were in the barn so she headed to the track kitchen, hoping they were there. Things were quiet on the backside now and most people had gone home for the day. Her heart pounded. There was no one there to protect her. Would anyone hear her if she screamed for help? She peered into each barn she passed to see if someone was there in case she needed help. But there was no one anywhere. She was alone.

Her heart continued to pound when, as she passed the next barn, she saw a dark figure standing in the shadows. There was a red tip of a cigarette that glowed brighter, then dimmed. She couldn't go in there. First, he could burn the whole barn down with that one cigarette. Second, he was creepy. She backed away and turned toward the kitchen. Her stomach turned sour and she thought she might throw up. She told herself she was being silly. *This is the track. I'm safe here. Nobody here would hurt me. Would they?*

When she looked back, she could see the cigarette glowing in the darkness. He was still watching her. Trying to walk straight and upright as she attempted to appear as confident as possible, she reminded herself of her goal. Still, she felt those eyes boring into her back.

Unable to resist, she looked back once again and the red glow was gone. She shook her head, frustrated with herself. Finally, she made it to the kitchen safe and sound, and scanned the place for her family. A few men sat reading their *Daily Racing Forms* but her mother and brother were not there. She feared they had gone home and had forgotten about her. Her heart beat quicker, but she had to be brave. She had to get back to her barn.

On her way back, she fought the urge to check in barn forty-two again to find out if he was still there. She couldn't help herself from looking, but the man was gone, or so it seemed. Still, she didn't feel safe. She glanced to the other side of her and found more shadows – places where someone might hide before jumping out at her. She avoided bushes and trees, trying to stay in the middle of the paths she took on her trek back to her barn.

She let her shoulders drop once she reached her barn. Of course, no one jumped out at her. She knew she was being paranoid. It was all a side effect of what had happened to her. She knew she shouldn't take those fears seriously. Now if only she was able to convince her body of the same.

"Rach, where have you been?" Julia asked as she came out of a stall, her voice raised and shaky.

"I'm sorry, Mom. I was looking for you. I didn't see you in the barn, so I tried the kitchen and you weren't there." By now, Rachel was also shaking. She went to her mother and wrapped her arms around her. That's when she realized her mother had been just as scared.

***

In school, Erick did his best to avoid Peggy, but they had classes together and their lunch period too. Therefore, most of the time, it was impossible to evade her. She was going to ruin him once he broke up with her, but he couldn't deal with her anymore. Her nasally, shrill voice, her incessant talking, her possessive touches. They had only been on four or five dates, and they hadn't gone out at all in the last month. Didn't she realize it was over?

However, by trying to stay on her good side, he knew he might avoid the drama of being ousted by every single friend he had made since coming here three months ago.

Every day, the same thoughts warred in his head on the way to and from school. First, he knew he had it bad for Rachel. Every second of every day was spent thinking about her, to the point of injuring his grades. Of course, he blamed it on having to start a new school halfway through the year, and his parents tried their hardest to understand. Truthfully, he knew it was Rachel, whose emerald eyes haunted his thoughts every hour of every day.

Second, Rachel wasn't ready for a relationship. She had stated that several times, making it very obvious. He knew it might take a while to get through to her. A long while. Nevertheless, it would all be worth it in the end. She was the perfect girl. What more could he ask for than a female version of himself? They seemed to be so alike that they might have shared the same soul. And something, some strange force, was connecting them. Erick knew Rachel felt it, too, but still, she resisted.

Third, he was simply unable to deal with Peggy anymore. It was time to end it.

None of those thoughts were particularly pleasing to him. He just wanted to be with Rachel.

"Hey, honey," he heard. He sighed with dread, dragged his feet, and scolded himself for not running his fastest from the school the second the bell rang. Peggy caught up to him and grabbed his arm, then weaved their fingers together. She stood close, obviously waiting for a kiss, but when he did not oblige, she kissed his cheek. It might have been his lips had he not turned his head at the last second. He did his best to keep walking. "What's wrong?" she asked.

Erick nearly groaned, but managed to stop it before it left his throat. *Leave me alone? I want to break it off? We haven't been on a date in over a month and you haven't noticed?* "Nothing."

"Aw, honey," she said, leaning her head on his shoulder as she walked next to him.

Suddenly, he couldn't stand it anymore and ripped his hand from her grasp. Peggy stuck out her bottom lip. "What are you doing?"

"I'm not feeling well. I have to go to work. You might as well go home. Not a good day today, Peggy." *It will be much better once I see Rachel.*

"Well, I could help you feel better," she said, reaching for him and rubbing his neck. He tried to shrug her off, but she had strong hands for a girl, and it felt good. "Hey, wait. Stop." She pulled him between two small buildings on Plainfield Avenue near the track and their school. Erick relented, stopping, though he wasn't sure why. He really wanted to run. He turned away, but she placed her hand on his cheek and brought his head back to face her. Moving closer, she set her hands on his shoulders, then slipped her leg between his. He hissed air into his lungs as she caressed him with her bare thigh from under her mini skirt. As she pushed him against the wall, he began to breathe heavily as she replaced her thigh with her hand. His heart pounded as desire hit him. This was wrong. Very wrong.

"No, no, no." He wanted desperately to pull away, yet wanted to stay at the same time. His body betrayed his mind.

"How come you never touch me like this, Erick?" she whispered in his ear, making him shiver.

"No, I can't." His voice cracked with desperation as he pushed her away and walked towards Belmont Park as quickly as possible, hoping the bulge his jeans was not too obvious.

"Hey!" she called. But he refused to stop.

CHAPTER TEN

It was dark. Late at night. No moon. No light. Rachel ran as fast as possible but was cornered in a dead end alleyway. Banging and screaming, she tried to get through a door with no handle, but no one answered. A man ran after her, and snatched her up easily as if she were nothing. She clawed, screamed, kicked, punched, anything to free herself, to no avail. He tossed her onto the bare metal floor of the van like a piece of trash, then tied her hands behind her back and tied her legs to keep her from kicking. Then he hopped into the driver's seat, laughing.

The scene became blurry and she wished she were in another world so badly that she saw herself somewhere else. It was her only way of escaping. She imagined she was home in bed, softly snuggled in a thick blanket and pillows. Her mom was there...trying to wake her up?

Maybe if she woke up, she *could* escape. She struggled to regain consciousness. Finally, she was free. Her mom was sitting on the side of her bed, obviously exhausted with her eyes half closed. "Honey, are you awake?" she was asking.

"Yeah, Mom, I'm fine. Thanks for saving me again," she said, trying to remain stoic. Her mom watched her for a minute, then patted Rachel's leg, got up and staggered back to her room.

Rachel felt awful for her mother. She had been through so much these last few months. She was unable to imagine the fear her mother must have felt the morning she hadn't come home last February. Mom had never said a word about it, but she knew it had to have been one of the worst moments of her life, the absolute worst being watching her husband fall from his horse during a race, breaking his neck.

Rachel had seen that race too, as she had been standing in her pram with her baby brother at her feet. She and her mom were holding the rail and jumping up and down as Daddy and his horse rushed through a pack of horses. His horse was going to win. Instead, another jockey's whip accidentally brushed his horse's nose, scaring him, causing him to trip over himself, fall, and take down two other horses in the process. Rachel remembered watching them fall, not knowing which one was Daddy, but the second her mother began screaming, she knew. Her mother's horrible shrieks of terror still rang in her head.

Tears drifted down Rachel's cheeks as it hit her that her only memory of her father was of his death. Even seeing herself as a toddler with him in pictures didn't spark memories. She never remembered posing for those photos.

That accident was the reason her mom didn't want Rachel to get her jockey's license, though Julia would never admit it. Rachel knew that Mom was scared to death to lose her, too, especially since it was such a new concept to have girls riding races. There had been quite a lot of aggression from the male jocks against the female riders, not caring how dangerous it was to themselves or the girls. The danger didn't matter. All that mattered was that the men did not want women in their business.

Despite the dangers, and despite the fact that only a few females in the entire country had jockey's licenses, Rachel desperately wanted to be one of them – "jockettes," the reporters called them.

Besides Rachel, there were three other girls her age who galloped horses in the mornings at Belmont. The four of them were known as the "gallop girls." It was fun to be a gallop girl, but she knew being a jockey would be even better. To experience the sensation of flying under the wire in first place would be the absolute best feeling in the world.

As her tears had dried up, she was no longer crying, no longer sad, no longer scared; she felt encouraged. She was determined, strong, and brave as she thought about her future. She had a goal, and was determined to make that goal a reality, despite the fear.

With a nod of affirmation, she sank back into her pillow and fell asleep.

***

Peggy's whole being was filled with anger as she glared at Erick in first period. Erick shook his head and continued his efforts in avoiding her scrutiny. When class was over, she popped up and grabbed his hand, then pulled him to the front of the room and out the door. He yanked his hand from her grip as his thick eyebrows nearly met in the middle.

"What's the matter with you lately?" she asked.

"Peggy, I'm sorry. You're so overbearing. You pull me around and treat me like a puppy dog or something. I can't stand it anymore."

"Well, why didn't you say something? I can be less...overbearing. I can give you your space, if you want. I guess your moves yesterday, abandoning me in my moment of weakness, were your way of telling me you need your space. That's fine. I need my space, too. We can do the space thing."

"We can?" He had no idea what she meant by "space thing."

"Absence makes the heart grow fonder. I bet anything you'll miss me after not being able to touch me for a day or two."

I seriously doubt that.

"Why don't we try that?" she asked as she reached for him, and then remembered not to touch him.

He stepped back, enjoying this "space thing" already. "Okay. Space thing."

Peggy nodded, then leaned in to kiss him, but did not touch him. Her hair flared out as she spun around, and the flowery scent of her shampoo drifted his way. It was the same kind Rachel used, and his heart burned.

***

Rachel's mom, Billy, and Grandma stood behind her as she took in every detail of the cake Grandma had made. It had eighteen candles burning on top, dripping multi-colored wax onto the icing. Written with green icing were the words, "Happy Birthday, Rachel." They sang to her, each with a tear or two as they thought about how close she had come to not making it to her eighteenth birthday.

"Make a wish," Grandma cheered as she brushed away a tear. The others nodded. Rachel paused for a moment, and then blew out the candles, prompting cheers and applause from her audience.

"What did you wish for?" Billy asked. He always asked her that.

"I can't tell you, silly. Or it won't come true," she answered as she always had. But she knew that he already knew. She had wished for her jockey's license. It had been the same for as long as she was able to remember, starting around the time she first got her pony at age five and had shortened her stirrups on her tiny pony-sized western saddle so she looked like a jockey.

"Let's open presents," Mom shouted, then headed for the closet and brought out a giant wrapped box.

Rachel popped with surprise and her jaw dropped as Mom placed it on the couch. Rachel and Billy ran to the living room and fell at the same time on the couch, nearly bouncing the box onto the floor. Rachel laughed as she caught it. Grandma followed and sat in her chair across from them.

"What is it, Mom?" she shouted as she held the box. It was lightweight, yet big.

"I can't tell you that, silly. Open it."

Carefully, Rachel opened the package, trying not to tear the paper because mom always saved it. She recognized this paper from Billy's birthday last fall. After managing to open it in one piece, she picked up the box. Mom slipped the paper out from under it, as she always did. Then, she folded it as Rachel took in the scent emanating from the box.

It smelled like leather, and anything leather meant something to do with riding. This was big enough to be a saddle. Within seconds, she ripped open the flaps and peered inside.

It was a racing saddle. Thin, lightweight, only a couple of pounds, barely anything to it but a seat made of leather, and there were stirrups, too. Underneath, it had pockets for holding the weights that she might need someday if she ever used it in a race. As she held her face with both hands, joy emanated from every pore.

"Mom!" she yelled, facing her mom again, who also beamed with joy. "Mom!" She didn't know what else to say. Tears formed and almost fell. "Oh my God, Mom. It's a racing saddle."

Julia nodded and pursed her lips to one side, indicating that she was closer to giving in one day, allowing her to race horses. One day. Maybe.

"I know you can't use this yet, and I'm not letting you get your license until later, but I thought you deserved this after all you've been through lately. You will eventually need it, and I had the money, so I couldn't resist getting it for you. Do you like it?"

Rachel was in full-blown tears now and almost sobbing. Blinking them away, she finally regained control enough to answer her mother. "Yes, Mom. I love it. I can't believe this. It's beautiful." She ran her fingers over the soft supple dark leather, taking in the leathery scent. "Wow." Then she held out her arms for a hug and Julia hopped up to embrace her daughter.

Billy griped, "I guess I won't need one of those, ever. I'm already too big to race." He chuckled as he inspected the saddle still sitting in the box. Rachel frowned at her brother, feeling bad that he would never realize his own dream of becoming a jockey. He would have to help train or become another kind of rider. He had hit his growth spurt and was already as tall as his mother at five foot six. He weighed one hundred twenty-eight pounds, soaking wet, and skin and bones. There was no safe way to force his weight to be as low as what is required to race.

"Well, I'm afraid she's going to hate my gift after something like that, Jules. I should have given her mine first." Grandma said out of nowhere.

Rachel laughed. "I'm sure I'll love it, Grandma. Can I open it now?"

"Of course, dear. Billy, would you hand this to your sister, please?" Billy hopped up, took the lightweight flat box, and handed it to Rachel.

Again, she carefully opened the gift, taking care of the paper. She gave her grandmother a quick wink and lifted the box top. Inside were, of course, hand knitted socks. Rachel's face lit up, as nothing could possibly ruin her mood now. "Thank you, Grandma. I love them. Thank you for making these for me."

Happy tears came again as she recognized how lucky she was to have these people in her life. They had gone through so much to help take care of her over the last few months. Not everyone was so lucky and she truly appreciated what she had.

If the same had happened to her friend Candy, she would never have had family such as this. The thought of it broke her heart as she wished she knew where Candy had gone.

Julia had driven Rachel past Candy's house one day recently but the house appeared to be abandoned. It had always seemed that way, but now it was obvious that no one lived there anymore. It killed her to know her best friend was out there somewhere, not knowing she was alive. Where was she?

CHAPTER ELEVEN

The only sounds she heard were outside. Traffic, mostly. Maybe the man had gone out or was asleep, and she hoped this was an opportunity to escape since he had left her untied, most likely thinking she was too weak to get out of that disgusting bed.

It took many painful minutes for her legs to get used to holding her up again. Her legs quaked as she made her way to the closet nearby. She ripped a shirt from its hanger, then slipped it on, her arms creaking with each movement. With a silent prayer, she peered at the doorway, hoping he was not on the other side. Still, she had to try. Blood was caked on her legs and pain shot through her mid-section as she inched out of the room toward another room, hoping to find a way out.

"Hey!" The monster was running toward her. She screamed as he scooped her up and threw her back in the bed.

"No! I have to go to the bathroom! I have to clean the blood off me. Please! Please! It hurts!" She curled into a ball as she writhed on the soiled mattress.

"Then you need more medicine!"

At that point, she remembered his attempts to persuade her into thinking she was his wife. Even while high on that medicine he gave her, she had never believed it. Maybe it was something she could use to her advantage. "No! I don't! I-I'm your wife! Don't you love me? Why would you do that to your wife? I need to go to the bathroom to clean up and I'll be okay. Then I'll be your...clean...wife."

That got his attention.

"You want me clean and fresh for you, right? I just need to freshen up a little."

"You're right, my dear. No reason why you shouldn't be allowed to go clean up. Here, I'll help you." He picked up her thin body again and carried her to the bathroom, sat her on the dirty toilet, and shut the door.

Silent tears of relief streamed down her bruised and battered face. She found a washcloth and reached to turn on the faucet without getting up. As she wiped dried blood from her legs, then arms, then stomach, she started to feel a little less sore than before. She looked down at her stomach to inspect the long cuts he had carved into her pale skin. Why would he do this to her? What was his obsession with blood?

There was so much blood caked on her body that she could never clean up with just a washcloth. To her left was a tub and shower. She doubted that her legs could support her weight during a shower, but she had to try. She had to wash away the blood as well as the disgusting stink he had left behind after...after...what he had done to her. With her feet flat on the floor, she leaned forward to put weight on them, and found them able to take the weight of her body again. Her legs wobbled a bit as she stood from the toilet but they held her.

With one quaking hand for support on the side of the tub, she turned on the water to the shower. Then she straightened with a groan and stepped into the warm water. It felt so good to be warm again that goose bumps appeared all over her skin and she closed her eyes to fully enjoy the water streaming down her body. A wave of dizziness hit her and she had to open them again.

He had given her a little water to drink here and there, but it wasn't nearly enough, so she opened her mouth and let the warm water spray in. She gulped the water down until she was full, and then sighed with relief. Her dizziness faded a bit.

Blood mixed with water and spiraled into the drain. It seemed she would never be able to get all of the blood and dried sweat off her body, but methodically, she used her washcloth to clean off as much as possible. Then, to her surprise, she found shampoo, and washed her hair.

The shirt she had been wearing was perfect for hiding in, so she put it back on while still wet, as she was unable to find a towel. Blood was dripping down her legs again, so she folded her washcloth and held it between her legs. Holding the washcloth with one hand, she opened the door, finally able to face the man, but praying he wouldn't be there. He wasn't, and she let out a puff of air. One step at a time, testing the creaking wooden boards, she padded down the hallway toward the back of the house, leaving a slight trail of water and blood. She looked, but found no other way out, so she made her way to the living room, which was outside of her bedroom. Fear struck her like a bolt of lightning when she saw him.

"Feel better, honey?" he asked. He was sitting on a dirty and tattered couch, holding a beer in one hand and a TV Guide in the other hand. The black and white television was on, show-

ing the Ed Sullivan Show. Aluminum foil posed as rabbit ears on the top of the television set.

"Yes...dear," she forced herself to say. "Is there, um, may I have something to eat?"

"No." He uttered a loud, guttural laugh that shot fear into her heart again. He stood as he ogled her, and then stalked toward her like a lion.

She shook with fear and backed into a wall as he slid toward her. He grabbed her hand, and then pulled her back to the bedroom. She screamed as the pain in her abdomen shot through her body with every step. Now, more blood escaped her body as she dropped the washcloth.

"No! Please! Don't tie me up again!" He hit her face and continued tying her arms, but he did not tie her legs. At least she had that. He left the room, came back with his syringe, and shot her in the hip with it. She cried, "No," weakly before the medicine took over her body once again.

Clouds appeared in the doorway and window and drifted into the bedroom, so slowly that she wasn't sure they were actually moving. Eventually they came to her, cradled her body, and made it feel all better again. No more pain, no cuts, no bleeding. The clouds softly caressed her skin like a lullaby, and she grew more and more sleepy. Finally, she fell asleep, contented, and peaceful.

It was still dark when she awoke. This dream was different. It wasn't exactly a nightmare but was more like a memory. She sat up as she tried to put the pieces together.

She wasn't sure why, but she felt the urge to write down her dream. She turned on the light and pulled her diary from her nightstand drawer. She hadn't touched the diary for a few years now, and the pages were full of talk about different boys – who liked whom, who had a crush on her, who she had a crush on... She chuckled as she skimmed through some of her writings.

A lot had changed in the last few years. As an eighth grader, she had her first boyfriend. Several months later, she was with someone else and had her first real kiss. She laughed as she read the words, "It was slimy and disgusting." Later, she grew to like kissing her boyfriends. Then boys, of course, tried to go further and further – first base, second base. But she never let them get past that. She had wanted to save herself for someone special.

So much for that.

It took her quite a while to write down everything from her dream. She wasn't sure why writing about her nightmares had become important, but she felt the urge to write down all of the other nightmares and dreams she'd had as well. For the rest of the night, she wrote everything she could remember and found that it became easier to do with each one. She felt lighter, not so scared, not so burdened – as if the ever-present dark cloud around her had somehow dissipated just a bit. She wanted to write more, but as the sun rose, she heard her mother moving around and knew it was time to get up.

Ah, the life of a track worker. She couldn't wait to get to work.

***

After workouts that morning, Erick appeared outside the stall she was working in. He was holding a large present wrapped in multi-colored wrapping paper. The excitement on his face told her he couldn't wait for her to open it, and she grinned back at him, despite her confusion.

He led her to two bales of hay, and they each sat on one. Then, he handed her the box.

She inspected it, not sure if it was appropriate to accept a gift from him.

"Well, open it, silly. Come on."

"Okay, okay, hold your horses." She chuckled as she glanced at him, and then tore into the paper, not caring if she saved it this time. Inside was a giant box with a picture of boots on it. *New boots?* Her old boots were pretty torn up and disgusting; it was time to get new ones. *Really? Boots?*

"Open the box." He reached over and poked her.

She smiled at him, then focused on the box again. Lifting the lid, she found a pair of beautiful new riding boots inside. They were brown leather, tall, with a western look. They were also soft, yet perfect for working horses in the mornings. She couldn't believe what she was seeing.

"You don't like them?"

She opened her mouth to speak but her words were lost. She had never had such nice boots. She had seen other people with boots like these, and had always wanted some like that, but mom could never afford it. Her rubber barn boots were plain, uncomfortable, and cold in the winter. Tears formed, and then spilled as she slipped one hand over the warm leather, taking in every detail of the beautiful boots. Still choked up, she smiled at him and moved over to his bale of hay to thank him. Holding her boots snug with one arm, she reached over to hug him with the other.

"You do like them." She nodded into his shoulder.

He wrapped his arms around her in a warm embrace, negating the early morning chill in an instant. He pulled her in tightly as her face burrowed into the warm crook of his neck. She sniffled as he drifted his fingers over her back and rested his head on hers. They both closed their eyes, savoring every moment.

She felt an overwhelming urge to kiss him. *Just a little thank you kiss is all.* Lifting her head from his shoulder, she pulled away and kissed him on the cheek, lingering for a moment longer than she had intended. His cheek was warm. It felt so good to touch him that she wanted to kiss him again and taste him fully this time.

Gradually, cautiously, he turned his head until their lips were only a whisper apart. His gaze drifted to her mouth. They could both feel the other's heated breath. Her lips ached for him. If only...

Peggy wouldn't like it. It would ruin everything if they kissed.

It hurt terribly to move away, as it went against everything inside her, every instinct, every need. Judging from the way he was taking her in, she knew if she let him, it would happen. For Peggy, though, she had to keep her distance.

To separate herself, she picked up the boots and tried to think of something – anything – to say. "I've never ever had anything so nice before. I can't believe you bought these for me. They're beautiful, Erick. I absolutely love them. How did you know what size to get?"

Erick blinked and came back to reality as she spoke. "Um, I had to sneak a peek at those old rubber galoshes you use for riding boots to get your size." He forced a weak smile.

Trying to lighten the mood again, she burst out laughing. Without thinking, she focused on his lips again, noting how soft and inviting they were, imagining herself touching them, knowing she might faint if she let it happen. She had to deny that he made her feel this way. She had to control herself, for his sake and for Peggy's.

She swallowed and forced herself to keep talking. "I *really* love these, Erick. I mean *really*." Holding the box at arm's length, she admired them. “They had to be expensive. It’s too much.”

“Nah, don’t worry about it. It was nothing.” This wasn’t the smile she loved so much, the one where his eyes lit up. Now they seemed to sag while he smiled with only the bottom half of his face. It absolutely killed her that she had caused his pain. “Well, um, I-I, gotta go. I have to help Mr. Watson with...something. I’ll see you later, okay?”

“Okay, Erick. Thanks again,” Rachel answered with a small, weak voice, as it felt as if all her energy had been sucked from her body. And when he left, she felt even weaker.

***

The next morning, before Erick left the track for school, he walked with Rachel as she led one of her horses to the grass to graze. She was a bit nervous about being alone with him. Peggy would be teed if she knew how much time they spent together when she wasn’t around. But this time, it was awkwardly silent for a few minutes as she felt a strange vibe coming from Erick.

“Rach,” he said, finally breaking the silence.

“Yeah?” she answered with a glance.

“Um, is Peggy setting you up with someone for the prom?”

“I don’t want to go.”

“Why not?”

“Do I ever answer that question?”

“No.”

“Maybe you could imagine, so I won’t have to say it. Maybe you could guess what I went through. But I don’t think you could even come up with anything bad enough.”

Her horse dipped his head into the thick grass as he repeatedly ripped it from the turf. Rachel focused on the ripping sound, then the chewing, anything to distract her from what wanted to happen inside her. She fought desperately to stay in the moment, outside, with Erick, with her horse, at the track. What should be such a happy and joyous time was turning into the opposite. She hoped her silent answer was just that – an answer. She hoped he knew what she was thinking, because she was unable to bring herself to say it. She had already said too much and was teetering on the edge.

Biting her lip, she put her hand on her horse's shoulder, hoping he would help her stand tall, hoping he would keep her from falling into that other world she so often fell into. Lately, it was mostly in her dreams, but during the day, many times she fought the feeling by turning her mind away the very second she felt it coming on. She was getting good at changing the subject instantly in her mind. As she told herself this, she woke up still in the real world, and was encouraged.

Then she noticed something else. Erick's hand was lightly resting on her shoulder. For how long?

She glanced at his hand as he yanked it away and mumbled an apology. Pressing her lips together in a tight line, she fought to maintain control as she gazed into his inquisitive eyes.

Then it dawned on her that she didn't need to worry about controlling her emotions right now. Instead of falling into the abyss of fear in the close presence of a man, she felt warm, safe, and secure, and knew without a doubt that she wouldn't fall this time. He was there to protect her, and she knew it. He was so close now but that only served to make her feel better. She never wanted to leave his side.

"Rach, I'm going to break up with Peggy. Once and for all."

What?

She waited, fully expecting him to say that he wanted to be with her. She tried to prepare words in her head to let him know she could never be with any man, but no words were right. No words were appropriate. There were no words to express what she felt. *Confusion.* That was the only word spinning inside her mind right now.

But, he never said it.

"Before prom?" she finally asked.

"Yeah."

"But she already bought a dress."

Erick lowered his face to the ground and knocked a rock around with his foot. "Then I'll give her the money for it."

"She'll freak."

Erick shrugged, and then settled his eyes on hers again and then on her lips. *No.* She had to resist because it would hurt all that much more when he learned about her. Then, not only would she faint as she felt his lips on hers, more importantly, Peggy would find out and accuse her of stealing her boyfriend. It would mean the end of their friendship. Peggy would also turn all of her friends against her. Not that she talked to them much, anymore.

He appeared to understand, though, and didn't touch her. She wasn't sure how she felt about that, but they continued to search each other's faces for answers. Time seemed to stop as they stood there in the grass.

***

Later, Rachel knew deep down that he was consciously trying to avoid scaring her. He had kept his distance earlier, avoiding kissing her, or holding her hand. He, of course, would know that he had to move slowly with her. What he didn't know about were all the things wrong with her – the things she referred to as her limitations. She had to tell him so he could decide, but she was afraid of what his reaction may be. *How do you tell someone these things? I can't have kids. I'm scared to death of sex. I'm scared it will hurt. I'm scared you will force me to do things I don't want to do. I'm scared you will see my scars and think I'm ugly. I can't even cook. What else would I be good for?*

Nothing.

CHAPTER TWELVE

The next day, Erick had it all worked out in his mind. He was going to talk to Peggy about breaking up in the afternoon at the track when she followed him to work. This time he had to be strong and not be worried about hurting her or dealing with her anger. He would keep his distance, too, and avoid her hands. And no distractions, no matter what she tried to give him a peek of.

Erick's hands were sweaty and he hoped he didn't appear too nervous. Peggy was going to be ticked. Nevertheless, he had the perfect spot. Somewhere where it was private, to avoid prying ears when Peggy started screaming.

As they walked together, despite not holding hands, Peggy was jovial and talkative as usual, most likely thinking their "space thing" had worked and rekindled their relationship. Erick knew everything would change in a few minutes. His heart thumped.

"Hey, let's go back here, I need to talk to you. In private." He felt as if his heart would jump from his chest as he directed her behind a barn.

"Okay," Peggy answered hesitantly, sensing his nervousness. The area behind Julia's stable had a secluded, grassy area lined with bushes. He waved an arm, inviting her to sit on a large rock next to a bush. She sat down without a word and reached up to twirl her hair with one finger.

"Peggy, this isn't working. I, I just want–," He meant to go on, but she interrupted.

"What?" she barked. "What? What do you want?" She hopped to her feet and backed up from him, steadying herself with her hand on the rock.

Erick opened his mouth, but nothing came out. *Now is not the time to freeze!*

"You want Rachel. I knew it!"

Erick shifted back and forth as he hoped Rachel hadn't heard through the barn wall.

Peggy continued. "I knew it. I can't believe you would do this to me, Erick. I can't believe it. You led me on for months and I knew it, I knew you were in love with her. Why aren't you going out with her if you're in love with her? Why did you even ask me out?" She burst into tears. "You shouldn't have even asked me out in the first place."

With both hands on his head, he searched the ground for answers, then took a breath to calm himself. "Peggy, I asked you out because I thought you were attractive, and I liked you, and gave it a shot. But it's not working. Rachel's not interested in me anyway. She's still trying to heal from this thing she went through. We're just friends and nothing more. It will probably never be anything more." His head almost dropped in anguish, but in an attempt to appear strong, he held on.

She filled with hatred as she believed his disappointment was caused by the thought of not being with Rachel. "You used me. You bastard! You used me to get to Rachel. I knew it!"

He had to stay calm in the face of her hysteria. Just as he did with his horses, he kept his voice calm and low. "Peggy, where are you getting this from? I didn't use you. I went out with you before I even met her. But now I can't stay with you because I'm not in love with you, and I can't stay in a relationship where I'm not in love. You shouldn't want to be in a relationship without love either. If you stay with me, you'll never find Mr. Right. I'm not the perfect man for you, Peg. You hate spending so much time at the track, for one. That alone is enough right there." He shook his head and paced for a few steps before coming to a stop again. Peggy stood with her hands clenched at her sides as she leaned forward toward him. Her lips pursed into a tiny pucker. "No, Peg, it's going to have to be this way. We're not right for each other and you should be with someone who wants to be with you as much as you want to be with him."

The tears had stopped, and as she faced the ground, she appeared to understand for the most part. But she was still angry and shot him a dirty scowl. "I wish you would have told me this before I bought that dress." Pushing him, she stormed by him, leaving him standing alone. He dropped his head into his hand with relief.

"Well, he's free, now. Go get him." Peggy waved an arm at Rachel over the stall door.

"What? What are you talking about?" Rachel asked as she ducked under her horse's head and approached Peggy.

"Erick. He broke up with me. You can have him. He used me, Rachel. He's a lying, cheating bastard and a no good...liar. He wasn't in love with me. But he led me on for months. Jerk! Well, fine. He's yours now. You can have him." She stormed off in a huff, her hair bouncing in all directions.

Rachel scanned the area for Erick but he wasn't there. She jogged to catch up to Peggy. "No, Peggy, it's not like that. Where did you get this idea?"

Peggy's eyes darkened as they glared into Rachel's. "Oh, like you don't know. Don't play dumb with me, Miss Googly Eyes, staring at him across the table all the time. Playing foot-sie. Yeah, I noticed. I knew this was going to happen sooner or later. Well, now you've got your chance. So take *my* boyfriend if that's what you want."

Rachel swallowed as the blood rushed from her face. *Oops.*

Peggy was crying so hard that she was unable to utter another word. Rachel tried to reach out to her friend, but Peggy pulled away with another evil glare, and then stomped away.

Still in shock, Rachel stood there staring but broke away when she heard laughter. A young man in overalls had been leaning against the barn with his arms crossed, enjoying the show. She glared at him and he instantly stopped.

She had to talk to Erick. She found him standing by the barn door with his hands shoved into his pockets. The expression on his face said, *Whew, I'm glad that's over*, and *I'm sad*, at the same time.

"You okay?" she asked him.

"Much better now," he answered, forcing a grin.

He left to do some work in another barn, leaving Rachel there to wonder if he would ask her out next, and the thought petrified her.

However, for several days, he never pressured her, never asked her out, and never even talked about it. Rachel felt more relieved and at ease as each day passed without the subject coming up.

***

Rachel and Erick made their way to the track kitchen to get lunch. As they passed by barn forty-two, she checked for the creepy man, as she always did. And, as always, the stocky man in overalls was there sweeping, and watching as the pair walked by. He caught Rachel staring at him and quickly turned away. *Strange*, Rachel thought.

Rachel nudged Erick's arm while the man was facing away. She nodded toward the man and Erick followed her line of sight. Rachel was glad Erick didn't say anything.

When they made it to the track kitchen, he asked, "What was that all about?"

"Do you know him?"

"I don't think so. I couldn't really see him. He was facing the other direction. Why?"

"Well, I feel so dumb saying this, but he gives me the creeps. He's always staring at me."

"Maybe he's got a crush on you," Erick said with a nudge and a grin.

Rachel peered at him with her chin lowered as she looked through her eyelashes. "I doubt that."

Erick only shrugged as he held back a chuckle.

After lunch, walking back, Erick saw the man in the exact same place. He was still sweeping, which was odd. Erick squared his shoulders and tried his best to appear unafraid and unfazed by the intense glower coming from the dark figure. Erick scrutinized him for several long seconds until they had passed him. Once Rachel and Erick were finally out of his view, they donned matching bewildered frowns.

"What do you think now?" she asked.

"I'm not sure. That was pretty creepy. He was watching us the whole time."

"Was he staring at you?"

"Yeah."

"Maybe he has a crush on you," she said as she laughed.

Erick shook his head and poked her arm, prompting her to poke back.

"Well, seriously, I don't think you should walk by there by yourself. I don't like him."

"I can take care of myself. No one will hurt me around here. Right?"

Erick pursed his lips and faced forward.

"You think I can't protect myself because I couldn't before."

He put his arm around her shoulders, forgetting that he was supposed to keep his hands to himself. He was relieved when she didn't stiffen. "I'm sure you can," he told her. "But I like to think I'm one of those heroes in the western movies, protecting the girl from the evil bandit who so desperately wants to tie her to train tracks. Why they do that, I don't know. I never understood."

Rachel laughed, and was disappointed when he withdrew his arm. "Well, there are train tracks over there," she said, pointing toward the train station on the other side of the grandstand.

"Yeah. So, you're going to need me to protect you from the man in the black suit and mask."

Rachel shook her head, still grinning. "Okay, cowboy. You can be my hero."

Erick nodded proudly from under his black cowboy hat.

CHAPTER THIRTEEN

He loved watching her ride and he admired her because she was so balanced, still, poised and low in the saddle, making her horse's gait as fluid as possible. At the same time, he struggled constantly not to imagine her on top of him in that position. She moved so effortlessly, yet he knew that her entire body was melding with the horse's form and they were moving as one. He wanted to be one with her and imagined...

"If you keep looking at her that way, you're going to fall off that horse. Be careful, man. He might bolt on you and leave you behind." The trainer he was working for had suddenly materialized out of nowhere next to him.

Erick glanced at the trainer, surprised and shocked. He tried not to appear that way, but it was useless. He lowered his gaze, knowing he had been caught, and it depressed him that he was staring at her like a lost puppy. What must the guys think of him? Was it that obvious how he felt about her?

The trainer continued as his horse shifted his weight. "She is cute, though, I'll give her that. Good rider, too. I like her form. It's good for the horse. She knows her stuff. But she'll never ride for me. Can't have a girl on my team. It distracts the men from their work, much like now. She's distracting you even though she's not doing it on purpose. You can't help but stare at her, can you?"

Erick smoldered with a hint of annoyance as the trainer talked about Rachel as a distraction. "Um."

"Yeah, I know. I was young once. Well, don't let her make you forget what you're here for. You're here to become a jockey and you can't let girls distract you." The aging man swiped his spotted hand over his mouth and mumbled, "They shouldn't be here in the first place."

"No. In fact, she helps me. She's taught me a few things," Erick said, sticking up for her. It was the truth. She was a more experienced rider and had been around the track her whole life. It was all she knew, and she had studied many great riders over the years and had put together the best of the best techniques.

"Well, let's hope she only teaches you how to be a better jockey."

His whole face lit up at the thought of talking about Rachel. "She has. For instance, she taught me about knotting the reins at different lengths, to make them longer or shorter depending on the kind of horse you're riding, and she also had me adjust my foot placement in the stirrups so I'm more on the balls of my feet and not the toes like I was. I was taught to ride more on the toes but she said it doesn't necessarily have to be that way, and had me adjust, and now I'm more comfortable and balanced. She knows her stuff," Erick continued, trying to give her all the respect she deserved. The men at the track never wanted to give her credit simply because she was female.

"Okay, Erick, okay. I believe you. Let's get back and get the next set going," he said, wanting to end the subject. Erick was grateful for the conversation to be over with as well.

As they made their way back to the barn, he realized that he was not going to last much longer like this. It hurt him not to be able to touch her, hold her, or kiss her. It was so painful that it wracked his entire body and sometimes even made him sick. Sometimes he was unable to eat, and would pick at his dinner, worrying his parents. Paying attention in school was next to impossible as he wished she were there sitting next to him, blocking his view of Peggy, maybe. How much longer would it take for Rachel to heal? Would she ever heal enough to accept him?

Just ask her.

***

"Hey, want to help me walk this guy?" Erick asked Rachel as he watched her coming out of the barn. He took in every part of her in just an instant.

"You need help with him?" Rachel grinned suspiciously. "I thought you were a better hotwalker than that, young man." She shoved her hoof pick into her pocket and fell into place next to him.

"Oh, this is one feisty horse. He needs two handlers in the gate and two lead ponies before and after a race," he exclaimed as he shook his horse's lead rope. The horse bobbed his head a little, but it remained low and exhausted.

"Yeah, I can tell he's a tough one," she laughed as she patted the horse's sweaty shoulder. Erick laughed at his horse, who wasn't helping his story any.

Once they were alone and out of earshot of other people, Rachel tensed at Erick's sudden silence. *Oh no, is he going to...?*

"Rach, I um..."

She hoped he wasn't going to say it. But when he stopped and faced her, she knew. Blood rushed from her head and she felt that familiar fear as the memories of the events that had made her this way flooded her mind.

This is it. Now is the time. You have to tell him. There is so much wrong with me, and he deserves a perfect girl, one without all of these issues. We can't be together. I know what will happen. He will get tired of me and my tears, my nightmares, flashbacks, the fear. It's time to tell him. Now.

But I can't.

He was so close that she expected him to reach out and touch her, or kiss her. And God, did she want to kiss him. Her heart beat quickly and a rush of heat swept through her as she imagined what it would be like to touch those perfectly shaped lips of his. But no, she had to resist, for him. *Remember your limitations?*

She opened her mouth, but was unable to utter a sound. She was floored. She was mesmerized by him, his perfect face, perfect body. Her courage dissipated, and she was unable to say the things she needed to say. Things he needed to know. Things he *deserved* to know.

As he glanced at her lips, she ducked her head, hoping to hide them. Still, his warm and slightly heavy breaths caressed her face. With one hand, he held his horse while he lifted her face with his other. His thumb drifted over her cheek, and despite his calloused hands, it felt soft and warm, and left behind a trail of sparks. Every bone in her body wanted desperately to taste him. It took everything in her power to speak. Or try to. She opened her mouth again, wishing for words, but they were stuck.

"You're shaking," he whispered, only inches from her face.

"I..." God, she wanted to kiss him. She wanted every inch of him. But it wasn't about what she wanted. It was about what was best for him. He did not deserve to be with someone like her. She was broken, bruised, scarred, and afraid, with the panic attacks and flashbacks that made her act like a crazy person who should have been locked up months ago and forced to endure shock treatments or a lobotomy. She dropped her head, allowing tears to fall onto the ground.

"What is it, Rach?" he asked as he wrapped one arm around her and pulled her into his chest.

Folding her arms in front of her, she tried desperately to keep some distance between them, and she was relieved when he loosened his hold. Despite what she had told her hands, they drifted down bumps and ridges of what promised to be his perfectly sculpted chest. She discovered her fingers drifting down his chest, but stopped them as she reached his toned abs. With a tiny whimper, she used her hands to push herself away.

He reached for her soft face. She leaned into his hand, though she didn't mean to. A touch like that from anybody else might have sent her into the darkness again, but not with him. With him, every touch set her entire body on fire.

"Tell me," he whispered, searching her face for answers.

I don't want to lose you. But I'm broken. I'm not perfect. I don't deserve you. Say it! "I..." The thought of losing him hurt so badly that she covered her stomach with her arms and leaned over. It was as if she had been punched in the gut, or kicked by a horse. Then she began whimpering as she felt the panic flooding through her.

Erick hooked his arm around her waist and helped her to a nearby bench. "What's wrong? You okay?"

As she leaned over her legs and tried desperately not to pass out, she shook her head. "I can't."

Erick leaned into her ear as he rubbed her back. "I understand, Rach. You're not ready. It's all right. I won't put pressure on you. Okay?"

It was such a relief to hear those words. Every moment, she had to cherish from now on, as she knew that as soon as she told him, he would have to move on. The longer she put it off, the more time she got to spend with him and avoid watching him with someone else. More than losing his love, she feared losing his friendship, which she valued more than anything. She had never had such a good friend, someone who was so much like her, someone on the same wave length, someone she connected with on a deeper level.

Finally, she sat up and faced him, searching his face for evidence of hurt. "Are we still best friends?" she asked, then froze as she awaited his answer.

"You are my best friend, Rach. And you *always* will be. Always. I promise." And there it was again, the smile she loved so much. His face lit with joy, his delightful blue eyes set on hers, and she was completely at ease. His happiness was the most important thing in the world to her at that moment.

***

"Detective Ritter?"

The detective ran his fingers through his thinning hair and leaned forward when he heard the distinctive accent through the black phone pressed against his ear. His heart skipped a beat as he hoped to hear good news from the vet. "This is Detective Ritter. How may I help you?"

"This is Doctor Senjin from Belmont Park. The veterinarian."

"Yes, sir. Good to hear from you. I hope you are calling with good news."

"Possibly. My assistant and I were discussing this subject earlier today and he mentioned that quite a few trainers had complained about the quality of the Ketamine in the month of

February. We called the manufacturer, and no other complaints had been filed. We think something happened in house."

"Like what?"

"Perhaps, since the drug is clear, someone replaced the Ketamine with water."

"How? Aren't the tops of the vials impossible to remove?"

"No, sir. It is possible to pop them off and put them back on without anybody knowing. Unfortunately, the vials in question will have been long gone by now. But I hope this helps somehow. We thought we should call and let you know, just in case."

"Who could have done such a thing? I've already talked with every vet at the track. I don't believe they were responsible."

"Neither do I. I can't imagine any of the doctors here playing any role in her disappearance. I can only speculate that someone sneaked into the office and did this."

Detective Ritter was silent as he pondered the possibilities. Perhaps this doctor was right. Perhaps someone sneaked in and replaced the Ketamine with water, knowing that they kept tight records of the drug. It had to be. It was the only logical explanation. At least, so far.

CHAPTER FOURTEEN

"Hey, guys, I'm going to get coffee. Who wants some?" Rachel asked before workouts. Erick raised his hand for a second before fitting his helmet over his head. Billy and one groom also indicated they wanted coffee, so Rachel headed for the kitchen. By herself. Without thinking.

Erick watched her walk away for a few seconds while he tried to decide what to do. He turned to Billy, who was also watching Rachel walk away on her own. They looked at each other. "I'll go," Erick volunteered. Billy nodded and with one last glance, he turned back to his horse.

As Rachel approached that barn with the strange man inside, she realized her mistake. Then she tried to decide whether she should go back or keep going, and slowed her pace. She didn't see him, so she kept going, hoping to avoid his creepy stare and shadowed face.

But, all of a sudden, there they were. Two dark eyes under a fedora. It was that man again. He hid his face in the shadows again, not allowing her to see him clearly. He seemed familiar, though.

The monster?

Before she knew what was happening, a memory came flooding back, sweeping her away in the undertow.

It was dark, raining outside, and there was thunder and lightning. She was sagging with the old bed again, and tied by her arms and legs. She felt hands on her breasts, hands groping, fingers in places where they shouldn't have been. She felt invaded, violated. The pain, physical and mental, was beyond manageable. Blood was coming now, and she smelled death, that familiar smell that put her back in that room again. It was too much and she had to get away. Then, all was dark.

Erick's voice was faint, as if he were on the other side of a long tunnel. Did she really hear him? Was that Erick? "Rachel! Wake up! Wake up!"

It is him. Where is he?

"Rachel? Oh no. Please, Rach. Wake up."

Wake up? Why?

She felt herself bouncing up and down. The man was attacking her again! Or was Erick attacking her now? Why would he do that? She screamed for help as she felt herself being carried, most likely back to that bed again, knowing that this was going to hurt. Panic kicked in as she screamed and grabbed at the man carrying her. Twisting her body, she managed to slip herself free of his arms and fall to the ground. She sat up and looked at her hands.

Where were the ropes?

"No, no, Rach," Erick called, his voice two octaves higher than normal. "Rach?"

Winded, confused, and wide-eyed, she had no idea what was going on, but she latched onto him, as she knew he was a beacon of light for her. Like her mother had done in the past, Erick spoke to her and waited until she focused on him.

By now, a crowd of people had gathered around. Finally, she was able to take in what was happening and peered up at a circle of men around her. It was terrifying. She glanced from man to man, and she became more and more frightened, even when she found Erick there holding her hand as he knelt next to her. Being under a crowd of men, all staring at her from above was too much to handle. She crawled between them, knocking away their hands as they tried to reassure her, and scrambled out of the circle. Once she was free, she stood and ran her fastest away from them.

As she ran, she began to realize what had happened. Blood pumped through her body, invigorating her. She focused. She slowed. Then stopped. It wasn't real. She was at the track. Those men weren't going to hurt her. The realization hit her like a brick, and she groaned with embarrassment. At the same time, she cried with relief as the fear left her body.

She heard someone running after her. She knew that sound and she was not about to let it happen again. She started to run again, but when she reminded herself that she was safe at the track, she gathered her courage and turned to face whoever it was. It was Erick. She let out two entire lungs full of air the instant he came into view.

All Rachel saw were two blue orbs the size of saucers on his face. "Rach," he said as he caught up to her and took her arm. "Let's get to the barn."

Without a word, she let him lead her to her barn. Once there, they sat down on a bale of hay as Rachel desperately wished she could sink into the ground and disappear.

"Your mom should be here soon. She's probably wondering where we are," he said softly, and she nodded in reply. When she flopped her head into her hands and leaned forward, he rubbed her back. Her muscles relaxed almost instantly, and she closed her eyes to enjoy his gentle touch to the fullest.

With caressing circles, he warmed her back, dissipating the stress, sending it away.

After a minute or two, she sat up and focused through her tears on those beautiful blue pools of his. He reached out for her. She hesitated, but then took his hand. He gently squeezed in reassurance. She watched his thumb tenderly tracing her knuckles. He did make her feel better, safer. His touch was a lifeline keeping her in the reality of today at the track, with Erick.

However, it wasn't right, and she denied herself again, though she was afraid of losing his friendship over all else. Telling him meant the possibility of losing him. Regardless, her needs didn't matter. He deserved better than her. He was so perfect, and he deserved a perfect girl. She had to tell him, and now, while she had the courage.

"Erick..."

Julia rode up on horseback. "Where have you guys been? I've been waiting for you at the track. What's going on?" She was obviously annoyed, which further upset Rachel. Ashamed and embarrassed, she sheepishly looked up at her mother. Julia's annoyance instantly became concern as she noted Rachel's expression.

"What happened?" Julia asked as she slid down from her horse.

Erick read Rachel's mind as he stood, and knew Rachel wanted to talk to her mother alone. With one last touch on the shoulder, he walked away.

"What was that all about?" Julia asked as she sat down next to her, still holding her horse's reins.

"I had another one of those...episodes."

"What? When? Just now?"

Rachel nodded. "Mom, I need to be locked up, I think," bursting into tears as she imagined the rest of her life in an insane asylum.

"No, honey, no. Rach, you know it's not going to go away quickly. It's going to take a while. This has been happening less and less lately. Right? So, hang in there. Keep trying. You're a smart girl. You know what's going on. You know what you need to do to fix it. And you will fix it."

Rachel shook her head. "I have no idea how to fix this."

"When you come out of these things, you always come out a little stronger. Each time. You always come out brave and ready to face the world on the other side. You're going to be so strong one day that you'll stop it before it happens."

"I hope so."

"Do you think riding will help?"

"Definitely," Rachel answered emphatically.

"Then, let's get to work."

***

Later, Erick found Rachel feeding a carrot to Old Guy. Her face lit up when he appeared. "Hey," she called. Deep down, she wanted desperately to avoid the subject of the incident this morning and hoped he would not bring it up.

But he surprised her by saying, "Let's go for a ride in the infield."

"You know we aren't allowed to do that." She knit her eyebrows at him, then noticed he was carrying a stack of plastic cups.

Erick laughed an impish laugh. "Good thing I brought my invisible horse. I brought one for you, too. They'll never see us now." He handed her two cups.

Rachel eyed the cups curiously.

Erick let her stew over them for a moment, then decided to fill her in on his plan. He held the cups with the openings together, then began clapping them together to sound like horseshoes on pavement.

Rachel pressed her lips together and snickered for a few seconds, then burst out in loud laughter.

"Come on. This way," he answered, then turned his horse toward the infield and clip-clopped away.

Embarrassed, but curious, she followed with her invisible horse, blushing at the people who stared. After trotting for just a bit, they settled into a walk.

Rachel stacked her cups, then grabbed Erick's and stacked them with hers.

"What are you doing?" he asked. He tried to take them back, but she protested and held them behind her, pulling them away whenever he got too close.

"I'm embarrassed," she admitted in a whisper. "Everybody was looking at us. We looked like crazy people."

"So?" he laughed.

"No way, Jose," she said as she shook her head with big motions.

Finally, Erick let her end their invisible horse ride with a sigh, but was glad to see the smile on her face.

They talked about what was going on at school, how Peggy had been treating him now that they had broken up. They talked about other horses around the track and their dreams of one day becoming jockeys.

"I just want to run fast with the horses, feel that feeling when you win, you know," Rachel said, motioning toward the track.

"Me too. And I can feel it. I know I'm going to get that chance once I graduate. I've been working on meeting as many trainers as possible and soon I'm sure I'll have enough people to work with that someone will give me a chance. I can't wait." Erick looked at her intently. "I know you'll get it too. I can tell. You're such a good rider, and with your mom as a trainer, she's bound to give you a chance, right? Do you think she will?"

"Actually, she's totally against me getting my license. Oh, exercising is fine. But racing is another story."

"Why?"

"Well, I guess because it's how my dad died, you know. I was three when his horse fell and flipped on him. He broke his neck and died instantly,"

"Oh wow, I'm so sorry. I knew he was in an accident, but that's all I knew."

It was a sunny but chilly afternoon and a breeze flowed across the open space of the infield. It was noisy, as the voices of hundreds of birds resounded at the same time near the ponds. The grassy, open area was peaceful, however, and promised relaxation. Nothing was in their way.

"Come on, let's race," he shouted excitedly when they stepped onto the inner turf track, jogging in front of her.

With a bright gleam in her eye, and a hint of rebellion, she said, "Sure," and immediately ran by him as quickly as she could.

Erick called after her, "Hey!" and caught up. "Give in! You cannot match my speed!"

"Never!" But soon, she was out of breath and had to slow. Meanwhile, Erick was completely at ease, hardly winded at all. Rachel marveled at him. "How are you not winded?"

"How are you winded?" he laughed.

She slapped his arm and then wiped her forehead with her sleeve.

They made their way through an opening in the hedges and walked to one of the ponds nearby. As a flock of birds flew away, their flapping wings and cawing combining in a deafening roar, Rachel and Erick could see that half of the pond was exposed and the other half was covered by algae. The other pond was in the same state, but once the weather warmed up, the algae would fully cover both ponds. Someone had recently planted flowers in a small memorial garden near the pond and the freshly turned soil was laced with the scent of nature's fertilizer – manure.

Nervousness set in, but she was determined not to appear nervous around him. Though she knew she had to tell him about her limitations, and soon, because he had been trying to get closer to her lately. She had to put a stop to it now, before it became too hard.

Unfortunately, it already was.

Erick plopped down into the grass and lay on his back. He glanced at Rachel and tapped the ground next to him. Honored to have his attention, she made her way over, then lay next to him in the grass. It was romantic, but it wasn't scary. It was comfortable and made her want to giggle a little. It seemed like the wrong time to bring up her problems.

"What do you see in the clouds?" he asked as he wrapped his arm under his head.

"I see….a white horse with one wing. He's half a Pegasus. I want a white thoroughbred sometime and I want to name him Pegasus."

"White?" Erick chuckled. "Good luck finding one of those. I've never seen one. Maybe a grey?"

"No, he'd have to be white. Pure white." She relished in the anticipation of arguing about the rarity of a white thoroughbred, and tried desperately to hide the sheer joy it caused by biting the inside of her lip.

"What are you going to do? Bleach his hair?" he laughed.

"If I have to."

He let out a quick laugh. "I wonder what the Jockey Club would say about that."

"They'd allow it if his name were Pegasus," she said, hoping to bait him some more.

"You're funny. There's no way they would allow you to bleach his hair." He laughed and then said softly, "You're a dreamer, that's for sure. A white thoroughbred *and* your jockey's license."

She sat up, suddenly defensive. "What's wrong with that?"

He was startled and glanced at her, but didn't sit up. "Nothing. Nothing at all. I have dreams too. Everyone does. Nothing wrong with dreams." He patted the ground next to him again and she complied, lying back down.

"As long as they're dreams and not nightmares," she said quietly. Slapping her hand over her mouth, she wished she could shove those words back into her mouth. She finally relaxed when he didn't say another word about it.

It was silent for a few seconds as they studied the clouds and tried to make shapes out of them.

"Do you see what I see?" she asked as she pointed.

"What is it? A cow? With horns?"

Rachel laughed. "No, silly. It's a giraffe. Don't you see the long neck?"

Erick turned to her with an incredulous look. "Long neck? On a cow?"

"Oh, is that the kind of cows they have in Texas? Long necked cows. Wow. I'd love to see one of those."

"That's the leg. What are you talking about?"

"Leg?" She burst out in loud laughter. "He's only got one leg but what, three horns?"

"Cows don't have horns." He scoffed. "Such a Yankee."

She pushed him and laughed. "I am not."

He reached over and tickled her side through her open jacket, causing her to squeal and swat his hand away. He flipped onto to his side and tickled her with one hand as she laughed. To avoid her swats, he kept moving to different spots on her body, until his hand brushed against her breast, trapping her nipple between his fingers. The laughter stopped and he jerked his hand away.

Erick's mouth hung open as he hoped his mistake hadn't ruined everything. The blood rushed from his head, blanching him. "Sorry," he finally whispered. His eyes were huge and round as he waited for her response.

She grinned, which thrust a giant breath of air from his lungs. He flopped onto his back as she snickered into her hand. "It's okay."

"Oh, so, I can do that again?" he asked, scooting closer to her again and wiggling his eyebrows.

Rachel playfully pushed him to keep him at a distance, albeit a slight distance. However, the laughter was over. Erick lay on his side and she faced him, also on her side. It was silent for several long seconds.

"Erick," she began, as he started to say her name. She had to speak first. This was it. He had to know. Soon. Now. She had to say something before allowing herself to give in to him. Erick sat up and faced her as she did the same.

"Go ahead," he said, obviously reluctantly. He wanted to tell her something. Bad. She knew what it was, though, and she had to stop it.

"Um," All this time, and she hadn't come up with the right way to tell him. She mentally slapped herself for not preparing the perfect words, memorizing them. And here he was, openly and patiently waiting for her. Waiting for her to tell him that she was a lousy catch. Waiting for her to tell him he deserved better. Though, she dreaded watching him with someone else again. Just the thought of it pained her terribly and her heart wrenched inside of her chest. Her jaw quivered and she nearly lost control of a tidal wave of tears, but pinched the bridge of her nose and quelled the waters.

"What's wrong?" he asked, scooting closer and taking her hand.

Spit it out! Now! "I'm," she started, and then stopped again. With a desperate groan, she forced herself to keep going. "...broken." The word came out in a squeaky whisper.

Erick shook his head, not able to understand her words. "What do you mean, 'broken'?"

It was too hard to meet his gaze and talk because every time she did, her heart skipped a beat. So she stared off into the distance at a flagpole.

Tell the flagpole. Now.

"I can't get pregnant."

Erick shook his head as he continued to search her face, but she was only able to stare at the flagpole. "Okay. Rachel, that's nothing. It's okay. There's always adoption. Hell, I'm adopted. I'm kind of an advocate for adoption." His eager face continued to search hers as she fought to stay focused on the flagpole. Not him.

She wanted to ask him about the adoption that he had never mentioned, but shook her head and kept going. *Get it out. Now.* "I have scars."

"So? Everybody does."

"Not like these."

"It's ok, Rach. I don't care about scars."

As the list began to compile in her head, her self-esteem plummeted and the tidal wave came crashing down. "I'm scared of s...," she admitted as she covered her face with her hands, pulling free the one he was holding.

Within seconds, he was next to her and had his arms around her. She wrapped her arms around his waist and sobbed into his muscular shoulder. His strength distracted her for a moment, but she reminded herself that she did not deserve him. She shook her head, denying herself once again.

"Rachel, please listen to me." With his finger under her chin, he lifted her head until their eyes met. She wiped her tears with her sleeve and sniffed. She hoped, prayed, and wished for him to accept her this way, but reminded herself that he was so perfect, and perfect guys always go for the perfect girls. It was natural selection.

"I'm not good enough," she whispered, interrupting him.

"Listen. Please? My turn." He ever so gently touched her lips with his finger, and she fought the overwhelming urge to kiss it. Then he ran his finger over her lips as he watched the path it took over her bottom lip to her cheek, then down to her jaw line. She held her breath as his touch made her whole body tingle.

"You're so beautiful, Rach. You're the most beautiful girl I've ever seen."

When she shook her head and closed her eyes in denial, he touched her face again, steadying her. He let his fingers trail from her jaw line and chin again, letting go despite his desire to stay connected with her.

"You are. Every time I look at you, my heart jumps. My insides do flips, I feel like I can't breathe. And it's not simply because you're gorgeous. It's because you're beautiful. And by that, I mean all of you. Your eyes, your hair, your body, but also your laugh, your silly jokes, your pokes on my arm, your sheer determination to pull through every challenge, even this one, the biggest one of your life, I'm sure.

"Over the last few months I've watched you change from a scared little girl clinging to her mother to a determined and strong woman. You went through hell, Rach. I don't know how, I don't know what happened, but you lived through something that nearly killed you, and might have killed anyone else. But not you. You're strong, and I deeply admire that."

Rachel sniffed as she felt a bit of pride in the realization of how she had changed. Erick placed his hand on her knee as he leaned closer.

"Rachel, your mom told me once that the doctors didn't think you would live when you first got to the hospital. When she said that, my stomach dropped because I imagined going through life alone. That's what would have happened to me, Rach, if you hadn't been so strong and determined to get out of that place and get back home. I would have gone through life without you, maybe trying one relationship after another, failing. I would have searched for you my whole life."

Rachel was almost sad as she imagined him going through life by himself. He did not deserve that.

"I know without a shadow of a doubt that we were meant to be together. There's chemistry and electricity between us. I can almost see sparks when I get close to you. The feeling is undeniable."

Huge tears puddled, clinging to her lashes until they blocked her vision and she was forced to blink them away. But she did not want to blink because it meant being separated from him for that split second. She almost couldn't believe her ears as he spoke the most perfect words she had ever heard. And they were for her.

"Don't you think?" he asked, leaning in.

She found herself nodding, though she didn't remember telling her head to move. He gave her his perfect smile, the one he saved only for her, and something hit her just then. He *did* accept her this way. He honestly and truly accepted her.

"So...you...you don't care if I can't get pregnant?" she asked, still not daring to believe it could be true.

"I love you unconditionally. It doesn't matter what you think is wrong with you. I don't see it as something wrong with you. I see it as something you lived through so we could be together."

"You love me?" she squeaked as she fought more tears.

"You love your parents. I'm in love with you." He winked.

Rachel giggled at his joke and wiped her tears again with her sleeve, then connected firmly with his warm, soft gaze. "I'm in love with you, too."

He was stuck between laughter and tears when she finally said the words she knew he had longed to hear for so long. When he scooped her up into his arms again, they laughed, not at anything funny, but simply from happiness.

He pressed her into his chest as the laughter died, and she felt his heart beating almost as hard as hers.

"Your heart is beating so fast," she whispered.

"It's taking everything I've got right now not to kiss you."

She lifted her head from his shoulder. "Why don't you want to kiss me?"

She almost hadn't said her last word when he eagerly dove in, nipping her jaw, her neck, her ear, then stopped. "Are you kidding me? I want to kiss every inch of your body," he moaned. He smelled so delicious that she surprisingly felt the urge to do the same to him. She very nearly fainted at the nearness of him.

As he reached up to touch her face, the electricity between them took her breath away as he gazed into her eyes. With his fingers caressing her loose curls, he cupped the side of her head and their lips touched for the first time. He traced her lips with his tongue and she opened to let him in. It was better than she had ever imagined. She knew then why people on television had fireworks behind them when they kissed. She became the fireworks, being sent into the air at breathtaking speed, then exploding into waves of color. She felt her whole body sparkling as they drifted together in the sky. Her head spun as he slid his hand down her arm to her hand and then weaved their fingers together. She knew in that instant he would never let go of her.

CHAPTER FIFTEEN

"So, what's it like being adopted?"

He glanced at her, then back at the road in front of his car as they made their way to the drive-in. "Well, I didn't even know it until I was sixteen."

"Sixteen?" Rachel blinked. "Why'd they wait so long to tell you?"

"I'm not sure they were ever going to tell me. But I had my suspicions because they're both tall and I'm...not." He winked at her. "They had to tell me when my biological mother decided to look for me. She found me and wanted to meet me."

"Wow. What was that like? Is she nice?"

"Yeah. She was nice, I guess. She lives in St. Louis. Married, has three kids."

"You have brothers and sisters, then."

"Half, I guess. They're a lot younger than I am because she waited another ten years to have kids."

"So you were...you know...it wasn't...I mean...,"

Erick laughed silently as he waited for her to stammer over herself. Finally, she gave up and poked his arm. "I was what they call an 'oops baby,' I guess."

Rachel smothered a grin.

"She was sixteen when she got pregnant."

"What about your father?"

"She showed me a picture. I look just like him, whoever he is. Wherever he is. I don't know."

"Do you want to know?"

Erick shrugged. "Not really. I don't know him. He doesn't know me. Might not even know I exist. It doesn't bother me, though. She gave me up because she was too young and wasn't ready to raise a kid. And look where I ended up. I've got two great parents who love me and treat me better than most parents treat their kids. They say they appreciate me all that much more because at one point, they had lost all hope. When they picked me up, they were extremely grateful to finally have a child of their own."

Rachel took his hand.

Erick drove on in silence for a bit and then he spoke again. "Can I ask you a question?"

"Depends on the question."

After a second's hesitation, he asked, "Why? Why can't you get pregnant? Was it...?"

"Yes. It was."

Erick dropped his jaw and shook his head as anger smoldered inside him.

"I wish I could chop his... Never mind. Well, yes. I wish I could chop it off sometimes."

"I bet," Erick answered, cringing at the thought. "And the scars?"

"Same reason. I guess you'll see someday."

He realized he had ruined the happiness he had seen on her face earlier. "I'm sorry," he started.

"For what? It wasn't your fault."

"I mean, I shouldn't have brought it up."

"No. You need to know. I mean, I've wanted to tell you for so long so you could, you know...decide."

He squeezed her hand. "Nothing to decide. We belong together. Remember? Besides, Rach, you can tell me anything. And it is best to talk about things like that. I'm not going to push you now, but some day, I want you to tell me everything. I want to know what happened to you, and how you lived through it. You can share that with me so you don't have to take on the burden by yourself. It will, I guess, take a load off. You know?"

Rachel nodded as she watched the scenery change from city to country in an instant. So much can change in the blink of an eye. One minute, she was happy, walking home from Candy's, the next, she was in a situation that nearly killed her.

"My friend, Candy, she's the one I was with that night. I left her house and I was going to go to the subway. But, you know, he, well, you know. Anyway, Candy was so upset that she quit going to work in mom's barn. She might have been Chiv's groom, too. But she left and never came back. And her house is empty. I have no idea what happened to her. She probably doesn't even know I'm alive. She probably thinks I'm dead."

"That's awful. No way to find relatives or other friends or anything?"

"No." Rachel gazed out the window, almost as if searching for Candy in the field next to them. "Her brother is gone, too. He was a drug addict. She lived with him because their parents died several years ago and left them alone. She worked, and he spent her money on drugs. I bet she left him, too. But I know she didn't have money to travel. She barely had money to eat. She was so skinny. I hope she's okay."

Erick winced. "Me too."

It was a warm summer evening, perfect for a drive-in movie. A chorus of crickets in the nearby woods chirped loudly as crackled movie soundtracks played over the rusty speakers sitting on their posts. Cars rolling over the gravel in the parking lot and the sounds of teenagers laughing as they climbed out of the trunks of cars surrounded them. Occasionally, friends honked their car horns at each other when they caught someone making out. In the back was a concession stand that reeked of day-old popcorn. Customers waited in line patiently to get their little box with the red stripes on the outside, and "hot buttered popcorn" inside. Kids played on a nearby swing set and teeter-totter.

Erick rolled down his window, hooked the metal speaker to the door, and twisted the volume knob, causing the sound to crackle and pop until he stopped. As Tom and Jerry filled the screen for the pre-movie cartoon, Erick slid the seat back and pulled Rachel in to lean on his chest as they shared the large driver's seat. She snuggled closer and watched the screen.

On the giant screen, Jerry hit the dog's leg and blamed it on Tom but Rachel was barely aware of the cartoon. She only thought about how good it felt to be in his arms, leaning her head on his chest as she had wanted to do for so long. The faint scent of leather drifted from him and she relished it, closing her eyes, and enjoying the moment. His head rested on hers and he took deep breaths, as if trying to take in every ounce of air around her. They had aligned, wanting the same things from each other at the same time. Still, they wanted more; they wanted everything. Touching and being in contact wasn't enough. They had to connect in every possible way. *Almost* every possible way.

In the past, her boyfriends had always done everything in their power to try to get under her clothes. She had always managed to stop them before they got too far. So, she knew to a certain extent what guys did and how to participate or to resist. However, beyond that, all she knew was rape. Violence. Logically, she knew that's not how it would be with Erick. It might not hurt since so many other people seemed to like sex. There must be something good about it.

Now, the urges in her body were unmistakable, though she had never felt anything like this before. She knew what she wanted. She wanted him, but at the same time, she didn't, for fear that whatever they did might conjure up images from the past, and of that monster. But every time they kissed, the need inside her became greater and greater, and at some point, resistance was going to be futile.

As he lightly ran his fingers up and down her arm, her back, into her hair and over her soft face, she surprisingly found herself yearning for that touch on the rest of her body as well. But he didn't. He was showing great restraint, knowing her nervousness. Under his gentle touch, she nearly fell asleep.

Finally, *Romeo and Juliet* started.

"Oh, geez. They're going to do the whole movie in Old English, aren't they?" she asked.

Erick laughed. "Yeah, but it's a lot easier to understand the movie than it was the book. Man, I hated reading that."

"Me too. I didn't understand half of it, honestly. Maybe more than half," she joked.

Then they heard something outside the car. Rachel started to scream but put her hand over her mouth to catch it. Then, her lungs stopped working, as if someone had knocked the wind out of her. She bent over her knees and rocked as she tried to suck in some air. At the same time, Erick turned to see a man with a flashlight standing outside the car door. As the man shone the light on them, they could only make out his silhouette.

"Everything okay in here?" the black figure asked.

"Yeah," Erick shouted, and then threw his arms around Rachel. "Oh no, baby, what's going on? Breathe, okay? Breathe out first. Breathe out."

"I...can't...." she mouthed.

He rubbed her back for a second, then picked her up and hugged her. She hid her face in his chest as he wrapped his arms around her. She finally started breathing again and gasped for oxygen. She whimpered as she tried to regain control of herself. He rubbed her back again as her whole body started shaking vigorously. "Shhh, it's okay. I got you. You're safe."

"What's going on?" the man said more firmly this time.

"Leave her alone, will you? Please?"

The man stood there, but turned off his flashlight. Erick tried to calm Rachel, but she knew the man was still there and continued shaking with fear. Erick glared at him for a second, and then whispered into Rachel's ear. "I have to get out for a minute and get this guy to go away, okay? I promise I'll be right back."

"No, don't tell him why," she cried softly.

"I won't, baby. I promise," Erick whispered with his lips on her earlobe. She reluctantly sat up, letting him go, but then bent down over her knees again. Erick kissed the side of her head and slid out of the car.

"Come here," he ordered. There was something familiar about this man, but Erick couldn't place him. The older man was wearing a theater uniform, complete with a grey hat that resembled Barney Fife's deputy hat. It gave him the impression the man was trying to seem more important than he really was. "Listen. You scared her. She's been through some horrible stuff, and you reminded her. Your standing here is making it worse. So can you please leave so she can calm down again?" He spoke firmly but quietly to avoid prying ears.

"Okay," was all he said. The theater worker stood still for a second, glanced into the car, and then crept away, wielding his flashlight. Erick shook his head and hurried back to the car.

"Okay, baby, he's gone." He wrapped his arms around her again as she started crying desperately with relief. She was finally able to calm down as he held her.

"I'm so sorry, I'm so sorry, I don't know what happened. It was his face…it was…it looked like…him." Rachel said between sobs.

"It was him? Or looked like him?"

"Yes. It looked like him. I think. Oh God, Erick. What if it was him?"

"Then, we need to call the police." Erick glanced in the direction the man had gone, but he didn't see him.

"No. I mean, I don't know for sure. It looked like him, but it might not have been him. God, please no."

"You want to go home?"

"Yes."

Her heart was still beating hard, and Erick could feel it against his chest so he continued to hold her in a bear hug to help her feel safe. "Okay, first, breathe deeply and slow down. You're going too fast. You're going eighty in a forty-five mile per hour zone," he joked.

She giggled and instantly her heart slowed to a more normal pace. "I am so happy you're here, Erick."

"Me too, baby. I love you."

He brushed his lips softly against hers. "I love you more."

***

A hint of energy, just a drop, bubbled inside her. It was enough to help her open her eyes, though the room spun as she did. She was so thirsty it hurt, but the hunger had given up on her days ago. How many days, she did not know. She had no idea how long she'd been in this smelly house, lying on this smelly bed.

She lifted her head. She was lying in a puddle of something. Blood? Urine? She mentally scoffed at herself. She hadn't had enough to drink lately for that. Suppressing a moan of sorrow and frustration, she squirmed to another part of the bed. Her arms were still tied to the headboard, but at least now they were together. He had gotten lazy and had tied them with one rope. Obviously, he didn't think her capable of untying herself in her state. He didn't know her very well.

Immediately, she went to work with her fingers, pulling at the knot. It didn't take long to loosen it, and then break free. From her last escape attempt, she knew that she couldn't go out the bedroom door again. He would probably be in the living room waiting for her. It was dark and quiet in the house, and felt like the middle of the night. But that meant nothing. He could be anywhere.

As she sat up, she peered out the window near the bed. She couldn't see the ground, which meant she was at least on a second story. The thought of jumping out and landing on the hard surface of the alley scared her, but she weighed the pain of a possible broken bone or two with the hell she was going through right now. If she broke both legs, though, she'd be out in the cold, naked, lying there in pain, unable to call for help lest he find her again.

Her eyes flicked to the closet where she had gotten the shirt she had worn the other day...or whenever that was. The long sleeves dangling in the moonlight gave her an idea.

Tie them together.

After checking the doorway, waiting for sounds in the house, she decided it was safe, and slowly slipped from the bed and to the closet. She took the shirts off the hangers without making a sound and set them on the bed. She found the other ropes with which he had tied her up previously, and used them to help join the shirts together.

Then she heard the most wonderful sound she'd ever heard in her life. A trash truck. It was far away, but it just had to come down this alley behind the house. It was a miracle! Holding her breath and checking the doorway again, she prayed silently for this to work. She tied one end of her makeshift rope to the headboard of the bed. Fortunately, the bed was close enough to the window so she could dangle her shirt rope out the window and climb down once the trash men got there.

Of course, she'd be naked, aside from the crusty layer of blood, but she hoped and prayed the trash men would help her despite her appearance. She'd had to use every shirt for her rope, and it still wasn't long enough for her to reach the ground.

Then, she nearly cheered when she saw the truck coming down the alley. Covering her mouth with her hand to keep herself quiet, she stood by the window, waiting for the perfect moment. She would have only one chance at this, for when she opened the window, he would hear and come running. She had to move fast. "Come on," she whispered to the trash truck, willing it to move faster toward her. It was two houses down when she decided she could not wait another second. She had to get out of there. Now.

With one final glance at the door, she threw the window open, then flung the shirt rope out. She heard stomping. He was coming. Grabbing the rope with everything she had left, she hurled herself out the window just as he came into the room. She slipped down to the end of the rope, but was still too high to jump. The monster began pulling on the rope and she was getting higher. She screamed for help as she saw the two trash men running toward her.

She'd have to make a choice. Wait until the men were below her and hope they could catch her, or let go now and fall to the ground. Before she could make up her mind, her hands decided for her, and gave out. She fell to the ground.

Rachel woke with a start and sat up sharply, breathing heavily, trying her best not to cry or panic from the leftover fear from her dream. She looked around. She was home. *Thank God.*

As she pulled herself together following the dream, she tried to picture the evil man's face, then the face at the drive-in. The flashlight in her face prevented her from getting a good look at him, but when she caught those eyes for a split second, she swore it was him. But, what if it wasn't? She couldn't put an innocent man in jail. She knew she had to be sure. Regardless, there was no way she was ever going to set foot at that drive-in again.

***

Erick's name was next to Chivalry's on the workout board in the barn. Rachel dropped her jaw and found her mother standing behind her. Julia dropped her shoulders.

"Mom..."

"I think it's best if Erick works Chivalry at least a few more times before he races. You guys ride similar, but he knows the difference. Trust me."

"Erick's going to ride him in his first race?"

"That's the plan."

"Okay." *Putting a new jockey on Chivalry?* Rachel knew her mother knew what she was doing. She had learned long ago never to question her mother about all things horse racing. Not because her mother punished her for it; Rachel had learned that her mom was usually right about things. Riding was Rachel's talent, while training was her mother's, and Rachel trusted her mother without question. And this meant Erick was going to race Chivalry!

With her hands clasped over her heart, Rachel watched Erick walk down the shedrow toward them. "What's up?" he asked, noting her expression.

"You're riding Chivalry today. You'll be racing him soon. Looks like you'd better get that license application going," Rachel answered as she wrapped her arms around him.

"What? Oh, man. Well, let's get to work." Erick eagerly led Rachel into the tack room to get their saddles.

Before she knew it, he had backed her up against the scarred wall of the tack room, with his lips on hers tightly, thrusting his tongue inside her. They moaned as they pressed their bodies together. She discovered his leg between hers, and the electric sensations shot through her. With his arm around her waist, he pulled her closer as he pushed his thigh up against her. Hers was in the same position for him, and she felt a lump against her leg. It was the sexiest thing ever that she had turned him on in this way.

Instead of being scared, as she had expected, she was so on fire for him that she didn't care if anyone walked in. She didn't care about anything but this feeling and she pulled him closer. He slipped his mouth to the nape of her neck, brushed his lips against the soft skin up to her ear, and a tiny cry of pleasure escaped her lips.

However, Rachel knew that Julia was waiting for them. Billy, too. Did her family wonder what they were doing in there?

Would they come in any second? Separating her lips from Erick's, reluctantly, she whispered, "They're waiting for us."

"I don't care," he replied, then dove for her neck again. She giggled and pushed him until he stopped, but she still wrapped her arms around him, reluctant to let go. He groaned into her shoulder, then straightened and pressed their foreheads together for a second. She fixed his hair, and he pretended to fix hers, though it was tightly braided in two long braids.

He sighed at his pants, "Down, boy."

Rachel laughed uncontrollably, so he tickled her.

Finally, they picked up their saddles and walked from the room. Julia flashed Rachel a look that said, "I know what you were doing in there." Rachel blushed and kept walking. "Oh, geez," she whispered under her breath.

***

It was a Saturday, and the Belmont meet had begun recently. Finally, they were able to watch races whenever they wanted. Erick, especially, wanted to watch, as he knew he might be riding some of these horses soon. He and Rachel went to the grandstand to watch and learn all they could about the horses.

Although she had always hated reading the past performances, Rachel knew it was time to get better at it if she were going to become a jockey one day. Jockeys always learned about their mounts before the race by studying how they ran in their last race and previous races. So, with Erick's help, they talked about each horse and compared them to the past performances in the *Daily Racing Form*. They then tried to predict each horse's outcome.

Rachel was surprised when they had guessed that the number two horse would take the lead and try to go wire to wire, but the number four would come up and snatch the race at the last second. In the next race, their predictions came true as well. Two in the row was good. But in this sport, unexpected things often happen.

In another race, one jockey flipped over the horse's head at the start as the horse fell to his knees coming out of the gate. The crowd gasped, but both horse and rider walked away unharmed. It was common for the horses to bump into each other regularly during the race, but a steward's inquiry was raised in the next race. One horse was disqualified for bumping and placed behind the horse that he had interfered with.

"He might get days for that," Rachel speculated.

"Probably three."

It wasn't unusual for a jockey to be suspended, depending on the severity of the accident or bumping, for three or more days. If the stewards felt as though the rider were careless or reckless, they were given a suspension. Even if a horse swerved on his own, the jockey could be suspended if the stewards felt that he did not work hard enough to straighten out his horse.

After the last race of the day, a stakes race, Rachel took Erick into the grandstand for a tour.

"It's amazing how little time I've spent inside this place since moving here. Do you come in here a lot?" Erick asked her.

"No, not too much. I've been to the betting area upstairs, the Belmont Café, and have been in the announcer's booth a few times. I also get to go places other people can't go and that's fun and exciting."

"Where else do you get to go?"

"Well, I'll show you."

She led him up every escalator until they were high up in the grandstand. The glass windows offered them a view of the entire racetrack, and Erick marveled at the enormity of it all. It was the largest track in the country and he could tell. From there, Rachel led him down a hallway where there were no people. Everyone had gone the other direction.

"Are we allowed to go this way?" he asked.

Rachel merely winked and kept going. The hallway stretched on forever, but they finally came to the end of the building. At the end was an enormous room. Rachel opened one of the doors and slipped inside. "This is the banquet hall."

"I see," he said, and suddenly knew why she had brought him here. Or at least, he hoped. "Show me around."

"Well, this is where they put the food," she said, pointing at a long row of tables covered with white tablecloths. "And this is where they put the tables where people sit," she said, waving her hand across the empty room. They came to a closet that was open, with stacks of chairs inside and one table. "This is where they keep the chairs." She led Erick inside, and as she held his hand, she placed it on her waist and faced him.

"This is where I lose my virginity," he joked. She laughed with one hand on her hip. "I know. I know. I'm joking. Don't worry."

She laughed again, covering her real thoughts. "I'm not worried."

He picked her up and set her on the table, then stood between her legs and held her hips. He leaned in and nearly touched her rosy lips, but stopped just a hair's width away. Rachel giggled softly, then touched her nose to his. He almost touched her again as he slid his lips over to her cheek, her jaw line, then the quickened pulse beneath her ear. One tiny and soft kiss at a time, he worked his way back to her now parted lips.

He sighed as he finally tasted her, then stepped closer to the table and pressed against her. She felt their clothes in the way, covering their heat, and almost wished she was free of them. Just as a fleeting thought passed through her mind about being with a naked man again, she sucked in air as he slipped one hand over her breast.

She wasn't ready for that. She wasn't ready for any of this, though she wanted to be. Her body wanted to be, but her mind couldn't let go and she was suddenly bombarded by memories of all the horrible things that man had done to her. The way he had touched her, had tried to kiss her with his ghastly ashtray mouth, the way he smelled. It came tumbling in like a wave over her, and she cried out in fear and pushed him away.

Erick's eyes were round, dark blue, and beautiful, yet haunted at the same time. His lips were swollen. His arms were outstretched as he tried not to touch her, and his jeans filled with lust and silently begged for attention.

"I'm sorry." She jumped down and into his arms again. Reluctantly, he held her until they both relaxed.

"What happened?" he whispered as he rubbed her back. It felt so good that an involuntary moan slipped out of her and into his chest.

"I, um, I started to see things. Um, you know. Things that happened. I'm so sorry, Erick. I know you're not him. I know it. I don't know why this keeps happening."

Just the day before, they had found a hiding spot in a shed near the track kitchen, reserved for tractors. They had kissed, touched one another, and it had caused images to flash before her. The images had come from nowhere, and she has been unable to stop them before they happened.

"I think I'm too eager. God, I want you so bad, Rach. It's my fault. We need to go slower."

She shook her head, but deep down, she agreed with him.

CHAPTER SIXTEEN

"She's done wonderfully, Mrs. McMahon. We've arranged for her to graduate with her class next week." Rachel's tutor turned to her and smiled. "How does that sound, Rachel?" The older woman put her hand lightly on Rachel's shoulder and looked upon her proudly, recognizing just how far Rachel had come emotionally as well as academically.

"I can't wait," Rachel answered, excited and worried at the same time. She still didn't do well with crowds, and was afraid of anyone being behind her. More so, she didn't want to run into Peggy again. Peggy was furious with Erick for breaking it off with her before prom. They had heard she never found another date, which made it much worse.

Erick was taking the brunt of Peggy's frustrations daily in school, and each day he arrived frazzled at the track in the afternoon. Rachel understood completely. Peggy could be ruthless. Still, he never complained.

"Hey," Rachel said, catching him as he arrived at the barn one afternoon. "Not much school left. You'll be done."

"What do you mean, 'you'll'? What about you?" he asked before grabbing her for a hug.

"I'm done. My tutor signed me off. No more school for me."

Erick pulled away so that he was face to face with her, and gave her a sideways grin. "Well, I only have a week to go anyway."

"She said she arranged for me to graduate with everyone." Saying those words sent butterflies to her stomach. Not only was she worried about dealing with Peggy, she was worried that she hadn't seen many of her friends for months. She was sure they were eager to talk to her and most likely hug her, but she just wanted to hide. And she especially didn't want to touch anybody but Erick while there.

"You don't seem too happy about it," he said, brushing his hand over her back.

"No. Not really. I'd like to do the whole graduation thing, but then again, I'm scared to death of people."

"Maybe we should practice."

"Practice? Practice what?"

"Being around people. We should go to Macy's. Or the Statue of Liberty. Or the Empire State Building. Some place where there are a lot of people. What do you think?"

Rachel thought about it. She didn't want to visit any of those tourist traps for the millionth time, and especially did not want to be around crowds. *Then again, facing fears is the best way to overcome them.* "What if I freak out?"

"I'll take care of you. I'll be there with you the whole time. Okay? And I know what to do if you do freak out. I talk to you until you come out of it. Right?"

Rachel nodded thoughtfully and reminded herself that it was time to be strong again. Jockeys are not weak. They're strong. They're brave. They live for adventure and thrills. That was the way she wanted to be. Not this fearful and shy person she was letting herself become. She drew strength from him through his eyes, and then nodded again, more confidently this time.

They agreed to try shopping first. "No train, though. Macy's will be bad enough. You'll have to drive me."

"Drive? Downtown?"

"Yes," she giggled. "Why not?"

"Parking? Traffic? Stoplights?"

Rachel fought the urge to snicker at the look on his face. "You scared?"

"Me? No," he laughed. "Of course, not."

"Then it's settled. We avoid the train and all those people. I'll help you find a place to park. I know a few secrets." Rachel winked at him. Erick raised one corner of his mouth in a weak attempt at a smile as he thought about driving in the most crowded part of the city.

***

"This your car? Or your parents'?" Rachel asked him as he held the door of his sleek, black GTO for her.

"Mine."

"What do you need with a car?"

"Check out the mileage."

As he walked around to the driver's side, Rachel leaned over to read the mileage on the dashboard. She covered her mouth to hold in her laughter when she found a bunch of zeroes, a six, and a five. But it was to no avail. She was already laughing when he slipped in and closed the door. He found her laughing so hard she couldn't speak. Erick lost control of his mock serious face and laughed with her.

When she finally slowed to a chuckle and a long, loud sigh, Erick shook his head. "Mom insisted on buying it for me. I told her people around here don't drive, but she didn't want me taking the subway. Too dangerous. But I wound up taking the train to Aqueduct last winter, and I'm still here."

Rachel's mouth and eyes opened as wide as her face allowed, prompting him to laugh again.

Finally, they were on their way, with Rachel directing him through the city and across the East River into Manhattan.

"Do you even know how to drive?" he asked her.

She tapped his arm and laughed, but answered, "Yes. I mean, I took Driver's Ed. in tenth grade but I haven't driven since I went in for my license."

Erick laughed, and Rachel shook her head.

"I'm going to have to take you out to reteach you, aren't I?"

"You might."

"You want to drive home when we're done?"

"No. No way. I'm not driving in the city. Are you crazy? I'd hit every car parked on the side of the street."

When they came to a stoplight, pedestrians just outside of their car walked a little too close for comfort. Rachel nonchalantly reached up with her elbow and locked the door. Erick glanced at her, noting the sheepish expression on her face, and decided to lock his door, too. She thanked him just as the light turned green. She felt a little foolish, but thought it better to be safe than sorry. You never know these days. Somebody might reach in and pull her out, or Erick, and steal the car with her in it.

The person behind them honked and swerved around them, irritated at Erick's careful driving. Rachel jumped high enough to scare Erick, and he jumped, too. She rolled her eyes and sighed as he chuckled at her. That angry driver only served to remind her of the volatile tempers of some New Yorkers. She wondered if it would be safe to get out of the car once they parked. Angry drivers, people everywhere, it just didn't seem safe to Rachel. After sneaking a peek at Erick, who seemed too relaxed given the circumstances, she told herself again not to be ridiculous. Erick felt safe. Maybe she should, too.

After directing him around the block twice, she finally found the nerve to allow him to park, and they found a place between two cars. Erick wasn't used to parallel parking. He had to try a few times, which angered other drivers as they waited behind him on the narrow street. Eventually, he fit the car into its spot.

Erick waited for the cars behind him to go around before opening his door, then got out and walked around to Rachel's side. Her hand was on the door handle, prepared to open it for herself, but in seeing so many people on the sidewalk, she froze. When Erick caught sight of her face, he wasn't sure if he should even open the door. But he had to get to her, so he opened it carefully and stepped directly in front of her, hoping to block her view for a moment to give her time to relax.

Her face was white, her breathing too fast. Her eyes darted back and forth as they scanned for danger. As she let loose a tiny cry of fear, she slapped her hand over her mouth. Erick held out his hand for her.

"I don't know about this," she said, trembling. "I mean, maybe we should have gone to Jersey or something."

"You can handle it, baby. You handle people at the track, right? There are people all over the backside."

"People I know."

"And one creepy guy in barn forty-two."

"There are lots of creepy guys around here. Check out that guy with the little balls hanging from his hat. What is that?"

Erick laughed as he tried to hide his face from the black man in a white bell-bottomed pantsuit, and what looked like a pimp hat, as he strutted down the street past them. Rachel laughed too as Erick stuck his face closer to hers inside the car to hide.

"Welcome to New York," Rachel said, now a bit more relaxed.

Erick held out his hand, she took it, and stepped up onto the sidewalk, feeling like she had won an enormous battle. As she gripped his hand, she spotted more people, and wondered what they were capable of. Erick wrapped his arms around her, setting her mind a little more at ease. Once he felt her body relax, they finally started walking.

"Have you ever been here?" Rachel asked as they walked by the Empire State Building.

"Yeah. Actually, my grandparents live around here. We moved here because my mom wanted to live close to them again."

"Your dad's parents are in Dallas?"

"Near there, yeah. We lived there my whole life, but moved here back in February."

Rachel was silent. *February*.

Fortunately, Erick kept talking, probably on purpose, and took her mind off the past. As they walked, Rachel held his hand and stayed as close as she possibly could. They had to pass people going in the opposite direction, as well as tourists stopping to take pictures with their Polaroids.

As they talked, Rachel learned that Erick's mother was from a wealthy family of real estate investors who had made their fortune investing after World War II when the market took off. His grandparents now lived in SoHo.

SoHo? Rachel couldn't believe it. She thought only movie stars and models could afford to live there. His father's parents, still in Texas, also had money, and when he described their ranch in northern Texas, she couldn't believe it. "Oh wow, I can't imagine getting on a horse and going wherever I wanted. All that open land. I don't even know what that's like. The biggest piece of land I've ever seen is the infield at Belmont. Or maybe Central Park."

"I'll take you there sometime, and we can run as long as you want. We can go anywhere."

She nearly teared up thinking of that much open space to ride in.

A man in a paisley button-down shirt rushed by, eagerly talking with someone, and bumped Rachel's shoulder. She turned cold as she eyed him sideways, expecting him to come at her. He apologized and kept going, moving on with his life as if nothing had happened. Rachel, though, thought her heart was going to explode from her chest. Erick pushed her closer to the building next to them. She leaned against the cool, stone wall as Erick shielded her from people walking by, and she tried to catch her breath.

"He's gone," Erick said needlessly. Rachel knew that, and told herself repeatedly that he wasn't trying to hurt her. She fought tears, bravely, and swallowed a lump of fear. Finally, she straightened and pulled away from the wall. Still hand in hand, they continued on their quest toward the giant store. It wasn't much farther.

Erick peered up at the tall building, and then at Rachel, who nodded his way. They went through the front door and found themselves in what most considered a shopping Mecca. Macy's. Rachel scanned the store for danger, and found everyone more focused on their shopping than on her. No one, absolutely no one, looked at her. Finally, her shoulders dropped and she lightened her grip on Erick's hand.

After an hour in the store, Rachel was encouraged that she hadn't been afraid. It was as if everything were back to normal again. The thought of being the way she was before was so exciting.

However, when Erick left her on an overstuffed brown couch in the furniture department so he could use the restroom, she fought against a rising panic from being alone. The restroom was close, but she stood and moved a bit closer, hoping Erick would come out soon.

A man came out and stopped in front of her. He ogled her up and down and whistled, probably thinking he had flattered her. He sauntered closer. Rachel wanted to melt into the wall and backed up until she was flat against it.

"Hey, little lady. Uh, you got the time?" he asked, now standing directly in front of her. He was so tall, her neck hurt to look up at him, so she opted for looking into his t-shirt clad chest instead.

"No. Sorry," she answered softly as she wished him gone. But he stayed.

"You lonely? How about we go..."

Rachel felt the blood drain from her head. She was about to faint, when Erick appeared from seemingly nowhere, walked between them, grabbed her hand, and pulled her away.

Fortunately, the man didn't follow or say anything else. Rachel wrapped herself around Erick's arm, staying as close as possible as he led her away from the man. Neither said a word until they reached the escalator and headed down.

"You okay?" he asked softly, leaning in closer.

She had been watching the floor the whole time, trusting Erick to lead them, and now she was staring at the silver escalator steps. Without a word, she nodded and leaned her head on his shoulder. She lifted her head and took a cleansing breath as she reminded herself how far she had come in the past few months.

It seemed a lifetime ago that she couldn't even handle standing in the barn without breaking down. Here she was now, in public, in a crowd of people, having to deal with strangers, and living through it all. With her eyes, she let him know that she was going to be okay. Erick wrapped his arm around her waist.

***

Graduation was difficult at first, as so many people wanted to talk to her. At the same time, it was so hectic that the busy-ness and confusion made it easier for her as the morning wore on. People were too busy to ask her too many questions about where she had been. She spent the morning helping friends with their hair and makeup, exchanging shallow small talk, and avoiding the subject she feared the most.

Occasionally, people asked if she was okay, and she always answered, "Oh yeah. I'm fine. Happy as a lark," or something similar. She knew that if she had gone back to school a few months ago, she would have said those same words, but they would not have been sincere. Now she knew that in saying those words, she could be.

Overall, being around her friends again was easier than she had anticipated. No one asked about the kidnapping directly, for which she was extremely grateful. Instead, they were more worried about themselves, for which she was also grateful.

Rachel latched onto Erick, leaning her head on his shoulder and relaxing. He wrapped his arms around her.

"You okay?"

After a nod into his shoulder muscle, she lifted her head. "Whenever you touch me, every bit of stress flies away."

"What are you stressed about?" he asked into her ear.

"Nothing, really. I guess I thought it was going to be harder but it's not. Everything's fine."

"Good." Erick pressed his lips into the side of her head.

"Oh, look. The wonder twins," they heard, and turned to face Peggy. Rachel and Erick said nothing, so Peggy rolled her eyes and left with a cackling new friend behind her.

Rachel shook her head. "You've been dealing with her the whole time like this?"

"Easier to ignore her, I've found. She won't stop. Ever."

Rachel silently snickered, knowing he was right. Immediately, they heard an announcement to line up and head outside.

They were seated on the football field in rows according to last name, so Erick was in front of her while Peggy was behind her. Rachel was glad for that, and when she stood to get ready to walk across the platform, she made sure not to look back at Peggy. She couldn't help but smile at Erick, who kept turning toward her from the front. He gave her the courage to stand up in front of the enormous crowd.

Just across the street, on the other side of the field, she could see her safe haven – the track. It was incredible to her how close she was to her school while at Belmont, and yet so far. Part of her wished she had forced herself to go back to school, while part of her was glad for her private tutor and the opportunity it had given her to avoid all of the crowds. She hadn't really been ready until this moment, just in time to walk across the stage with her friends.

"Rachel McMahon," she heard, and then started up the three stairs to the stage to meet the principal and receive her diploma. Sudden cheers and applause erupted, startling her enough to make her stop for a second. She wasn't sure they were cheering for her, but when the principal took her hand, she knew. For an embarrassingly long time, she stood on the stage, holding the principal's hand and peering out over the crowd in disbelief. It normally would have scared her to death to have everybody focused on her, but not now. Now she was hardly able to contain her joy, and a tear slipped from her eye as she found her mom in the crowd, also crying.

***

As joyful as her day had been, her nighttime was just as horrible. She woke up to find her pillow and sheets soaked with sweat. As she sat up and caught her breath, she tried to think back on the nightmare she had just had. Of course, she'd had this one before, and she knew being in a crowd today had triggered it.

The man had multiplied himself into hundreds of evil men, all smoking, choking her, laughing at her as she cried with pain. She had begged for the drug, whatever it was, because it always helped her escape into another world. Sometimes he would oblige and give it to her, but sometimes not. That's when the agony would rise to almost unbearable levels. In this dream, as in so many others, she lay in the sagging bad, staring at the yellowed ceiling, focusing on one crack in the plaster. She had used that crack to distract herself. She focused on it, memorized it, analyzed how wide it was, how deep it was. Anything to distract herself. The hours were never ending, but fortunately, her extreme hunger and dehydration, and later, blood loss, helped her sleep through much of it. It was strange to think that the very things that nearly killed her had been keeping her sane at the same time.

For months now, these nightmares had plagued her. Her diary was full of descriptions of the events, most of which were physically painful to put into words. As she thumbed through, she found only one page left. The padded purple cover with a tiny lock enclosed tattered pages, some full of doodles or scribbles, but most full of words. Horrible words. Each time she had written down a dream or nightmare, she had hoped it would help. She tried to convince herself that writing it was helping, but she wasn't sure.

CHAPTER SEVENTEEN

June 1969

After having lost ten pounds in order to make the weight, a skinny one hundred and five pound Erick dressed in his silks and tried to pass the time by playing cards with the others. They had accepted him as one of the guys, teasing him and shouting, "It's about time," or "Just try to stay on the horse, kid." Once the ribbing was over, they gave him pats on the back, hand-shakes, and well wishes before heading out to the paddock.

Though they wished him well, they all knew that once they hit the track, it was all about winning. Friends or not, they were all there with the same goal – to win. No matter what, they weren't about to give Erick a break because it was his first race. It was every man for himself. And every horse.

Erick's valet carried his saddle and pad for him. He didn't have his whip since he was a newly licensed rider, and was not allowed to use it for the first three races. That was okay. He didn't need it with Chivalry.

Rachel held Chivalry, and Julia stood by quietly as Billy took the saddle from Erick's valet and put it on the horse. All were silent because of their nerves, but also to give Erick plenty of space. His face reflected his tension and he was silent, knowing what he had to do and knowing he could do it well. All he had to do was ride the way he knew how to ride. The horse would do the rest.

Julia had told him that a win was not the most important thing here, which surprised him. It was also Chivalry's first race, so they were more concerned with judging his performance in a racing situation and creating a positive experience for him. Working out with other horses in the morning was one thing. A real race was another.

The race was six furlongs on the dirt and the track was fast. The short storms from the night before had had no effect on the track, thanks to the excellent on-track drainage system. Not many people were in the stands, just the usual railbirds.

Rachel mounted Old Guy and clipped a lead line to Chivalry's bridle as he stepped onto the track. Erick sat still in the saddle as he allowed her to lead his horse in the post parade. He let his legs hang down around the horse's girth in an attempt to relax as much as possible. Chivalry, like any horse, was quick to pick up vibes and feelings from his rider. Their goal was to keep him as calm as possible.

Tossing his head from time to time, Chivalry pranced with eagerness as Erick held on with his legs. Finally, he decided to put his feet in the stirrups and quietly slipped his toes in. He glanced at Rachel as he stood, straightening his legs. She clucked to her horse and led both horses off in a canter as they warmed up. Rachel was afraid to say anything because he was so quiet, but he broke the silence by speaking. "This is a dream come true, baby." Her heart warmed despite her nervousness for him.

"For me too."

"Nah, not yet for you. Soon, though. I'll make sure you get your chance."

Rachel wondered how he could possibly make that promise.

As they neared the gate, she reluctantly handed him over to the assistant starter. "Good luck. I love you."

"Love you." The corners of his mouth rose, then straightened. His thoughts were already back on the upcoming race.

Then, he was out of her hands. Rachel nervously watched them being led in circles behind the gate while they waited their turn.

Chivalry was ninth in the field of twelve. Erick's horse had always schooled well in the gate, but today he was fidgeting as the starter held his bridle tightly. Erick thought his own tension might be adding to the horse's nervousness, so he willed himself to relax. He gathered up a tuft of mane to help him hold on for the break. He never heard the announcer say, "The horses are in," but he knew the start was coming as he kept an eye on the other horses with his peripheral vision. He was ready; Chivalry was ready. Sitting as still as possible, he waited for the doors to fly open. *Any second now*. He felt as though he was waiting to be shot out of a cannon and into a war zone.

The gates flew open, the bell rang, and the horses were off. This was a two-year-old maiden race, so no horse in the race had ever won anything before, and many of them were running their first race ever, including Chivalry. The horses wobbled as they all found their running space. Their long legs appeared a little too long since their bodies and necks hadn't filled out completely yet, and the awkward colts bumbled down the backstretch, heading for Belmont's wide turn.

Erick had settled into a safe and easy fourth place. There was one colt ahead of him on the rail that almost tripped over himself as he changed leads without prompting from his rider. The others were further ahead. The colt in front of them wasn't budging, and Erick needed room to let his horse run. He didn't have much time left since it was a short race, so he took Chivalry to the outside and asked for more. The expected surge of power never came. He had run much faster than this in his morning workout the other day, and before that, too. What was the matter with him? Nothing felt off underneath him, the horse was travelling smoothly, and the kickback from the horses in front of them was almost non-existent now that they had angled out.

Erick felt the urge to use his whip, but as he didn't have it, he had to slap the horse's neck with his hand and shake the reins. As the horses in the lead tired and slowed, Chivalry drew even with them. Then he began to slow along with them. Chivalry refused to leave the other horses, even though Erick knew his horse hadn't even started running yet. He tried pushing on his neck in encouragement, but that wasn't working either. Chivalry continued to slow along with his new-found buddies. Under the wire, he came in second by a head.

Julia caught up with him and asked, "What happened? That was a terribly slow time for him. He could have done much better. Was he waiting for the stick?"

Erick shook his head and said, "He wanted to stay with his new friends, apparently. He didn't want to run and...well, I couldn't get him to fire. He didn't even try. No matter what I did, he just loped along."

"Ah, okay. We'll work on that. Don't worry. We can fix that," she said, calming down. "We have to run him again, another maiden race. I want to get him in something at Saratoga but he has to win first. Sorry, Erick, I need you to carry one eleven. You're so skinny. Are you going to be able to do it? If not, we can let you go over," Julia said, wincing. She hated contributing to the weight issues jockeys often have, but she didn't have much of a choice. Once Erick won a race, he could carry a few more pounds. Then, after he rode in forty races, he could get his full license and not have to worry about being ten or seven pounds lighter than the rest of the riders.

Erick replied, "Oh yeah, I can handle it. Don't worry about me. It'll be hard for the first few races, but it will get easier once I don't have to worry about that ten-pound allowance thing. I'm more concerned that I couldn't get him to put out any effort today. If you want to get a more experienced rider, I understand. Whatever it takes to get this guy to win."

"No, Erick, you can handle it, I have no doubt about that. This guy is a bit too friendly."

"You said it," he said shaking his head.

"Don't worry. We'll get through it. He's still immature and a little green. I have a good feeling about the next race, though. We'll run him in ten days to two weeks and see what happens."

"Sounds like a plan. We'll get it." Erick nodded with enthusiasm.

***

Chivalry's workout a few days later was on his own, and Rachel tried to stay away from other horses on the way to and from the track. She had to show this colt that he had social time and work time, and now it was work time. Fortunately, he did exactly as he was told, and worked well, responding when asked. Thinking back to other workouts, Erick remembered that Rachel had not touched Chivalry with the whip lately. Was it because he was distracted on crowded race days? Or did he prefer Rachel? Erick watched Rachel on him and knew she should be the one to race Chivalry. He seemed to respond to her better.

But what would the other riders think of her riding in races? A few other women around the country had tried it and had run into extreme resistance. They had hurtful words tossed at them, which only served to motivate them further, and things like food or rocks that hurt them physically. Men had even threatened to kill them. They had vandalized the girls' new changing trailers. For the first female jockey's first race, the rider had to have a police escort just to get to the paddock. What would happen here at Belmont? The same? Would Rachel get hurt?

Another jockey was standing on the rail watching a horse he was scheduled to ride soon. Erick asked the tiny but tough Hispanic man, "What would you think if Rachel were to get her license and ride Chivalry?"

The jockey made a strange face and said, "That's crazy, man. Girls don't become jockeys in New York. Too dangerous. She's tough, but not that tough. She'll get hurt way faster than any man out there. If you cared about her, you wouldn't let her race."

Well, I just had to ask. He was silent for a few seconds, not sure how to respond. Finally, he said, "She wants it so bad. Any of us could get hurt out there. We're all risking our lives. I think she'll get her license sooner or later. She's determined to get it one day. Not right now. I don't think she's ready, but she will be, and I don't want to stop her because it's something she wants so badly. She always has."

"You know her mom tried that and failed, right? That's why she's a trainer and not a jockey."

"Yeah, I know, but that was almost fifteen years ago. Things were different then. A lot different. These days everybody's pushing for equal rights and all that. She shouldn't run into the same discrimination her mother did."

"She *shouldn't,* but she will. Mark my words, if she gets that license, guys around here will be ticked. They don't want an overly emotional woman screwing things up in a race. They also don't want to have to worry about accidentally bumping her, or running over her if her horse falls or something. No. Take it from me, she doesn't want it. She doesn't understand."

Erick thought about it. He knew the older jockey was right, and that the others strongly disapproved of females in the business. The guys here assumed Rachel was a typical, overly emotional female. The issues she had been dealing with lately and her reactions certainly didn't help that image. If she started riding races, were they going to be mad enough to hurt her? Not only with words, but physically?

Rachel and Chivalry trotted up and greeted the two men. "Hi there, Mario. Erick," she said, winking at him and sitting in her saddle as her horse stopped. "He looks good. I think he's getting the idea. There's work time and play time, and he's learning the difference. Mario, you watch, next time he runs, he'll win." She nodded with confidence and allowed her anxious horse to head back home.

Erick savored the excitement emanating from her as he thought about her future as a rider. It was obvious Mario resisted that feeling.

"She's too confident," Mario said, watching her lope away. "Good rider, but she shouldn't think that way. He might not win and she'll be disappointed. Typical woman."

Erick was becoming irritated, so he decided to leave before he lost his temper. "Yeah, I'll tell her. Thanks, man."

***

"You're so good with Chivalry. You should be the one racing him," Erick told her, though his mind was somewhere else. He scanned her body, noting his favorite parts of her, categorizing them, ranking them, memorizing them. As he pulled her closer, despite the fact that people were everywhere around them, he pressed his lips against the side of her head and took in the faint scent of her flowery shampoo. The sound of her nearly silent moan rumbled in his chest. A spark ignited inside him and he felt his body spring to life.

One of her arms was around him and she drifted her hand from his hips, up his back, and to his shoulder. She squeezed his shoulder lightly and kissed him. Just for a second. Then they stood still, holding each other with their faces nearly touching, but denying themselves the pleasure.

He felt her strong, racing heartbeat, felt her breaths caressing his face, and relished in the fact that he was finally able to be close to her this way. As she angled her face, she nearly touched his lips, but resisted. The temptation was getting to him, and he was beginning to shiver with need.

"Rach," he whispered. Her eyes were closed now, but she moaned a tiny acknowledgment. "Let's go off track for lunch."

Tightening her hold on him, she nodded into his shoulder, and he felt a weight lift from him.

***

In the car, she held one hand as Erick steered his GTO from stoplight to stoplight. "This is why people here don't drive, isn't it?" he asked her, glancing her way for just a second.

She winked and nodded.

"But this way, we can go wherever we want."

She nodded again.

"And do whatever we want," he added as he winked.

She nodded, but her smile faded.

After searching for a private place, they decided on their school parking lot since school was out. He put the car in park, slid his seat back, and reached out for her. He took her hand, which was cold, despite the heat of the summer. The air conditioning blasted through the vents of the car, but it was still warm inside.

"I'll never force you to do something you don't want to do, Rach. I promise. I'm not like that animal."

Rachel tilted her head as she touched his arm, then she slipped onto his lap, straddling him. "I know, baby. I know. You're not like him and will never be like him. You're beautiful, kind, and so gentle with me. I will never equate you to him. It. The monster."

"Is that what you call him?"

She nodded.

He reached for her face and softly touched her with the backs of his fingers as to avoid his calloused fingertips, hard from work at the track. "He *was* a monster. But you're right. I'm not. I love you, and will always do everything I can to protect you. I promise."

She nodded an almost imperceptible nod, and then leaned into him. Wrapping her arms around his neck and the back of his head, she sighed softly as she touched her lips to his. She withdrew and kissed his bottom lip, his top lip, the corners of his mouth, his cheek, jaw line, and then felt his strong pulse with her lips on his throat.

He grabbed her shirt and pulled her body closer to his until they touched. Her kisses launched him into another world, one where it was just him and her luscious mouth as she tasted him. He relaxed for as long as possible before losing some of his restraint, and then swept his tongue in to meet hers.

As he slid one hand around from her back to her stomach, he felt a fraction of a second where she tensed, but then relaxed. Hoping for more, he slid his hand higher until it was just below her breast. He waited for a reaction, and found the one he wanted. She was breathing hard and anxious for him to touch her. His thumb slid over a hardened nipple, prompting an involuntary flinch from her, though she tried her hardest to keep their lips together.

He pulled back. "You okay?"

She nodded, but sought to reconnect with him, and pressed their lips together again. As he brought his other hand up in the same way, he felt her quivering as the heat rose between them. Was it fear? Or eagerness to be with him? He was not sure.

He was even more confused when she reached for his shirt to unbutton it, but stopped herself. With her fingers on his top button, she shook her head, though her fingers touched bare chest through the opening above the button. She caressed his smooth and hairless skin, drawing circles and swirls, tempting him and setting fire inside him.

He knew she was torn, just as he was, but he also knew he had to keep trying, for it could take months. Each time they kissed, his body screamed for more and more. It was becoming harder each time to stop when she needed him to stop. But he had to. He didn't have a choice. It was either this, or break her fragile mind and heart.

CHAPTER EIGHTEEN

Erick watched her from across a crowded barn. Her long curly hair bounced as she walked with her long-lashed eyes focused on him. He tried his best not to appear too eager for her. The others loved to tease him about the way he looked at her. They always had. And now that everybody knew they were together, it had gotten worse, as if somehow their relationship had given permission for everybody to tease them like kids on the playground in grade school.

As she drew closer, Erick nonchalantly scanned the area for those who might bother them. Not only were the jokes becoming annoying, he wanted privacy. However, on the backside of a racetrack, that was impossible. It had to be worse than any small town.

Finally, she was directly in front of him. They stood face to face as he ran his hands up her arms to her shoulders, and back down to her hands. With one final glance around their surroundings, he pulled her into an empty stall.

Snickering, they hid in a corner near the front and checked for people passing by. *Nope. All clear*. Erick sat against the corner and Rachel knelt next to him, facing him.

He knew what was going to happen, and tried his hardest not to get his hopes up again. Though, it had become increasingly difficult each time she had asked him to stop. He wondered if his frustration before they were together was easier to deal with than this. He had felt he carried the weight of a Clydesdale on his shoulders as he tried to hang on long enough for her to come around.

He searched her face, and knew again that he had to continue being patient and strong. Strong enough for her, and strong enough to keep his hormones under control.

As she touched his chest, she watched her fingers trace the ridges underneath his shirt. He loved when she did this, but at the same time, it drove him close to crazy. The need that she invoked felt like a lake of fire in his groin, and he did everything he could to keep the fire from getting out of control.

Finally, he pulled her closer for a strong and needy kiss. All that did was make it worse. His hands quivered, and all he could think about was how to get her to touch him the way he needed. The throbbing became painful. It was almost too much to handle. No, it was *definitely* too much to handle.

And for the first time, he pushed her away.

Rachel knew instantly why he withdrew from her. He didn't have to tell her. She knew.

"I'm sorry," she whispered. "I'm so sorry." She noticed he did not look her way. He was obviously frustrated, which made her feel like a heel. It was all her fault.

"It's okay, Rach," he answered as he ran his fingers through his thick hair. She suppressed the urge to fix the lock of hair that was now out of place and sticking out awkwardly. He thumped his head against the wooden wall of the stall as she bit her lip with embarrassment and shame.

"Sh-should we, um," she started to ask, but stopped herself by shaking her head, as if answering her own question.

"Should we what?" Finally, he met her gaze, and it was such a relief that she nearly laughed.

She took his hand, held her breath, and shook her head again. "Nothing."

Rachel was so afraid of disappointing him. She wanted desperately to give herself to him fully just to make sure he did not get too frustrated and leave her. *What about the memories? What if they come all at once?* So far, it had been gradual, and she had only had to fight one bit at a time. All at once might send her over the edge. She didn't think she could do it. However, most of all, it pained her terribly that she had hurt him like this. She had to do something.

"Erick," she started. When he didn't reply, she continued, "I want to try again. I want to try as many times as it takes. I want to be with you so badly, it hurts. But I know it hurts you, too, whenever I get afraid. I don't know what to do about that. M-Maybe we sh-shouldn't, you know. Kiss. Or anything."

And go back to the way it was before? No way. Erick knew that he was not strong enough to deal with that again. Having had a chance to taste her and be with her, at least this much... *No way. I would die, maybe literally.* "Rach, I cannot handle going back to that. But I think I have an idea."

"Anything." She shifted closer to him.

"I read something in one of my dad's medical magazines about how vets are dealing with life after the war. It might work for you." He sat up straight as hope and excitement coursed through him. "You need to talk about it and deal with the violence in a controlled situation rather than waiting until we're...you know. Hot and heavy. It's better to deal with those memories when you're talking and not making out or something. I want you to tell me everything. And I mean, everything. Because, obviously, it's not working this way."

Fear of telling him about it released a flood of tears, but she knew he was right. Erick was always right. She also knew he would be there to pull her away from the edge if it was too hard. He had done it before and all he had to do was talk to her and hold her until she realized where she was again.

She nodded, though reluctantly.

***

Erick's mother had gone out to a charity event while his father was at work. Rachel told her mother they were going to lunch again, but they went to Erick's house in Floral Park, also near the track.

He parked the car in the garage, and then opened the car door for Rachel.

"I've never parked a car in a garage before," she joked as she stepped out into a two-car garage. A door in the back of the garage connected it to the house, making it near impossible for neighbors to figure out that he had sneaked a girl in while his parents were not home. Erick chuckled as he led her inside.

Goodness, look at this place, Rachel thought. The house was not large, as space in the city was scarce, and homes were only so big, but it was impeccably decorated. It resembled something out of a magazine to Rachel.

"Did your mom hire a decorator?"

"Yeah," he answered, as if it should have been obvious.

They walked into a formal living room with parquet floors, a huge, furry white throw rug, and a perfect and seemingly untouched couch surrounded by a coffee table and two end tables. The matching lamps framed the setting perfectly, as if someone had measured the exact and perfect locations of each piece for it to be uniform and symmetrical. A large starburst mirror hung on the wall above the couch and a grandfather clock adorned another corner of the room. A long, wooden hi-fi stereo cabinet sat just under the bay window.

"Things don't fit in this house as well as the last one. Our last house was bigger."

"Well, I just cannot be seen in a house of this size," she joked as she flapped her hand in the air, and then laughed at his reddened face.

"It's not easy for the rich kids, either, you know," he answered, and playfully stuck his tongue out at her. She threw herself into his arms and he obliged by squeezing her. "Okay, let's sit down."

She blew out a breath, hoping to relieve some of her tension. She grasped the notebook he had told her to bring, and her diary. Her innermost thoughts. She couldn't believe that she was about to share these painful experiences with him, to talk openly and graphically about what had happened to her, but most of all, it was surprising that it did not bother her as much as she expected it to. What bothered her most was that she was going to have to remember things, confront them, and somehow figure out how to send them packing. Was it even possible?

He had told her to write down everything in one place, not disjointed like in her diary where she had written down dreams as she had them. Instead, her assignment was to write the entire story from start to finish.

It had taken her a week, and tons of tears, but she had done it.

They sat together on the couch. He slung one arm around her shoulders, pointed at her books, then touched her nose. “You ready?” he asked.

Pursing her lips, she answered, “I guess.”

“Candy and I walked to her house from the movie theater at about 10:00...”

CHAPTER NINETEEN

Erick held her tight, unable to hold in his tears any longer. The respect he had for her increased tenfold, and he was so proud of her strength that he told her repeatedly how honored he was to know her.

"You've helped me so much, Erick. If it weren't for you, I'd be in an insane asylum right now."

"It wasn't because of me, baby. You were already healing when we first met."

"You inspired me to keep going. I looked forward to being with the horses again, but I looked forward to being with you more."

"I love you," he whispered, and kissed her forehead. When he released the kiss, he held her close. He wanted to be with her in this way all the time, close, and not just physically. They had a connection deeper than anything he'd felt before. Peggy and other girls had tried to force this feeling on him, making him want to run in the other direction. With Rachel, though, it was not only natural, it was irresistible. He wanted to be with her, always.

"I love you, too," she whispered in reply, and squeezed his ribs.

He sighed, then spoke again. "I hate to say this, but I think the more you read this, the better you will feel. The story won't sound so scary after a while. It's like a horror movie where if you keep watching it over and over, it becomes less scary over time. Right?"

She nodded.

"It will happen, baby. I know it. It works for vets and it'll work for you. You'll be over the nightmares and flashbacks soon. Real soon."

"I hope so. I'm tired of being this timid and afraid person. That's not me."

"I know. I can tell."

"How is it you can tell who I am through all this fear?"

"You're not always afraid. When you're riding, you're so brave and strong. That's you, too."

"Yeah," Rachel mused. "That makes sense. I do feel that way. But it's also when I'm with you. You make me stronger."

"That's because we belong together."

"You believe in fate?"

"Yes. I do now. It's as if we're on the same path together, and we are meant to be on this path. Do you ever feel that way?"

"I do." Lifting her head, she sucked on his bottom lip, lighting him with joy. "I can't believe I'm so lucky to have you. You're the best looking guy in the world, and the sweetest, most caring guy in the world. How did I deserve this? Are you real? Or am I just imagining all of this?"

"Do you feel this?" He tickled her ribs, and she squealed as she squirmed and writhed. He wrapped one arm around her and pushed her flat onto the couch as she continued to giggle.

CHAPTER TWENTY

Ten days after his first race, Chivalry was entered in another maiden race and Erick had to make sure his weight was low enough to fulfill all of the allowances. He still had to be careful with his diet, even though he naturally weighed less than some of the other jocks. He felt lucky to be only five feet tall, too, because it still meant an easier fight to maintain a constant one hundred and fifteen pounds over his career. What used to be a curse back in school was now a blessing.

A seven-horse field paraded to the gate in the backstretch, preparing for a six-furlong run on the dirt. Once in and all horses were ready, Chivalry broke well. He ran comfortably and easily for most of the race, able to stay out of trouble by avoiding being closed in. They stayed in third for most of the race. When Erick let him go as they rounded the turn, Chivalry sped up, but only until he drew even with the horse in front of him. Erick had finally raced in enough races to use his whip, so he twirled it from under his arm and raised it just above the horse's shoulder. He gave his horse a few taps, but nothing happened. They were running out of room. The horse in the lead had slowed, and Chivalry and his new friend passed him. Erick switched his whip to the left side and tried hitting him in stride. Chivalry was surprised and pushed himself forward just enough. Under the wire, they won by a nose. Chivalry had broken his maiden, and so had Erick.

Rachel rode up on their lead pony and helped slow an eager Chivalry. Erick was beaming from ear to ear. "You did it, babe. Your first win!" Rachel could tell that he had forgotten about the initiation ritual for new jocks who won their first race. She certainly wasn't going to remind him. She hoped he wasn't reading her mind again. With her lips drawn into a wicked grin, she wished she were a man for the next few minutes so she could watch.

After the celebration in the winner's circle, Erick headed toward the locker room, still unaware of his impending doom. Just before he walked in, he was accosted by several jocks who dumped a bucket of root beer on him. Then, in the jocks' room, they came at him with bottles of baby powder, clouding up the entire room and choking them. They were laughing so hard they were unable to talk or even see straight.

After cleaning powder from his ears, he finally made it back to their barn to find everyone standing in front of Chivalry's stall. Even the horse was peeking over his door. Each and every person he saw had their hands behind their backs. Erick didn't see any root beer or powder, but he froze in his tracks well away from the motley crew. Willy, Julia, Rachel, Billy and several others all raced toward him, but he spun around and took off running.

Rachel yelled, "Honey, come back," but he never slowed. They made it all the way to the track kitchen when they finally caught up to him and sprayed Reddi-Whip all over him. Erick screamed with laughter as he grabbed the can from Rachel and sprayed her with it. In the end, it was all over every one of them, the bushes, and the ground, angering the staff inside the kitchen.

***

"Erick, I'm nervous."

"Aw, come on. I've met *your* mom."

Rachel tilted her head. "That's different."

"Come on. They're just normal parents. That's all. Don't worry. They're very nice." He started to open the front door to his house, but she stopped him.

"But I'm not, you know, I didn't grow up learning how to be proper and all that."

"They don't care. Trust me. They're very down to earth."

"Will you tell me which silverware to use? Oh, I'll just watch you. I'll do what you do." Rachel nodded confidently.

"Go from the outside, in. But we're only going to have forks and knives, anyway. I'm sure she didn't make a whole seven course meal." He tried to open the door again, but she stopped him.

"Does she cook? Or do you guys have a chef?" Rachel thought it was funny when he messed up her hair, but then she realized that it had been transformed into a rat's nest. "Erick!" she scolded quietly, then ran her fingers through her curls, trying to tame the knots he had just made. Her fingers became stuck several times, and she panicked. "I can't do this."

"Nonsense. Here." Erick helped her with her hair, then pulled her in front of the glass window on the side of the door so she could see her reflection.

"Okay. Oh, wait. If I do something wrong, just kick me under the table."

Erick playfully rolled his eyes and took her hand, then opened his door. Diane Bennett, Erick's mother, greeted them with open arms. Even so, Rachel still felt as though she might throw up. It was a good thing Mrs. Bennett was wearing an apron over her blue dress.

"Pleased to meet you," Rachel said, then attempted something like a curtsey. Out of the corner of her eye, she saw Erick's face fill with surprise, and she froze, but thankfully after she had straightened again.

"Oh, you're a doll. Come in, please," Mrs. Bennett offered.

Rachel had been here before, but couldn't let on. She looked around. "You have a lovely home, Mrs. Bennett."

"Thank you, Rachel." Mrs. Bennett offered drinks, then invited Erick and Rachel sit in the kitchen while she finished dinner. "Your father will be home soon, Erick."

"Okay."

"Rachel, I suppose Erick's told you about his jump from a fairgrounds racetrack to the most prestigious track in the country?"

"Yes, he's told me a little. You know Erick. He doesn't really like to talk about himself. Every time I try, the subject somehow winds up on something else." Rachel winked at Erick. He took her hand.

"That's Erick, all right. Modest and unselfish. I'm not just saying this because I'm his mother, though I could be biased. I think he's become quite a young man. Mature, smart, empathetic and caring. Rachel, you are one lucky girl."

Erick blushed and dropped his head to hide his face. Rachel ran her fingers through his hair to fix an out of place lock.

"I agree, Mrs. Bennett. I completely agree."

Erick was glad to hear his father coming in from the garage because it meant they could change the subject. Erick's father came into the kitchen and Erick introduced Rachel to him. By now, she was feeling more confident and made sure to grip his hand tightly when they shook hands.

"Quite a grip you've got there," Dr. Bennett remarked.

"Thank you," Rachel answered proudly.

Dr. Bennett sat with them at the table, then leaned forward toward Rachel. "Erick tells me you ride horses, too."

Rachel relaxed even more at the mention of horses. This was something she could talk about for the rest of the evening, if given the chance. "Yes. Sir. Um, I do. I exercise my mom's horses in the mornings."

"Do you two ride together on the track for these workouts?"

"Sometimes, yes."

"Erick has always wanted to be a jockey. I hear girls are riding races now, too. Is that something you want to do, too?"

Rachel's heart soared. "I feel like that's what I'm meant to be. Like it's in my destiny or something. I can't imagine doing anything else."

"Dangerous work."

"Yes, but we all go in knowing that. We try to be careful and avoid accidents, but we accept that sometimes things happen." Rachel shrugged. "Broken bones aren't all that bad. They heal."

Dr. Bennett sat back. "They seem pretty bad to me."

"It hurts. Sure. But people heal. I mean, as long as the accident isn't too bad, most of the time, we're okay."

"Have you broken many bones?"

"From a fall off a horse, just once, actually. Lots of cuts and bruises, but only a broken arm."

"Erick's broken his arm and got kicked once. Broke a rib."

Erick nodded. "That hurt."

"But he's not afraid of it happening again." Dr. Bennett shook his head. "Crazy kid."

"If you ride enough, you're going to have something happen sooner or later."

"How old were you when you broke your rib?" Rachel asked.

"Twelve. It was at my grandparents' ranch."

Rachel imagined him falling from his horse and being left in the middle of a giant field all by himself, no one to help. "What happened?"

"We were herding cattle and my horse stopped without telling me. Well, without me telling him to. I flipped over his head, or so I was told, I don't even remember it. Then the horse kicked me and ran off. Wasn't very nice of him," he remarked, rubbing his rib.

Rachel winced. "Ouch. Did someone help you?"

"Oh, yeah. I got up. Didn't realize it was broken until later. Dad, of course, felt it and knew it was broken, so I went to the emergency room."

"Yeah, which was, unfortunately, an hour away," Dr. Bennett added.

They compared past injuries before dinner with Rachel avoiding anything to do with her kidnapping. That would be a major topic, she knew, and definitely not good dinner conversation. Besides, she didn't want to talk about it, anyway.

Later, though, Erick had promised to sneak her into his father's office where they could look for information on dealing with nightmares. Erick had read a little about it, but Rachel wanted to know more. She wanted to know everything about any treatment there was available besides shock treatments. Erick assured her they didn't do that anymore. Her mother had said the same thing, so she let her mind relax about it. At least she wouldn't have to endure that.

Dinner was delicious, Rachel thought, and had told Mrs. Bennett numerous times. Mrs. Bennett offered to share her recipes with Rachel. She graciously accepted, but knew with certainty that she would never be able to make these things. Rachel could not bring herself to admit her faults in the kitchen as she remembered burning things like grilled cheese sandwiches, eggs, or boiling soup until it was completely evaporated, leaving nothing but burnt remnants fused to the bottom of the pot. She'd even melted the bottom of a copper bottomed pot before. That was something she wasn't about to bring up, though.

Fortunately, the subject turned to riding horses again.

"Erick's told us all about this horse your stable has now. What's his name? Chivalry, right? Yes. He seems to have a lot of potential," Erick's father mentioned.

"Yes, he does. He just won his first race."

"Oh, yes, Erick mentioned that it was his first win, too."

Erick and Rachel laughed, remembering the whipped cream initiation. Erick had told his parents about it, of course, and they shared a laugh about it again.

"It was tough getting him to pass the other horses, though. He's capable, but friendly, and would rather stay with his herd. He doesn't want to be in front."

"He didn't want to win?"

"No. Somehow we're going to have to fix that."

After dinner, they watched television together, but Rachel was anxious to check out that library. She whispered in Erick's ear. "How are we going to do this?"

Without answering, Erick asked his father, "Dad, we're going to sit by the pool, okay?"

Dr. Bennett was half-asleep in his chair while his wife intently followed Walter Cronkite's every word. NASA was getting ready to send men to the moon. "Fine," Dr. Bennett mumbled.

Erick led Rachel to the back door, fortunately out of line of sight of his parents. He opened it and closed it again without going through. Rachel held her breath to keep herself quiet as she followed him down a hallway. They came to a room completely filled with books, from floor to ceiling, and on every wall. Rachel filled with awe and she went right to the shelves to touch them. The wooden shelves matched the floor, which matched the trim around the windows of the curved wall behind the desk. Between the bookshelves were cushioned benches and pillows, perfect for reading.

"Oh, wow," she whispered, touching a sculpture of an elephant on one shelf.

Erick flashed her a quick smile but went right to work. He pulled out a stack of magazines. "This is where I found that article on the vets. In here, somewhere." He thumbed through a magazine while Rachel looked over his shoulder. Finally, she picked one up herself and began searching.

Erick found one article, left it open, and sat it aside. "Keep looking. Let's get as much as we can, then take them somewhere else to read them. He doesn't like me in here."

"Why not?" she asked, still leafing through.

"I don't know. Some silly rule he's had since I was a kid. I mean, come on, I'm eighteen years old. You'd think he would trust me not to break anything by now."

Rachel nodded and glanced at him, then went right back to her work.

After they had stacked several magazines and books on the floor, they put the rest back on the shelves, just the way they found them. While Erick was straightening one section, Rachel glanced at the article on top.

"**Are rape victims really victims**?"

The headline horrified Rachel and she was suddenly swept with anger. She had to read this one and yanked it closer. *How dare they say such a thing?* She skimmed quickly past the introduction to get to the meat of the article.

"Women of today are promiscuous. They dress provocatively to attract men, and it works. Unfortunately, when men give them the attention they crave, they pretend not to enjoy the attention. In turn, this frustrates men, who then fall victim to their testosterone. Sometimes they lose control..."

Rachel's eyes widened more with every word. She shook her head as she covered her mouth with one hand.

"What is it?" Erick asked.

"I-I can't believe this. How could they say such a thing? I wasn't dressed provocatively. I was in a coat. Mittens. Boots..." Without warning, the memory of walking in Queens that night flooded over her. The room darkened and she was suddenly on that street, a van approaching from behind. *The man inside offered to give her a ride home. When she refused, he became agitated. When she started running, he went crazy, chased her, trapped her, then...*

"Rach? Rach? Wake up." Erick patted her face. "Come on, Rach?"

She awoke to find herself lying on the floor of Dr. Bennett's office, wondering how she had gotten there. But she knew – it had happened too many times before. Erick was holding her hand and brushing the hair from her face. She gripped his hand and sat up.

"You okay? You sure you want to sit up?"

"I'm fine. Like all the other times," she added waving her hands in frustration, then slapping them onto her legs.

Erick's touch comforted her as he brushed a tear away with his thumb.

"That article, Erick. It's teaching doctors that women are asking for it. I didn't ask for that man to beat me, or rape me, or tie me up like that. I nearly died!" Rachel began sobbing and Erick held her close. "My mom would have lost me too. I would never have seen my family again. He almost killed me and I didn't ask for it. I didn't want it. I didn't deserve it!"

"No, baby, no. You didn't deserve it. That article is wrong. You did nothing to provoke him. He was crazy."

Rachel nodded into his shoulder. "It wasn't my fault."

"It wasn't your fault," Erick affirmed, and tightened his hold on her.

They heard footsteps approaching on the wood floors. Erick loosened his grip on Rachel. He looked up to see his father, then lowered his gaze, defeated. Rachel hid her face from him.

"How much did you hear, dad?"

"Enough."

Much to their surprise, instead of being upset with Erick for being in the office, Dr. Bennett stooped down to meet them on the floor. He touched Rachel's shoulder. "Rachel, no, it wasn't your fault. Erick's right. That article is wrong. Just because the writer said that doesn't mean it's true." Rachel wiped her face with already wet hands. Erick pulled some tissues from a box on the desk. She took them gratefully. "I remember your story from when we first moved here. Horrible. It's a miracle you're still with us. It must have been very traumatic."

Rachel nodded, sniffed, and wiped her face again.

"Rachel, I can help you with this, if you want."

Sudden relief washed over her and she wiped away fresh tears. "How?" she asked, looking up at Dr. Bennett.

"I have a friend. She's a psychiatrist. I can give you her number. She's is good at helping with things like this. I'm sure she can help you."

"But Dad," Erick started. He stopped, but then hesitantly continued. "Her mom can't..." he stopped himself when he saw Rachel's expression. He knew she didn't want him to say it. But he had to. He tried to apologize silently. He tried to tell her to trust him. He hoped she could read his mind as easily as he could read hers. He looked away, not able to stand the look on her face another second. "They can't afford it."

Rachel's face contorted into an angry scowl and her bottom lip thrust out, just enough to make Erick want to kiss it and make her feel better.

"Don't worry about the cost, Rachel. We'll work something out."

Rachel glared at Erick for another second, then hesitantly turned to Dr. Bennett again. "Work something out?"

Dr. Bennett nodded. "Yes. As in, you won't have to worry about a thing."

"Oh, no, I couldn't."

"Yes, you could, Rachel. I insist."

Erick had relaxed and he finally met Rachel's gaze as Dr. Bennett stood to go to his desk for the phone number. Rachel looked a little less apprehensive now, and looked as though she may forgive him for his comment. He hoped, anyway. When he took her hand, she didn't pull away. That was encouraging.

Rachel had to ask for details, though. As Erick drove her home that night, she couldn't stop herself. "What did he mean by that?"

"By what?"

"You know. He said I won't have to worry about a thing. Will the doctor do it for free? Or is your dad paying for it?"

"I don't know." Erick glanced at her. He really didn't know what his father meant, but at the same time, did not want to find out. If his dad were paying for it, Rachel would surely find out, and then refuse the treatment. "He probably meant she would do it for free."

"Okay. Good. If your dad pays for it, though..."

"I know. But, you know, doctors give free treatment all the time."

"For charity."

Erick didn't see it, but heard the eye roll in her voice. "It's not charity, Rach."

"Yes, it is."

"It's not. But even if it were charity, why not accept it? It's like refusing a gift. You'd be saying no to something that could change your life. For the better, even. And I know that whether he's paying or she is, it is a gift. Would you say no to that gift?"

"Gift," she repeated.

"Gift."

Rachel thought about it from that aspect. Refusing a gift is rude. They would be disappointed if she did not accept it. And besides, Erick was right. This could change her life. "Okay. I'll do it."

***

Now that Chivalry had won a race, he qualified for an allowance race at the end of July at Saratoga, five hours north. They stayed at Belmont and drove up for the race that morning.

In the tree-lined paddock before the race, Julia went over her instructions with Erick. "Keep him on the lead, if you can. Keep him far enough away so he doesn't focus on them." Julia inspected the blinkers, a hood with small eye cups, which she hoped would keep him focused ahead. This was his first race with the blinkers and she knew it was going to be one of two reactions with Chivalry – he would either slow so he could see the other horses in front of him, or the blinkers would keep him focused on the track ahead, and he would run the way he so loved running.

With his ears pricked, Chivalry shot out from the gate, ready to run. After a perfect break, he hopped to the lead right away and stayed there. Other horses tried to keep up, but they wound up slowing down while Chivalry ran at the same speed for each quarter. As a result, Erick never had to show him the whip, never had to hurry him. He ended up winning by nine lengths, hardly breaking a sweat. The blinkers worked.

Erick cheered and laughed with joy as he patted Chivalry's neck. As they slowed, Erick marveled at Chivalry's run. *This horse is amazing*. Normally, horses slowed down each quarter, but he was able to keep up a steady pace without even being pushed. There was no way he could lose if he kept that up.

The press swarmed Julia when they realized Chivalry's times, knowing that Erick wasn't pushing his horse at all.

"Honestly, guys, I don't know. He's doing great now, but I will never try to predict the future when it comes to horses. Things can change on a dime. Right now he's doing well, I know that much. I've never had a horse like this in the fifteen years I've been a trainer. I must admit, I'm enjoying his success, but I'm also prepared for anything. I won't get into what could happen." Julia wasn't about to remind them of all the little things that might take a racehorse out of commission. It would be bad luck to even think about those things.

***

Later, driving home from a celebratory dinner, Rachel and Erick stopped along the river to enjoy the lights of the city.

"It's beautiful," Erick remarked as they took in the skyline across the river and the reflections on the water. The sparkles in the river made it seem so clean. Nothing like it was during the day. When Rachel didn't reply, he caught her watching him. He took a moment to drink in her beauty. Everything about her was the most gorgeous work of art he'd ever seen. Porcelain skin with a few freckles, cute little Irish nose, slightly turned up, and of course, her eyes. He loved her eyes. They were so expressive. He could read her mind just by peering into their depths. He reached for her, but she was too far. He slid his seat back and pulled lightly until she was on his lap, facing him, straddling him.

The riverside trees in the moonlight shadowed their bodies, but he focused only on her face as he reached for her. He trailed his fingers up her silky, soft arm, prompting goose bumps in their wake. He followed the lines of her shoulder to the base of her throat, then to the hollow crater between them. He traced its circular shape and drifted down lazily between her breasts. With one hand, he unbuttoned her first button, studying her, taking in her reactions. When she didn't stop him, he unbuttoned one more. His other hand moved up her side, pushing her shirt out of the way. His thumb searched for bare skin and found it. When he touched the ridges and scars on her belly, she flinched and became stiff.

Inch by inch, he flattened his palm to her side and slid his hand to the front, over her scars. Rachel tried to remind herself that he did not mind her scars. He accepted her this way. Despite knowing this, she was incredibly self-conscious and wanted him to stop. Yet, she didn't.

Without warning, a flash of the knife that had caused those scars appeared before her. Erick hesitated as she shook her head to rid herself of the rusty blade. It worked. It was gone, and Erick resumed his slow and soft movements. The way he was worshiping her body turned her on more than anything. His barely-there touches only served to make her want more.

When he unbuttoned more buttons, he was slow and careful, still taking in her reactions, knowing she was scared, but also knowing she wanted to share herself with him. By the time her shirt was completely opened, her chest heaved, partly from fear, partly from her eagerness for him to touch her.

Absorbing everything bit by bit, his eyes followed his hands again down to her scars. He traced each one with his softest touch, replacing the knife with him. The purple marks ran from underneath her bra down into the waist of her pants. Overwhelmed at the sight and thought of what she had gone through, he shook his head and scowled at the scars with a frustrated tear in his eye. "I'm so sorry, Rach," he whispered.

"Sorry?" she asked. She grabbed her shirt and pulled it closed again. Was he going to dump her? Had he decided now that she was too ugly? *No, not him.*

Erick was calm and slow as he reached up to her hands, keeping his gaze on hers. As he lowered her hands again, her shirt fell open. "That you had to go through this. It's...it's not right that he did this to you. I've never wanted to kill someone. Until now. He deserves it. Or better yet, he deserves whatever punishment they put him through in prison."

"If they ever find him."

"They will. They will." As he touched the scars again, Erick thought about that man marking her like this, trying to make her his possession. Erick's eyes narrowed with hatred, but he wiped it away as he tried his best to stay positive for Rachel.

"I can never wear a bikini again," Rachel said, lowering her head.

"My dad's a doctor, Rach. Maybe he can fix it. Maybe there's some sort of medicine to help it heal better. Maybe soon they'll go away."

She merely shrugged, refusing to give herself hope, afraid to be disappointed. Her thoughts were swept away as Erick resumed his movements, and she only focused on his hands, and how good it felt. His hands not only felt good, his acceptance of her felt good, too.

With both hands, he smoothed over the soft, ivory skin on her chest. "You're so perfect," he whispered. Did he truly feel that way? Or was he trying to make her feel better about herself? That thought also vanished the instant he reached the top of one breast, and then drifted his fingers lower and lower, tracing the shape of the tiny bump beneath her silky bra.

Her chest heaved as he cupped her in his hand. She sucked in air and closed her eyes as his thumb made circles, each one like a vortex, spiraling her body deeper into need for him. When he leaned in and replaced his thumb with his tongue, she cried out, raked her fingers through his hair, and held on for dear life.

With his hands free, he slipped her blouse from her arms and let it fall to the floor. She arched her back as he slid his hands up her back, unhooked her bra, sliding the straps off her shoulders and down her arms and then tossing it on top of her blouse. With her breathing still ragged, her eyes wild with need, she reached for his shirt. Sliding it up his rippled chest, as if savoring every moment, she watched as inch by inch, his sculpted chest came into view. He allowed her to lift his shirt above his head, and toss it onto the pile on the floor behind her.

Her fingers drifted down his pecs, to his abs, to the slanted muscles on his hips that pointed into the waist of his jeans, beckoning her to follow their lines. Oh, she wanted to, but she didn't, at the same time. *This is Erick*, she reminded herself. *Beautiful, perfect, caring, and loving Erick.*

He softly nipped at her neck, placing kisses from her shoulder to her throat where he felt her strong and eager heartbeat. His lips found hers, and he nipped at her bottom lip. Then, taking her in, the faint scent of sweat and lavender, tasting her skin, he worked his way to her ear and below as he barely touched her.

She shuddered with need as he brushed his hands over her, her skin erupting as every nerve was set ablaze. Unable to wait another second, she grabbed his head and kissed him deeply again, tasting the wine from his dinner, kneading his tongue with hers. Acting purely on instinct, she pressed herself against him and felt him shudder. His head tilted back for a second, separating their lips. Grabbing his lips again with hers, she let him continue the motions with his hands. The goose bumps came again and she moaned into his mouth, which excited him even more.

She wanted, no, *needed* him inside her so badly it hurt. The ache was undeniable, persistent, desperate, but no. It was too soon. Or was it?

With a tormented cry, she pulled away from him, leaving them both breathlessly gaping at each other with swollen lips, flushed cheeks, wild eyes. His gaze flashed to her bare and heaving chest, then back up to her face as she still sat on his knees. He looked so desperate; she hated to get him worked up, and leave him that way. She couldn't do that to him. Or was that an excuse? Hell, she was worked up, too. Her insides ached almost enough to hurt by now.

She wasn't sure how or why, but she discovered her fingers working on the button on his pants, and once that was free, she slid down the zipper to reveal his boxers. Relaxed and with his head pressed against the back of the seat, he let her explore. Methodically, she roamed with her fingertips, learning every bump and ridge through the fabric. He gripped her thighs with strong hands as he tried his hardest to stay in control. As he filled further with need, he tilted his hips and pushed himself into her hand, desperate for more.

He was moaning, panting, needing more and more, yet knowing she might stop at any moment. He grit his teeth as she lightly ran her short fingernails up his length, still through his boxers. Once she reached his waist again, and that tempting arrow of muscle, she hooked her fingers over the top and slid them down. He sighed with relief as he lifted himself and as she helped undress him.

"Oh, God, Rach," he whispered, but was quieted when she wrapped her hand around him. She felt his heartbeat right there in her hand, wild and fast, concerned and scared as well. He sighed loudly as he pushed himself into her hand, and then stopped. "I don't want to stop, Rach. I'm not going to be able to stop."

Silently begging and pleading for more, he gripped her waist, then her hips, wanting desperately to pull her closer again. His whole body shuddered as she let her fingers trail off the tip of him.

Then, without a word, she slid from his lap into the passenger seat.

He cried a lonely cry as he writhed almost in pain and clenched his fists, trying to calm himself. But seconds later, she was back, wearing nothing, on his lap.

"Rach...Are you sure?"

"I don't want to stop, either," she admitted, then slid forward again, taking him inside of her, savoring every inch as it filled her. They cried out together, holding on to each other tightly for several long seconds, relishing in the sensation before moving again. Each new touch, feeling, sensation, was better than the last. How much better could it get before they either exploded or melted – or both?

Though they tried, they were not able to get close enough. When she began tilting her hips in motion with his, she gazed at him, connecting in a new and intense way. Fighting the urge to involuntarily close their eyes, they continued to watch each other, taking in every breath, every goose bump, every sigh, until every nerve in their bodies sizzled.

The intensity of her gaze was too much and he could not hold on any longer. With reckless abandon, he pulled her deeper and deeper over him, and then stopped with a sigh of pleasure.

She felt his rolling waves inside her and felt every hair stand on end. Her body quivered above him as goose bumps covered her. The sensation and emotion of sharing this moment with him was so powerful that a tear slipped from her eye.

He pressed his forehead into her chest, heaving breaths against her skin. Every breath sounded almost pained until the pulsing stopped, and he finally rested his head on her shoulder.

"I'm sorry," he said as he tried to control his breathing, as well as the rest of his body. "I couldn't stop, baby. I couldn't stop."

"It's okay." She assumed it was all over, but he slipped his hand between them and touched her with a gentle finger. She sucked in lungs full of air, and then almost purred as he massaged her. She briefly wondered how he knew to do this, as she hadn't even known. Had he been sneaking around in his dad's office again? But she couldn't laugh. It felt too good. Despite his inexperience, he filled her with the most unbelievable feeling she had ever felt.

Then, as she moved her hips just the right way, she felt a rush as she neared a cliff, held her breath, and jumped. Waves of pure rapture took over her body from head to toe, and she allowed herself to soar. After a few seconds of feeling muscles she didn't even know she had flexing in waves, gripping him tightly, she realized Erick's face was pained as he tried so hard to hang on for her.

It was just too much. With his eyes closed, and as she quivered around him again, he moaned, and burst in pleasure once again. They sighed together as their waves worked in unison for what seemed like an eternity. Finally, they crashed, holding each other tightly again, him breathing into her chest while she did the same into his thick hair.

When he finally calmed himself, he moaned softly, rumbling into her chest. She kissed the top of his head, moist with sweat. Rachel raked her fingers through his hair, lightly massaging his head, holding him against her heart as if protecting him.

The realization fell upon her that he had saved himself for her, and she was honored to be with him. A guy like him could have had any girl he wanted, but he chose her to share this moment with. Then, she realized...

She was his first, but he wasn't hers.

"You okay?" he asked as he held her secure in his arms. How did he always know when something was bothering her?

She continued to run her fingers through his hair as she thought of the best way to say it. "I wish I could have saved myself for you," she said, tears spilling before she was able to stop them. As she rested her head on his shoulder, he held her tightly. Silent sobs wracked her body as she tried not to cry and ruin the moment. Despite her attempts at fighting them, the tears flooded his shoulder until she picked up his shirt and wiped them away.

"But baby, you did."

She shook her head as she patted his shoulder with the shirt again, then sniffed. "I always wanted..." She was unable to say another word, and she hoped he knew what she meant.

"That didn't count, baby. That wasn't making love. This is making love. And you saved that for me." As he wisped his fingers up and down her back, she stopped crying and nodded as she understood his words.

Maybe she hadn’t been ruined after all.

CHAPTER TWENTY-ONE

"One of these days I'm going to have to learn to drive again. How did I ever get around without you?"

Erick shrugged. "I'm not sure. I don't think you could have gotten here by train. Does it go up this far?"

"Of course. Goes all the way up Long Island."

"You're kidding."

Rachel laughed. "It's called the 'Long Island Railroad' for a reason. It goes all over *Long Island*."

"All right, smarty pants."

The psychiatrist's office was in a hospital surrounded by golf courses. Rachel thought that was hilarious, and laughed even harder when Erick told her that his father had never played a round of golf in his life. "That's like a cop never eating doughnuts. Come on, really?"

"What?" he laughed. "No, a cop not eating doughnuts is way stranger than a doctor who's never played golf. Where would my dad have learned to play golf on a ranch?"

"Well, I just thought maybe his doctor friends would ask him to go with them on Wednesdays."

"Wednesdays?"

"Yeah. That's the day they all play golf. "

"Really?" he laughed again.

"Yes, really."

Finally, they made it to the psychiatrist's office inside the hospital on the top floor. It had been a long walk from the parking lot through the hospital, up the elevator, then wandering the floors looking for the office. Rachel was surprised they were not late.

"Good afternoon. I'm Doctor Franklin," a woman in a straight navy blue dress said as she held out her hand. She offered Rachel a seat in the waiting room and gave her some forms to fill out. The doctor waited in her office while Rachel worked on her forms. There was no secretary or nurse to give them to, which Rachel found strange, so she knocked on the doctor's office door.

"I'm done, Dr. Franklin."

"Ah, very good. Come in, please."

Before walking in, Rachel glanced back at Erick. Erick smiled and waved, then told her he would be fine waiting for her. He picked up a magazine. Rachel forced a grin and went inside with the doctor.

Erick took one look at the magazine selection and gave up. All women's magazines. Although, he was curious. *What do they talk about*? *Probably fashion. Men*. He picked up a Glamour magazine and read the headlines on the cover.

"**How to do the new wear-it-wet headsets**"

"**How to find the right pants look for your figure**."

Erick chuckled silently. The girl on the cover was pretty, despite reminding him of Peggy, but he tossed the magazine aside and decided instead to take a nap.

"Erick, I'm done."

No response.

"Erick?" Rachel jostled his shoulder.

He awoke with a start. "Rachel," he said simply. Erick stood and took her hand, and they started on their trek back to their car. "So, what did she say?"

"She said that activity you made me do was a good idea. Then she said that I should tell the story again, so she made me tell her everything. God, that was hard."

"You were able to tell the whole thing without reading it?"

Rachel nodded. "Yeah. I mean, it was disjointed, but I got through it."

"Good. That's awesome, Rach."

"At the end, she said it was important for me to forgive him for doing this to me." She scoffed at the idea. "Funny. Mom said the same thing. I told the doctor that I didn't know how to forgive him. I can't just let it go. I mean, look at what he did to me."

"But that's the thing, Rach. You *are* able to let it go. It might take a while, sure. But you will get to the point one day, hopefully soon, where you won't be so mad at him. Then, you will feel better."

"That's what's causing the nightmares, she said. My anger toward him. I told her that I thought the nightmares were because I wanted to change it. Each time, I'm hoping for a different ending. She thought that was interesting."

"What else did she say about that?"

"She said that I won't get that other ending until I forgive him."

"Wow."

"Yeah. Wow." Forgiving him would be the hardest thing she would ever have to do.

***

Rachel's second visit to the doctor was tougher than the first. The doctor had asked for more details this time, causing her to nearly faint as she recalled the specifics. Somehow, she managed to stay in her chair and stay awake. After recovering, the doctor asked her to take another huge step.

"Rachel," She took Rachel's hand "It's time to forgive him."

"He nearly killed me!" Rachel ripped her hand free.

"Listen, Rachel," she started in a soft and low voice. "If you don't forgive him, he still holds you prisoner." She waited until it sank in and she saw the look of understanding on Rachel's face. "Don't you see? He *was* crazy. There was something wrong with him. But you have to forgive him because holding those hate-filled feelings inside you will eat you up. He still has you trapped, unless you forgive. It doesn't mean you won't ever be reminded of it, or won't ever be mad or upset about it. It just means that you didn't let them win. *You* won. Does this make sense?"

"It *has* been eating me up inside." Rachel was looking at the floor, deep in thought.

"Exactly. Now it's time to forgive. You won't forget, but you can forgive because he was insane. He wasn't thinking straight. No one in their right mind would do such a thing."

Rachel nodded as she thought. *Now, how do I forgive?*

As if reading her mind, the doctor answered, "It may take time, but tell yourself again and again that you forgive him. Think about what it means to forgive. It means you let the resentment go. Let the hatred go. Remind yourself that you are winning by not letting them get to you like this. Besides, your hatred toward that man does nothing to him. It's not hurting him at all. It's only hurting you."

Rachel nodded thoughtfully and straightened her back. "You're right. It doesn't affect him at all, does it?" She took a breath and held it for a second. "Okay. I'm ready to forgive him. I'm ready to move on." It was such a relief just to say those words, whether she believed them completely or not, that she welled up with tears before she could stop it from happening.

***

Curiosity got the better of her. She couldn't take it anymore. The strange man seemed to live in that barn. All he did was rake the dirt floor inside the barn or sweep straw from it. Did he stand there all day waiting for her to walk by? Did he know her schedule and know when to watch her walk by on her way to the track kitchen? She was about to find out.

Rachel knew if she told Erick or her mom where she was going, they would want to go with her. Rachel also knew that if they went with her, the man might hide.

She found herself within steps of his barn as the sun rose from behind it. However, she hardly noticed the pink and orange colors in the sky. She was focused solely on the barn's entrance. As she peeked from behind a bush, she watched as he emerged with his rake and began raking the same spot. Over and over and over. For several long minutes, she stood and watched him, and wondered if he felt her eyes upon him as she had felt his so many times.

Still, she couldn't get a good look at him, even when she squinted and refocused. He was a silhouette in the darkness as the sun rose behind the barn. His shape was portly, that much she knew. He had short hair, a flat top. Just like the monster's hair. She had to get closer. Rachel eyed her surroundings. No bushes were close enough to sprint to. Several minutes later, he was still in the same spot, and she knew now, without a shadow of a doubt that he was waiting for her.

What if this man was the monster? Certainly, he wouldn't be right there in front of her, watching her, taking a chance that she could turn him in. Right? Maybe it was just someone who had a crush on her. It had to be. She just had to explain to him that she was with Erick now, and not looking for anyone anymore. Ever. *Well, that's not a good way to word it,* she thought. She didn't want to break his heart. *Don't flatter yourself, Rachel. Goodness. He's probably not even waiting for you. He's probably waiting for someone else.*

Still, she had to know for sure. She found another bush in back of her and ducked behind it. Next to her, there was an entrance to a barn that was out of the man's line of sight. Fortunately, this allowed her to slip in the side door. She hoped to avoid questions about why she was there. Just in case, she came up with something to say. Sometimes Erick rode for this barn in the mornings. Perfect. *I'm looking for Erick. Is he here?* she rehearsed silently.

Keeping the bush between her and the man, she slipped into the barn. No one said a word to her as she sauntered confidently down the shedrow, looking in each stall. When she came to the middle door, she ducked outside again and stopped. Her stomach burned with uneasiness, but it was time to be strong. After all, Erick said she was strong. Time to live up to it.

As if plunging into a pool of cold water, she took a breath and set off toward barn forty-two and the man. After squaring her shoulders, she headed right for him, even keeping her eyes on him. He stopped his raking when he saw her coming. He backed up. The closer she came, the more he backed away. Rachel quickened her steps, almost desperate to talk to him now. The man twisted and scurried down the row just as she reached the side door. As she walked in, she watched him turn down the middle aisle and head for the other side. She quickened her steps and turned the corner behind him. He grabbed her arm and their eyes met.

It was him! The monster!

Rachel screamed and struggled to free herself from his grip. He pulled her toward a stall as he glanced back and forth for people.

"Help! Help me!" Rachel screamed, and then kicked his leg as hard as she could. She kicked him again as she tried to pull her arm free. She lost her balance and fell to the ground with his hand still firmly around her upper arm. As he bent over, trying to pick her back up again, their eyes met again.

The last time he had seen her, she was scared, broken, helpless. This time, Rachel was filled with rage and determination. He wasn't going to get away with this again. Now, she was strong, physically and mentally. This time, she was determined to put a stop to this man.

In an instant, her body filled with adrenaline, she lifted both legs, shoved her feet into his chest, hurling him away from her. He fell into the wall just as two men came running. Rachel scooted away as the men dove for her attacker, but missed. With agility no one would have suspected from him, the monster leapt to his feet and ran. The men ran after him, leaving her alone in the barn.

Rachel's breathing was so fast, she was sure she'd hyperventilate and pass out. Despite the feeling, though, she had to get back to her barn. Using the wall behind her, she stood on wobbly legs, took a breath, and ran her fastest toward her barn.

"Mom? Erick? Mom?" she called as she ran inside.

"What's...?"

"Where's Mom? Where's Erick?" she asked Mark, as she grabbed his arms.

"I don't...there...over there."

"Thanks," she yelled and turned in the direction he was pointing, and then ran outside again. "Erick!"

"What? What's wrong?" he asked with panic that mirrored hers as she ran into him just outside the barn. He wrapped his arms around her to steady her trembling body.

"We gotta call the police. Now. It's him. That man. It's him. Oh, my God, I'm gonna be sick." Rachel bent over, holding her stomach, then fell to her knees. Erick bent down to hold her, but she stopped him. "Go. Call the police. Please."

"Okay. Okay." Erick rushed into the barn and into Julia's office.

Mark approached Rachel cautiously. "You okay?"

"No," she cried. "No."

"Let's get you inside out of this heat."

"I'm not hot."

"Come on," Mark said as he tried to lift her by her arms. Reluctantly, she allowed him to help her stand, and walk back into the barn where Erick had run. "Let's go to your mom's office."

Rachel was hyperventilating again and whimpering. She tried to stop it from happening as they walked. "It's him," she whispered.

"Huh?"

"It's him," she repeated, louder this time, her volume growing with each word. "It's him. It's him!"

"That man that took you? Here? Where? Where is he?" Mark straightened and looked around.

"I don't know. He ran off."

Mark helped her into Julia's office. Erick was on the phone and Julia was just running out to help her daughter. Julia and Mark helped Rachel sit at the chair next to Julia's desk.

"Yes, she said it was the man that kidnapped her. He's here on the Belmont backside. You need to send police over right now...Okay. Thanks. I will." Erick hung up. "Did he see you?"

"Y–," she started as she nodded. "H-he grabbed me, but I pushed him away. Two men ran after him. I don't know where they went."

Erick and Julia looked at each other incredulously.

"I can't believe...I can't believe...he was here. He was here. The whole time," Rachel continued, crying out with desperation heavy in her voice.

"Are you okay?" her mother asked. Erick was still in too much shock to speak.

"I don't know," Rachel answered with her hand over her heart. She took a deep breath, trying to calm herself.

***

"We can't find him, ma'am," one officer said coldly. "He's gone."

"What?" Rachel screamed, making everyone jump. "He was right there. Where did he go?"

"We will keep looking, ma'am. Don't worry. We know his name now."

"What's his name?" She almost didn't want to know the answer to that question.

"Victor Watkins."

"Oh! Ch-check the theater. The drive-in," Rachel shouted as she remembered the man outside the car.

"You think that was him?"

"Yeah, it had to be. Erick, he's been watching me this whole time. Right under our noses."

Erick clenched his jaw in anger and peered out the window of the barn, wishing he could get his hands on this man. He could do nothing about it now, though, which frustrated him terribly. He slammed his fist down onto the desk.

***

Police checked with the drive-in, and sure enough, it was him. They learned that he had not shown up to work for several days. They had assumed he quit. Another dead end.

Police also questioned the staff in barn forty-two, where he had worked. Victor had worked in that barn for about a year, and several co-workers now admitted that they had felt something strange about him. His incessant questioning about Rachel's disappearance and then reappearance at the track annoyed his co-workers, but they had dismissed it, as their main focus was work and not the eccentricities of a fellow worker. Those employees then put the pieces together once they learned that he was the one who had taken Rachel that fateful night. Unfortunately, by then, too late.

"That sick bastard's been watching her this whole time," Mark grumbled to one of the grooms in barn forty-two. The groom shoved his hands in his pockets and shook his head in disgust, silently wishing he had seen it earlier. He didn't like the fact that Rachel wanted to become a jockey, but still, she was one of them, and you gotta protect your own in tumultuous times.

***

"Good afternoon, Ladies and Gentlemen, and welcome to the Belmont fall meet. Today, several Kentucky Derby hopefuls will be competing in the Rockefeller Stakes, including our own hometown favorite, Chivalry."

With his neck arched and tail held high and flipping around behind him, Chivalry pranced onto the track, led by Rachel and Old Guy. Chivalry was right at home at his own track and pranced around as if he owned the place. He was the big man on campus, the one the other colts looked up to. Or so he thought.

Chivalry was eager to start the race, and hurried into the gate, knowing this meant it was time to run soon. His muscular body quivered with anticipation as he kept an eye on the other horses. He knew now that his job was to lead them, to run in front, show them which way to go. He knew that whenever he did that, everybody praised him and loved him. He loved having his picture taken with his owners and rider, and then there was the quick wet sponge full of water over his head, which he loved in this heat. There were the hugs, the rubs between his ears, the scratching on his withers. All things he loved.

He waited for the gates to open, his enormous heart beating strong with anticipation. Then, they let him go. He was free! He thundered down the backstretch, pulling against the bridle, knowing his rider wanted to hold him back, but not knowing why. He just wanted to run. But he also knew when his rider would let him go – the turn – and it was fast approaching.

As he carried his rider to the front of the herd, they turned for home, and he set his sights on the winner's circle just past the crowd of people. That's where everybody wanted him to be, and he was going to be there soon. Just a bit further. He was free and running as fast as he wanted with his herd behind him now, following him.

But soon, too soon, his rider patted his neck and stood in the saddle, creating more wind resistance, pulling on the reins, trying to slow him down. He didn't want to slow down. He wanted to go around again and lead his herd, but no. Sadly, it was over. His old friend was coming to get him, and while he knew he would be restrained soon, he also knew that this meant it was time to be adored.

The old dappled grey approached and Rachel took hold of Chivalry's bridle. Chivalry tossed his head to prove that he could run more if he really wanted. Reluctantly, he allowed Rachel to hold him, and as the grey eyed him with a warning, he settled. He was so excited that he pranced sideways all the way to the winner's circle.

***

In October, they traveled to Maryland to run in the Pimlico-Laurel Futurity at Laurel Park, between Washington, D.C. and Baltimore.

Rachel led Chivalry to the long chute for the mile and sixteenth long race.

"Don't know what to tell you. Stay out of trouble, I guess," Rachel told him needlessly. Erick didn't seem worried. She didn't want him to become complacent, though. "Hang on tight, okay? Be careful. You still never know."

"I know, babe. I love you."

"I love you more," she answered as she admired his strength and courage, and his devilishly good looks. The wink he gave her sent a little tug to her heart and she blew a tiny kiss to him in reply, trying to remain inconspicuous to save him from being teased in the jocks' room later. Reluctantly, she unclipped the line and rode away, still finding it hard to believe that someone like him could be so in love with her, given all her troubles.

From time to time, she had to remind herself that this was real, true love, and those things did not matter. As he had told her, you don't choose who you fall in love with. It just happens, and you cannot deny its power to hold two people together. As she moved her horse further down the chute and out of the way, she watched him rub Chivalry's mane in encouragement as the assistant starter coaxed the horse into the narrow stall.

Soon, the horses were loaded, the bell rang, and the doors banged open. Six horses pounded down the chute to the main track. The dirt was different going from the chute and Chivalry stumbled as he crossed onto the main track. In one gigantic thrust, Chivalry regained his footing and Erick analyzed his horse's strides for signs of lameness. His heart pounded as he tried to decide if he should pull up or keep going. The answer came to him when Chivalry shook his head, asking to run. Erick had been holding him back, and they were now in last place, but at least Chivalry was fine.

No problem getting around this small field. It's okay. We can do this. Not much of a chance to get boxed in unless he wasn't thinking, and set himself up, but he did need to make up ground. Chivalry was pulling Erick's arms, wanting to run, but there was a group of five other horses in front of him, tightly packed. Erick moved Chivalry closer to the rail to save room, ducking in behind another horse as they neared the pack.

Bahama Dream, a horse that had recently begun winning races, was further ahead in second but started moving up. Bahama's rider had taken the lead by the first turn, and was now slowing the pace ever so gradually as they pounded down the backstretch. Erick could tell that he and Chivalry were gaining on the others even though they had kept a steady pace. Something told him the other jockeys could not tell that the pace had slowed. It was a trick many jockeys used to try to save their horse for later, yet stay in front to avoid dirt in their horse's face. Erick was glad he noticed, and he knew what to expect later. Sometimes they called it, "putting them to sleep," as the slow pace would calm the horses in the pack, effectively calming their excitement and urge to run faster.

The rail didn't open as they rounded the turn for home, and Erick knew he was going to have to hurry around them on the outside, losing ground in the process. He was confident that his horse would be able to make it up, though. He headed to the outside for his move, going wide, making their trip longer.

The front-runner, Bahama Dream, was now running strong, even pulling away, and as Chivalry approached the front of the pack, it was obvious they would have to hurry to beat Bahama. For the first time ever, Erick whipped Chivalry in stride to push him. He didn't have to use the whip for long, however. He felt Chivalry give him another gear as the horse flexed and stretched his muscles in faster rhythm. Chivalry was flying down the homestretch, gaining on Bahama Dream. Even so, Erick wasn't sure they were going to make it. Stride by stride they moved closer and closer, and finally passed Bahama just as they passed the finish pole.

CHAPTER TWENTY-TWO

"Rachel, we need you to come to the station and identify the suspect," Detective Ritter told her over the phone.

The blood rushed from her head and she covered her face as if to hide. Rachel shrieked, "What? Who? Did you arrest him? Oh, my God. I can't do it. Oh, God."

Billy caught the phone as it fell from her violently shaking hands. While trying to hold the phone, he helped her sit on the chair next to Julia's desk. She bent over her legs as she tried to regain control.

"Hello?" Billy asked, finally putting the phone up to his ear.

"Yes, who is this?"

"Billy. Rachel's brother. Is this...?"

"Detective Ritter. We need your sister to come in to identify a suspect. Can you bring her now? Or soon?"

"I don't know. I don't think she can handle it."

"No, wait, Billy. I think...I think I can do it. Ask him if he will see me," she said, touching his arm.

Ritter heard her and answered before Billy spoke. "No, he will be behind a one-way mirror. Or some people call it a two-way mirror. He will see a mirror, you will see inside the room. Promise her she will be safe."

"Okay," Billy answered, then tilted the phone. "Rach, he says you will be safe."

Rachel nodded as silent tears fell along with a silent sob as she covered her mouth with both hands. Billy left Rachel there while he went to get the others, and they headed to the police station together. Rachel clung desperately to Erick in the back seat as Julia drove.

Once there, an officer led them to a small room with a table and four chairs in the middle. A large glass window showed the contents of the white room next door, which was nothing. Rachel was relieved for now, but knew soon that she was going to have to face the evil man once again.

"Okay, Rachel, please sit down," the officer said as he waved his hand toward the table.

After sitting and facing the window, Rachel took Erick's hand and squeezed tightly. Erick jiggled his hand and she apologized and loosened her grip. Rachel peered up at her mother, who stood behind her. Julia nodded and blinked, trying to relax Rachel. She put her hands on Rachel's shoulders.

"Ready?" Ritter asked as he walked into the room.

Rachel groaned and answered, "Yes, sir." Looking through the glass, she saw the door to the tiny room open. It took several long seconds for them to shuffle four men in chains and prison uniforms into the small room. Those seconds were torture to her as she felt each one as if it were an eternity. Tightly squeezing Erick's hand again, she whimpered as the second man's face came into full view.

As they were positioning them against the white wall, she smothered her sounds in Erick's shoulder, afraid he could hear her through the glass.

"He almost killed me," she whispered. He kissed the top of her head and tried not to give that monster the satisfaction of his attention. The story she had read to him back at his house that day replayed in his mind. The horror was unimaginable, and Erick then glared at the man with fury.

For Julia and Billy, seeing the face of Rachel's nightmares was unbearable. Julia broke down and sobbed. Billy turned away to hide his tears. Erick had a hard time controlling his emotions as well.

Her fear and misery turned to anger in an instant and Rachel stood up. "He's been watching me." She clenched her fists. "He's been watching me for months. Sick son of a..."

Erick stood up with her as Rachel slapped her palms onto the glass. "Rach," he started as he placed his hands on her shoulders.

Rachel interrupted, screaming. "Chicken shit, ugly, fat, candy-assed pervert! You kidnapped me. You almost killed me and didn't even care. You and your sick, twisted obsession with blood. Your stupid drugs. You're crazy, you sick bastard. Can't get a girl so you have to steal one? Loser! You're the one that needs the lobotomy and shock treatments. I wish I could cut *you* with a rusty knife. Then I'd cut off your..."

Rachel stopped herself. "Wouldn't do any good. He'd probably like it. No. I couldn't do what he did. I refused to become what I hate." Rachel took several breaths and clenched her jaw. "I f...I for...forgive...you." Those three words were the hardest she'd ever said.

"Rachel," Erick moved his hands to her hips, reminding Rachel that he was behind her and bringing her back out of the darkness. She turned and fell into his arms, sobbing and thumping her fists on his shoulders. Erick rubbed her back as tears slipped down his face. Julia and Billy came to them to be close and cry with her.

***

"The trial is set for next summer. August fourteenth," Detective Ritter told Rachel over the phone. It had been three weeks since she had identified the monster. She was grateful that he had been caught, but now she was going to have to face him in court. The thought nearly stopped her heart.

"All right," she answered barely loud enough to be heard. Erick placed his hand on her back as she hung up the phone. She relayed the court date to him, and he nodded.

"He will rot in jail for the rest of his life, Rach. I guarantee you that. Ritter said they have plenty of evidence. After that trial, you'll never have to see him again."

"I don't want to do it."

"You have to. You don't want him back out on the streets, do you? He could do this to someone else and they may not live like you did."

Rachel lowered her gaze and nodded, knowing he was right. She couldn't give up now, as badly as she wanted to. She couldn't let this happen again.

CHAPTER TWENTY-THREE

The gray sky was a sign that winter was coming. But it was also Chivalry's break, and he had been sent to Hanover Farms in upstate New York to rest for the winter. The Hanover Team at Belmont missed him, but, fortunately, they had other horses racing at Aqueduct, only a few miles from Belmont Park.

Erick had an idea. "It's a day off. Come on. Let's go. I have something to show you."

"But I'm not dressed," She looked down at her muddy jeans and sweatshirt.

"What you're wearing is perfect. Ready?"

Rachel chuckled at his eagerness and looked at her mom, who nodded. It was a dark day, a day without races, and there wasn't much to do. So, with a shrug, Rachel followed Erick to his car.

"Where are we going?" The city had been left behind twenty minutes ago, and she had never been this way before. Leaving behind the security of familiar surroundings, she felt a twinge of nervousness. She's spent so much time at the track that it was always a little scary to venture out.

Erick only smiled without answering, no matter how hard Rachel tried to get answers from him about where they were going. He was smart, and recognized each one of her tricks.

They eventually slowed and turned. Her eyes were wide as they drove up the long driveway lined with fencing and paddocks on either side. Erick hadn't noticed, though, as he closely watched the driveway, choosing the best path as to avoid being stuck in the muddy tracks left over from a tractor.

"Trail ride?" Rachel asked eagerly. Erick smiled silently, and she knew. She bounced in her seat and clapped.

Erick and Rachel leaned patiently on Erick's car while a family with two children were helped to mount their horses. As one boy sat on his horse with a proud smile, his brother laughed hysterically from behind as he watched his brother's horse lift his tail and let poop fall into the mud. "Look! It's steaming!" he shouted as he pointed. His mother rolled her eyes and hid her face as the rest of the family laughed. They were sent off with a guide soon after.

Rachel's horse was a gentle gray named Abigail and Erick rode a paint named Tonto. Finally, they were tacked up and ready to go after being told which trails to use. They walked side by side, hardly holding the reins as they relaxed in their big western saddles. At first, they joked about how docile their mounts were, but then appreciated the opportunity to take in the scenery.

A few ducks bobbed under the water in a small pond, and smoke rose from the chimney on the old colonial-style house some distance from the red barn. A mound of hay sat next to the barn, complete with a pitchfork poking out of it. It was as if they had stepped into an old painting from a hundred years ago.

A mosaic of multicolored leaves decorated the path ahead of them and the nearly naked branches created an arch above their heads. Rachel looked around and wondered if she had entered a fantasy land or a movie set. She had never been in the woods before, had never seen the darkened and empty limbs of a forest. She had never even seen them with leaves in the summer. She had never ridden on a country trail, only on a never-ending oval track where the scenery never changed. She'd never had a chance to see things like this. It was a whole new world for her. This was different, exciting, and exhilarating. Despite her cold and reddened cheeks, she had the overwhelming urge to laugh. She didn't fight it, and Erick was glad to have given her the opportunity to get away for a change.

Soon, they came to a smaller trail that was obviously not as traveled as their current trail.

"Want to try it?" Rachel asked as she stopped her horse.

"Well, I guess. If it doesn't bring us around in a circle, we'll turn around. I don't want to be lost in the woods. It's too cold."

"Okay, deal." Rachel clicked her tongue, squeezed her knees and Abigail set off again. They heard a stream, found it, and decided to dismount. They sat next to each other near a large rock after tying the horses to two separate trees. The horses went right to work scraping the bark with their teeth.

Erick leaned closer and kissed her. "If it weren't so cold I'd rip all your clothes off and have my way with you," he joked. He slipped his cold hand under her shirt and she squealed as she swatted his hand away. He tried from another angle and managed to get it under her shirt in the back. She squealed again.

"Ahhh." He relished in the warmth of her body. Erick grabbed her by the waist and pulled her onto the ground on top of him. He kissed her again. "I can't resist you."

She answered with a giggle, and straddled his prone body. The faint scent of his cologne only made her crave more of it, and she burrowed into the crook of his neck. He opened to let her in, arching his neck for her, begging for more. Tickling him with her lips, she drifted up and down from his ear to his shoulder, side to side along his collarbone, drifting over his Adam's apple, eager to taste every inch of him, wishing the clothes were not in her way.

She felt his need for her as he lifted himself to meet her, and pushed her hips into him. Rachel teased him, rocking her hips forward and back, caressing him. It was too cold to be without clothes, but she desperately wanted him to lose control again. The sexiest thing she knew was him losing himself to her. Every nerve and fiber of her being wanted him, but was it was too cold to get naked. She whimpered in disappointment.

As she adjusted her leg, she felt something sharp in his pocket. She knew it wasn't the car keys because they were in his coat pocket. She slid her hand down over his hips as she raised one eyebrow at him. Without a sound, he let her feel through his jeans and try to figure out what it was. *Small, sharp edges, a circle*. She gazed into his eyes. *Is that what I think it is*?

He reached into his pocket and pulled out a ring with a half-carat diamond and two quarter-carat diamonds on either side set in gold. "What's this?" he joked. Her mouth opened wide with amazement and she laughed with pure and utter joy.

After sitting up, he held one of her hands and held the ring in the other. His voice was calm and smooth in contrast with her now quivering body. "I love and respect you so much, Rach. I'm honored to be a part of your life. You deserve so much more than I can give. But I promise I will always be here for you no matter what. I promise I will never take our relationship for granted. I promise to always love you and appreciate you. I promise to spend my life only with you, making you the happiest woman on earth because you deserve it. You're the best thing that's ever happened to me, Rach, and I want to spend the rest of my life with you." Big round tears welled in both of them.

"I love you," she squeaked as she held his face, running her thumb over a dimple in his cheek.

"I love you too, baby. Marry me?"

"Yes," she sobbed as she wrapped her arms around his neck. She held onto him for so long that he had to remind her that she had to put the ring on for it to be official. Laughing as warm tears dripped from her face, she held up her left hand and he slipped the ring onto her finger, a perfect fit.

"Oh, my goodness," she exclaimed at the sight of all the diamonds. "I've never seen a ring like this before. It must have cost a fortune."

"Don't think about that, baby. It was worth every penny."

Rachel shook her head, unable to believe he had bought her something so fancy. "I feel bad, though. You know I'm not Marilyn Monroe or something. I would have been fine with a smaller ring, you know."

"That's why I made sure to get the nicest ring they had."

"I love it, baby. It's absolutely beautiful." She kissed him again as her fingers dug into his hair and pulled him closer.

"We'll have to get married before Chiv starts racing again, you know."

"The sooner the better. We'll be together forever."

"Forever."

They sat together in a pile of leaves next to the stream as the horses slept or spent time digging around in the leaves. They talked about their entire relationship together, the good times and bad, even the confusing times as he waited for her to finally give in and allow her feelings for him to override her fear. Fear of losing him, fear of intimacy, fear that her body wouldn't work the way it should, fear that he wouldn't accept her when he saw her scars and heard about the damage the monster had caused. But as he had shown her, his love was above all of that. It didn't matter that her skin was not perfect, nor did it matter what restrictions she had. It only mattered that they wanted to be together, and when she finally understood, he was there for her with open arms.

"One more thing you need to know about me," Rachel added hesitantly.

"What's that?" he asked with a contented smile, the one reserved just for her.

"I um, I can't cook."

"We'll hire a chef for our mansion."

Rachel laughed loudly as she tossed her head back, and he dove into her chest, knocking her over. She wrapped her arms around his head.

"You have the patience of a saint," she told him as he sat up again.

"I love you so much that there was no other option. The thought never even entered my mind that I would give up on you. I was going to wait as long as it took because that's the way it's supposed to be. We're supposed to be together."

She nodded and kissed him in reply. "I love you for that, baby."

***

When they finally made it back home, they shared the news with Julia, Billy and Erick's parents. They arranged for all six of them to go out to dinner that night and she displayed her hand on the table for all to see the ring. Julia gave Erick an incredulous look. Erick was amused by her expression, and then made sure to thank Chivalry again for helping pay for the ring. Speechless, she shook her head at herself for reacting that way.

"It's just unbelievable, Erick. I've never seen an engagement ring like that before. It has three different diamonds," Julia remarked as she stared at the ring some more while holding her daughter's hand up for a better view.

Diane answered, "He wanted to make sure she got the best one because she deserves the best." She smiled and patted Rachel's shoulder as she blushed and thanked her.

"You two are young, but I know everything will work out just fine. You are both very mature young people, and I think you will be just fine as a married couple," Dr. Bennett added.

"Agreed, though I married at eighteen myself," Julia answered.

"I suppose we were only a bit older than that, weren't we?" Diane asked her husband.

Rachel and Erick silently watched the interaction, turning their heads to each person who spoke.

"I was twenty, she was nineteen. We were young, too, I suppose. Though, at the time, it certainly didn't feel that way," Dr. Bennett said.

Julia nodded. "That's exactly how I felt. But I now know the difference as I look back." Julia turned to Rachel. "I'm not worried. Erick has been so good for you over the past nine months. Without his help, I'm not sure you'd be where you are today."

Rachel nodded, suddenly too emotional to speak.

"And your help, too, Steve. I am forever grateful to you for helping her find Dr. Franklin."

"You're quite welcome. It was a pleasure."

***

One year after her abduction, the worst day of her life, she had the best day of her life. The date was February 8, 1970, before Chivalry's next big stakes race at Aqueduct in March. They held the wedding at the church closest to their house, the same one Rachel's parents had been married in twenty years earlier.

That night they went home to Rachel's house, where they planned to stay while looking for an apartment close enough to the track. Julia's house was extremely convenient, as it was just across the street from the entrance to the backside of the track, and they weren't sure if they even wanted to find their own place yet.

"How are we supposed to stay quiet in here? This isn't fair," Erick whispered into her hair, and moaned quietly.

Rachel shoved her face into his shoulder, trying to stay quiet, as their bedroom was next to Billy's. *Talk about awkward,* she thought. "Just...I don't know...smother it in the pillow?"

"You're kidding me, right? You'll suffocate."

"Me? What about you?"

"I can stay quiet."

"Yeah, right. You cannot."

"If you start making too much noise, I'm gonna plop a pillow on your face, and then I can use it, too."

Rachel then stuck a pillow on her face, in between them. He had been resting on top of her after having dove into bed after her, making the headboard hit the wall. Erick bit the pillow and flipped it away from her. In mock surprise, Rachel went to grab it again, but Erick stopped her by holding her hands.

He was able to hold both wrists with one hand, and push them above her head. But, instantly, the giggling stopped and Rachel's expression went from jovial to petrified in a split second. She sucked in air as she tried to pull her arms out of his hand. He let go and lifted his weight from her, having seen the terror on her face.

"I forgot. I forgot, baby. I forgot. Are you okay? I'm so sorry. I forgot."

Catching her husband's eyes, she fought tears, fought fear, and felt awful for making him feel this way. She wrapped her arms around him and pulled him down onto her until his protective weight was upon her again, then she wrapped her legs around him. "It's okay." Shaking her head, she continued. "I am so tired of being afraid of everything, Erick."

"You're not afraid of everything. Just certain things, which are understandable, considering everything you've been through."

Then, she thrust her hands up toward her headboard again. "I'm going to learn not to be afraid of this. Let's go."

Erick grinned and kissed her. "Well, I might need some convincing since you just scared the crap outta me. Sort of...you know...not ready anymore."

Rachel tilted her hips, brushing against him as she felt him growing again. She closed her eyes for a second, still keeping her hands above her head, in much the same position she had been in while kidnapped, refusing to let it bother her. It had been nine months now of overcoming hurdle after hurdle, but she had done it. This was just another hurdle to beat.

He sighed in awe of her as he slid his hand from under her arm down her side and to her hips. With his fingers drifting back up her thighs, he worshiped the curves of her body. She lifted her legs, curling them to his sides, and he reached under her legs, supporting them as he slipped himself into her warmth.

Rachel's eyes closed involuntarily, but when the horror of the constant torture came back to her, she snapped them back open again and focused on Erick. Erick glanced up at her hands and Rachel asked him, "Wondering how long I can keep them this way?"

"You're strong, baby. One of the things I love so much about you. You can do this."

He nodded with affirmation as he let go of her legs and lowered himself to nuzzle her neck, and then feathered his lips along her collarbone. Her skin erupted in goose pimples as her body shook. Rachel pushed him deeper with her legs and they both suppressed the urge to cry out with pleasure. Rachel stopped caring about the position of her hands and arms, and grabbed the pillow next to her, arching her back into him as he slid his tongue over her chest, circling, teasing her. As silently as possible, she sighed.

***

"No!" Rachel struggled to catch her breath. "No, no, no...,"

She scrambled away from Erick, out of the bed and onto the floor.

Erick reached for her and she screamed again, slapping his hand away. She backed up against the wall, trying to get away from him.

"Rachel. Rachel." Erick's voice finally reached her and she woke up. She grabbed his arm and pulled herself back onto the bed, then threw her arms around Erick. He wrapped the blanket around her and held her shivering body tightly.

"I haven't had a nightmare since... I don't know. Months? I'm sorry, baby. Did I scare you?" she asked as she huddled as close to Erick as she possibly could.

"Scare me? Don't worry about me. Are you okay?" he asked.

She drew a ragged breath. "Yeah, I'm okay. I should be used to it. Well, not so much anymore, but it used to happen all the time. Did I hurt you at all? Did I scream?"

He lightly touched her cheek. "Yeah, you screamed but you didn't hurt me. Scared me, though."

"Sorry, honey. Sounds like this one was mild compared to the others. God, I hope that doesn't happen again. I don't want to hurt you." She reached from inside her warm blanket to take his hand. "You're going to be scared of sleeping with me soon."

"No way, I'm not afraid of that." He kissed her messy curls and pushed them out of her face, then kissed her cheek. "Do you feel better now?"

She took a cleansing breath. "Better," she said as she rested her head on his shoulder.

CHAPTER TWENTY-FOUR

During the Aqueduct meet, Erick hired an agent who began securing races for him. Erick spent the winter trying to stay warm with layers, but still make the weights for each horse. Each race had different conditions, including weight allowances and requirements. Horses could carry as little as one hundred five pounds including jockey, saddle, and pads. Erick weighed one hundred thirteen comfortably, and losing enough weight to wear extra clothes was a challenge for him, as well as any jockey. When Rachel suggested using panty hose under his riding pants, he scoffed.

"I'll get a liner, thank you," he joked as he messed up her hair.

"The other guys wear 'em. You know you want to," she said, then hopped up from her seat next to him on the couch, baiting him into chasing her. He fell for it, and wound up chasing her around the tiny house and bumping into Billy.

"Watch it," Billy mumbled as he shook his head.

***

Erick was doing well this winter as an apprentice, and was already in a respectable position in the jockey's standings. He was sixth out of twenty jocks so far.

But he was exhausted. The added riding in the afternoon coupled with his morning exercising jobs was getting to him. He had not grasped the reality of his exhaustion until after the races one day, when he could barely stand. His arms were sore, his shoulders tight, and he limped home with Rachel after work.

"What's the matter? You get hurt?" she asked as she watched him walk unevenly.

"Nah. Just exhausted, I guess. I'm riding what, ten, fifteen horses every morning, then going over to Aqueduct for five or six races in the afternoon. I'm wiped out."

"You shouldn't be riding so many in the mornings. Don't worry about mom. She can find somebody, Billy included. She wouldn't mind putting him up since he weighs more."

"You think? She won't be upset with me?"

"No way. She's been in the business a long time, babe. She knows how it is for you guys. I'm surprised she hasn't suggested it herself."

"What about the other trainers? How many races I would lose?" Erick was often promised a mount in a race in exchange for exercising the horse in the mornings.

"Talk to your agent. Ask him what to do. I mean, think about it. How many times do the other jocks ride in the mornings? It's rare. They spend all morning in the stands with the trainers and their agents."

"I guess."

"It's Roger's job to help you get races. You shouldn't have to break your neck doing someone else's job. You'd lose more than a few mounts if you got hurt, too, you know."

"I'll stop if I get too tired."

"I think you're too tired now."

Erick didn't say anything.

"Sorry. Guess I sound like a nagging wife already."

"No, you don't." He lifted her hand and kissed it. "I know you're just trying to help."

"Do what you think is best. I just want you to be safe, that's all."

***

"Hey, Roger," Erick called, approaching his agent.

"Hey. What's happenin'?"

"Roger, something has to change. I'm wearing myself out with all these workouts in the mornings plus riding all afternoon. I go home every day with Jell-O for legs. I have to slow down."

Roger pursed his lips as he thought. "You'd lose some mounts taking away the free exercise rider deal."

"I know. But it has to happen. I'm not worried about the money. I'm more worried about causing a spill."

"You're not gonna cause a spill. Listen. Your body will rise to the challenge. You've been easy on yourself for so long that once you have to work a little, it's tough. You're not able to rush into it quickly like this. But you'll catch up."

"I've been riding races since last summer."

"Not regular like this meet. See?"

Erick shrugged. "I need to drop a few horses in the mornings, that's all."

"You want to lose half your races, too? 'Cause that's what's gonna happen."

"Is it the money? I can pay you –,"

"Not the money, kid. You'll never make it as a big time jock like the others unless you work your ass off." He shook his head. "Kids these days, I swear. Think everything's gotta be handed to 'em on a silver platter."

Erick walked away without another word.

Rachel noticed the anger written all over his face the moment he returned to the barn. "Baby, what happened? What did he say?"

Shaking his head for a few seconds, he was silent. Then he lifted his downturned face to her and answered, "I'm getting a new agent."

***

A few days later, an exhausted Erick was still working in the mornings and all afternoon. He was unable to find someone to replace Roger, and hadn't told Roger his plans to fire him. Yet. However, he knew he had to do something soon. He shook his head as he dressed for the first race, slipping panty hose over his hairy legs. Roger had no idea. The others didn't work all morning like he did. They'd had to when they first arrived at the track, but once they started riding races, they stopped exercising, or at least slowed significantly.

The big name jocks only rode the big name horses in the mornings, or the occasional working horse so they would get to know their mounts and uphold a relationship with a certain trainer. Chivalry and a few of the others still had regular exercise riders, but in order to get that big race in the bag, the more successful jockeys made sure to exercise the better horses as well. It was all part of the game. They didn't have to hop off one horse and immediately jump onto another, spending four hours pulling on reins, cutting off the circulation in their fingers, jamming their feet into the stirrups to hold strong horses back for slow workouts.

The morning workouts were much harder than the afternoon rides, although the races took a lot out of him, as well. They caused more mental stress than physical. Making quick decisions, some being life or death, all while balancing perfectly as the horse stumbled or was bumped, it wasn't easy in any way. But it was still easier than four hours of constant pulling in the mornings.

***

Julia's friend, Paul, hired Erick to ride a horse named Admiral Joe in the last race of the day after he had ridden in five other races. Erick had won one race and finished in the money twice. It wasn't bad, but it was exceedingly difficult as his muscles faltered.

The mile-long race included Admiral Joe and nine other horses in the field. Erick got a leg-up and made his way to the track, anxious to get this race over with, go home, drink some water, and relax. His back muscles were sore and his legs were tired. He worried about his ability to ride well because of his exhaustion, but tried to will himself to hang in there and get the job done, and done well. His job and his goal were still to be first under the wire at the end, regardless of how he felt.

Rachel stood next to Billy, who was mounted on their new lead pony, Indian. They had sent Old Guy back to the farm to retire, and had brought Indian in to take over, knowing they would be traveling more now that they had Chivalry. They stood just off the track near the saddling paddock. Rachel had been worried lately about Erick's exhaustion, and knew it wasn't good for him. But this was the last race for him today, and they were going to get something to eat soon and relax.

"Hang in there, baby," Rachel said softly.

"What's that?" Billy asked.

After a slight pause, she answered, "One more race today. I think he needs to stop working horses in the mornings because it's running him into the ground and he'll be no good to anyone if he's too exhausted to ride. Plus, he'll make mistakes, and trainers will replace him in a heartbeat. They're just waiting for him to screw up since he's only had his license about a year and every other jockey here is more experienced."

Billy nodded. He knew she was right. Absolutely right.

The starters loaded the horses into the gate, the bell rang, and they were off. Admiral Joe stumbled coming out of the gate but righted himself. He was in last place, but Erick knew his horse would be able to work his way back up if he was patient with him. He just had to find the room. While he was looking for an opening, he felt something out of place.

Did the saddle slip? He rocked from side to side and found the saddle to be snug and in place. *The stirrups. Left one is longer. Something must have happened to that strap. Must have been the stumble. Maybe the buckle wasn't latched all the way and it slipped in. But the left one is longer.* And he normally did not ride that way. His heart pounded and he grabbed a tuft of hair in his horse's mane, along with the whip and reins. *Is this thing going to break any minute? Maybe I should pull up. If I do that, it'll surely break from the extra pressure on it. Let's win this race first, then get an outrider to help.*

He flipped his whip around in his right hand and lifted it high into the air. Before he could bring it down again, the horse next to them bumped them. Hard. Something told him that he was going to go down. The stirrup wasn't going to make it, and neither was he. In an instant, as he anticipated hitting the dirt, he tried to remember all the things the other jocks had told him about falling. *Duck your head, roll, fold your arms over your chest to protect it, try to roll off the track...* None of that mattered now, though. He didn't have time to plan his reaction.

The stirrup leather broke and the cold metal stirrup slipped away.

He slipped his other foot out of its stirrup to equalize himself. His horse was confused by the rider's change in stance and slowed. Just as he slowed, he was bumped again and Erick slipped to one side. His legs were exhausted. He tried, but was unable to pull himself back up and onto the horse's back. He felt himself slipping.

Erick felt someone grab his silks for a second, but knew it would be to no avail. He slipped out of the rider's hands. *You're going down.* He felt his left leg buckle underneath him as it hit the ground. Sharp pain radiated up his leg. Then, before he knew it, his face hit the sand, filling his nose and mouth with sand.

It was eerily quiet as the horses pounded off toward the finish line. As he lay there with his face buried in the dirt, he realized first that his leg was broken, and that he shouldn't move it. He lifted his head as he unlatched his helmet. He stripped it off, along with his goggles, tossing them aside.

He boosted himself onto his elbows just as the ambulance pulled up, and spit out blood and sand from his mouth.

Rachel heard screaming and gasps from the grandstand behind her. "Billy, what happened?" She jumped several times, hoping to catch a glimpse of something, but all she could see were horses and jockeys thundering toward the finish line.

"A spill. Not sure who..." his voice trailed off. Billy craned his head to try to see who fell, but the answer came to them when Erick's horse sprinted past them at full speed and continued around the clubhouse turn. An outrider gave chase.

"No!" Rachel grabbed her head with both hands. "Pull me up! Pull me up!" Rachel reached for Billy's arm. He pulled until she was seated behind him on their horse. Billy shouted and kicked Indian into a run toward the ambulance. *We must be idiots to participate in a sport where an ambulance has to follow behind picking up injured people*, Rachel thought as she willed the horse to run faster.

Coming from the grandstand, Julia and Paul ran behind them on foot. Rachel jumped down from the horse to find her husband conscious, sitting up, and holding his leg. *Oh, thank God. Thank God*. The EMTs were assessing the situation. They were preparing to cut off his boot.

"Are you okay? What happened, baby?" She fell to her knees beside him.

"The stirrup fell off. Dammit this hurts," he yelled between gritted teeth, then spit out more blood. With a groan, he flopped backwards onto the sand. Fighting tears, Rachel lifted his head into her lap then brushed sand from his hair and face.

"Try to stay still, sir," one EMT said calmly. Erick pounded his fist in the dirt but did his best to stay quiet. Rachel stuck the whip in front of Erick's mouth, and he grabbed it and bit down hard into the leather wrapping.

Julia paced in circles next to the ambulance thanking God he wasn't hurt worse. Paul tried repeatedly to hold her, but she refused and kept moving. Visions of her husband's fateful accident fifteen years ago rushed through her head as she paced in circles. She shook her head repeatedly to rid herself of the horrible scenes. *This sport is just too dangerous. I knew this would happen sooner or later. Just not this soon.*

***

Erick was on his way to the hospital, so Rachel asked Billy to go into the locker room to get Erick's wallet and clothes.

"Here you go."

"Thanks."

"I gotta get back to the barn. You're going to drive Erick's car?" Billy was doing his best to smother a grin.

"Yes," Rachel said, slapping his arm. Billy laughed, then left, heading for the barn.

Rachel stuffed the clothes into Erick's duffle bag and was just about to leave when Mario came out of the locker room.

"Come here. I gotta tell you something," he said with his thick Puerto Rican accent. She stepped back when he moved too close. The fiery glint in his eyes was not one she had ever seen before. Despite what she wanted to do, she moved out of the way of the door and into a quieter area so they could talk.

"What is it?" Rachel asked cautiously, not sure if she really wanted to know the answer to that question.

Her heart nearly stopped when he drew closer to her, close enough to smell his sour breath, most likely due to flipping, vomiting to lose weight. It was also obvious which jockeys flipped because of their teeth. Mario had the blackened and rotten teeth most of them had. She wrinkled her nose and tried to turn her head without being rude. But he had no qualms about being rude, and drew even closer, backing her into a wall.

Trapped. Her breathing quickened as she tried to hide her fear. He seemed to like the fact that he was scaring her. Just like the monster had. She slid sideways, but he put his hand on the wall, blocking her path.

Then it hit her. Mario was nowhere near as large as the monster. In fact, he probably weighed exactly the same as Erick, and she could pick him up. Easily.

She stood a bit taller. Mario let his arm drop as Rachel scowled at him, but he kept his intensity.

"You start riding to replace him and I'll make sure you never ride again. The others agree. We don't want you in the way. You understand?" It didn't sound like Mario. He sounded evil, as if he had been possessed.

Something came over her that she hadn't felt for a long time. She wanted to hit him, push him, punch him, yell at him, and her face flushed with anger. Her green eyes burned into his as she spoke. "You hurt me or my mother's horses and I'll make sure *you* never ride again. Understand?"

He ogled her up and down, sizing her up, but when he didn't respond, she pushed him with her shoulder and stormed away.

Once out of view of him, her whole body shook and felt weak. She pushed herself to move faster toward the car. By the time she hit the asphalt of the parking lot, she was running. Fumbling with the key, she finally slid it into the lock and opened the door. She threw the duffle bag onto the passenger seat, slipped behind the wheel, and shut the door. She pushed down the lock with her elbow and checked to see if he was following her. Thankfully, he wasn't.

As the GTO engine roared to life, she debated whether she should tell anyone about Mario's threat. Was he serious? Would he hurt her? Or was he just trying to scare her? After swallowing what felt like a watermelon, she started to cry, but stopped herself immediately. *No!* She was not going to let fear take hold. She refused to imagine all the horrible things he might do to her, though she knew exactly what those things were from her past experience.

Her husband was in the hospital and needed her. For now, that was more important than focusing on the past. So she put the car in drive, and slowly and carefully headed to the hospital, driving for the first time since she was sixteen.

***

Erick was resting comfortably in a cast below his left knee, watching the television on the wall with Rachel seated next to him on the bed. The two watched the news as reporters talked about his injury and speculated on who would ride Chivalry. A reporter interviewed a backside worker as they stood under a tree.

"I heard Julia's daughter, Rachel, might ride him. She's always wanted her license. And now, since other girls around the country are trying it, I bet she might try it, too."

"Is that something you approve of? Women riding in races?"

"Ha. No. Definitely not. They just don't have the upper body strength, you know? They're the weaker sex. They're too fragile."

"What would happen if Rachel did try to ride Chivalry in a race?"

"There'd be quite an uproar, I tell you that." The man put his hands on his hips and shook his head. "It ain't gonna happen in New York, though. They'll never let her. New York is where all the best riders in the country ride. They'll never let a woman in. Never."

"Who do you think should ride the horse?"

"Well, not sure they'd ride for a woman trainer, but I was thinking somebody like Bill Shoemaker, or Laffit Pincay. They need to ride a horse like that. Not some amateur and especially not a girl."

Rachel's blood boiled as she glared at the man she knew to be a groom in another barn.

Erick rubbed her back. "You can do it, Rachel. You do have the upper body strength. Not that you need it much. You can't physically hold the horse back with the reins. You ask, and they give. This man has no clue what he's talking about. He's just a groom. Probably never ridden a horse in his life."

"I guess." Rachel let out a breath of air and lowered her head into her hands.

"If your mother knows what's good for her, she will put you up on him. You know that horse as well as I do. Or better. It only makes sense, other than the fact that you don't have your bug yet. I say you apply now and see what happens."

Rachel thought it might be the pain meds talking. He should have known what mom would say to her applying for her apprentice, or bug, license. She would say no, for sure. She knew she could make her own decisions, but she did not want to go against her mother's wishes. Besides, there was that threat from Mario. Rachel mused for a minute as she sat next to Erick on the bed. She wanted to help the stable by taking over for him, but at the same time, she had never ridden in a race. It would definitely be different from morning workouts.

But this could be it. Her big chance. The thought both excited and petrified her, though she didn't show it, choosing to think about it later, if it even happened at all. Rachel pasted on a smile and agreed with her husband. "Yeah, I guess. She, of all people, should be the one to give me the chance. But she doesn't want me to ride." Rachel paused, thinking for a second. "I wonder if she's not letting me because she doesn't want to appear to be favoring her daughter. Or maybe she's scared I'll get hurt. Either in a race, or…," she stopped the thought from crossing her lips.

"Or what?" Erick asked as he desperately tried to stay awake and pay attention to his wife. The drugs made him feel as though he was in a plastic bubble full of water, but he took her hand and set it on his leg.

"Well, the others wouldn't do anything to hurt me, would they?"

"Who? Other jocks? No way. They wouldn't do that to you."

"Well, I don't know."

"Why? Why would you think that?" Erick asked, sitting up more. His voice rose as he finished his question.

"Well," Rachel started. "Um," She squeezed his hand, and decided to tell him. "Mario came up to me and told me if I ever got my license and started riding, he would make sure, well, you can imagine."

"What did he say, Rachel?" he said as anger pierced his dark blue eyes. He sat up a little more, his mind clearing now that his blood was pumping.

She held her head as she stood up and walked in a circle, trying to calm her beating heart. "He said he would make sure I never rode again. No specifics. I don't know what exactly he meant by that."

Erick's face filled with surprise, horror, anger, and concern for his wife's safety. He looked back and forth as if trying to find the answer somewhere in the room. "He threatened your life, baby. Oh, my God. I'm gonna punch that bastard."

"We should let it go. He probably didn't mean he would do anything. It was only a threat to scare me. I shouldn't let it get to me. He wouldn't do anything to hurt me, would he? He doesn't seem like the type."

"No, but he also didn't seem like the type to threaten someone like that either, especially not someone he's worked with and known for what, six or more years? I think he's jealous. I think he is worried about you taking his rides because he knows you are a better rider. He sees you and your perfect form up there on mom's horses, he sees how you handle them, and he's jealous. The only way he can feel better about his sorry self is to threaten someone," Erick barked. She tried to calm him down by rubbing his arm and patting his hand.

"It's okay, don't worry about it. We'll see what happens later. We can talk to Mom about who's going to ride Chivalry. But I swear if she picks Mario, I'm gonna be pissed."

***

Julia was deep in thought while Rachel bounced her knee nervously and waited. Finally, she couldn't wait any longer.

"Mom," Rachel started.

Julia knew what was coming and put down her fork. "No," she simply stated.

"Mom, it doesn't make any sense why you won't give me a chance. No one else will either. How are we supposed to make this move for women if you don't help me? You're the only one who can help me. And help women. Are you afraid I'll get hurt or something?"

"Yes, of course, but I know that's part of racing." Julia sat back in her yellow chair. "Honey, I need to tell you something." She paused to gather her thoughts. "Someone threatened me that if I let you ride, he'll make sure you don't ever ride again. He was so...evil when he said that, and it...just...it scared me." Without another word, she closed her eyes and clenched one fist as if fighting tears. In only a second, she regained control and relaxed again.

Billy, Rachel, and Erick all stared, open-mouthed. Rachel was the first to recover and speak. "He threatened me too, Mom. Mario, right? Same thing. Same words."

"What?" Julia slammed her napkin onto the table. "I'll kill the little bastard myself if he lays a hand on you."

Rachel looked at Erick. "I think you're right." She stood up and announced, "I'm going to ride that horse, win, then spit in his face from the winner's circle. I can't let him push you or me around, Mom. That's it. I'm riding."

Julia's heart sank as she realized it was time. This was it. Rachel was going to do it. Her stomach burned with nervousness and she fought the urge to tell her it was too dangerous. It was, but Rachel already knew that. She was going to do it regardless of the dangers. Watching her daughter stand there bravely declaring that she would take on this fight, Julia was petrified, yet proud at the same time.

Rachel had always assumed that she would have to sue the New York Racing Association to force them to grant her an apprentice license. But now the concern was the time needed to go through the judicial process. Mom had races coming up and she wanted to ride those horses. The Derby couldn't be her first race. She had to get in as many races as possible before the Derby. She needed experience before the big race. She had to get moving on this.

Rachel filled out the application the next day, took it directly to the stewards at the track, and waited for her answer. She included a letter explaining their situation and urging them to allow her to take over for her husband while he was injured. She also added a letter of recommendation from Julia as a trainer. The stewards knew her, knew this was coming, knew she was a good rider, but also knew that the male jockeys could make things difficult, if not impossible for her.

CHAPTER TWENTY-FIVE

The stewards had seen her exercise horses nearly every morning since she was fourteen years old, but they decided to watch her again to judge whether she was skilled enough. She told herself it was just a formality and to think of it like any other workout. Even so, she had to try to keep her heart from beating out of her chest.

Since she was working Chivalry that morning, she invited them to watch her on him. She double-checked the saddle and stirrups, bridle, reins, everything, just in case. Because of her husband's accident, she had been worried about someone sabotaging her equipment and causing another spill. Billy helped her get ready and checked it as well. "You're good, Sis," he said, patting her on the back. He gave her a leg up and as they walked away, she knotted the reins and shoved her toes into the stirrups. Balancing on the balls of her feet, she straightened her legs for a second to make sure the stirrups were the correct length and the saddle was secure. She hooked the helmet strap under her chin and sat up straight, trying to relax as Billy led them to the track. Chivalry was calm for now, but she knew he was going to become excited as soon as he set foot on the dirt.

Rachel was nervous but told herself to remain calm, and act as if everything were perfectly normal. *Nothing different, just another day on the track.* Her horse trotted and side-stepped his way to the chute where the stewards had told her to break the horse from the starting gate. Another routine move.

Her horse loaded well with the help of an assistant starter. Rachel held on to Chivalry's mane, and with a loud ring, the gates flew open, freeing three horses. She lowered her hands and held him back after he broke, not wanting him to run all out in the beginning. Julia had asked for a mile breeze with a push at the end. Chivalry liked longer workouts, and was always slow to start, fast to finish. Her form was tiny and perfect as she moved in unison with her horse, hiding in his mane. Then she relaxed, allowing him to run comfortably, not pushing him, yet not holding him back.

For the last quarter, she fully let out the reins and allowed Chivalry to run as fast as he wanted. She concentrated on her form, balance, and where she was on the track. The other two horses that had broken with her had been left behind long ago and they were nowhere near. She ducked down as low as possible while staying perfectly balanced, making her horse's run easier. She found joy and happiness in the eagerness of her colt as he floated over the track. She heard four quick thuds in the dirt with every stride, and silence as he soared in between. Rachel found nirvana as the long-legged three-year-old stretched out for the last furlong and shot under the wire.

She slowed her horse and made her way to the stewards, who were standing near the outside rail. She stopped directly in front of them and waited for their next move. They were going to either ask her questions about racing, tell her she was approved, or tell her she was denied. She wasn't hopeful, despite knowing that she had ridden perfectly and the horse ran well. After all, she was female. And while the stewards knew she would win a court case, she also knew they could deny her just to delay the whole process. They also knew she was poised and ready to go.

Rachel walked her horse in circles to cool him as the stewards talked amongst themselves. Her heart was pounding and she was worried about passing out or hyperventilating while waiting. *Wouldn't that be a sight? The press would love that one. "Future jockette passes out and falls off her horse before stewards can give her an answer. Another reason why girls shouldn't be jockeys."*

The oldest man in the group finally called her to the fence. "Rachel, we've talked it over, and we've decided to approve you for your apprentice license."

Rachel almost fell off her horse at the news. It was much better than she could have expected. Words jumbled in her throat, but she had to speak, and soon. *Say something. Now.* "Thank you," she managed to get past her lips. "Thank you," she repeated. "Um, Julia thanks you, too. Wow," she said, trying not to laugh in her excitement. The three men walked away without another word and Rachel pushed her horse into a trot back to her family. Her face beamed with excitement.

Everyone cheered when they saw her face. But Erick's face was stern as he thought about Mario and his true intentions. Erick swallowed hard and peered up at his wife. "Word will get out about this, and fast. In fact, I bet the press have already been notified. We need to be extra careful now, okay?"

Julia responded, "We will. We have all of us together, all keeping our eyes peeled."

Rachel took Chivalry back to the barn, expecting angry people along the way. But track workers were hanging out around their shed rows, talking and cleaning. No one said anything to her about her test with the stewards. She knew that they hadn't heard yet, because there certainly would be some kind of reaction when they did.

The others caught up to her soon.

"Everything okay, babe?" Erick asked as he hobbled up with his crutches.

"Yeah, so far so good. I'm paranoid, though. Waiting for something to happen is almost worse than having it happen."

***

She felt as if she were being shunned. It was like a wall of heat when she walked onto the track ground the next morning. Hardly anybody outside her own stable wanted to be anywhere near her. But she had to go through with this. There was no turning back now. This was it. It was as if she had been thrown into the deep end of a pool full of tar. She hoped to figure out how to swim through this thick mess soon.

Security had been posted near their shedrow. "Gary, what is this?" Julia asked.

"People aren't too happy about this, you know." Gary, one of Belmont's oldest security guards, had been there from the beginning, from the time when Rachel's father died. He had watched Rachel grow up on the backside.

"Have there been any threats?" she asked him, trying to catch his eyes behind the reflective aviators.

"No, ma'am. Not yet. They're just not happy, that's all. The stewards told me to stand here and keep an eye out," he said folding his hands in front of him, standing with his feet apart, and sporting the air of a Secret Service agent. Julia was confident Gary would do his best to protect them. If she had to describe Gary in one word, it would be "loyal."

No one spoke after that. They didn't have to speak. They each knew what the other was thinking. Would it be worth it?

***

Rachel stared at her name in the program next to Summer Rain, her favorite filly. The race was at Aqueduct, and they had vanned the filly over that morning to prepare. There wasn't much time to prepare herself, though. Just a few days ago, she wasn't sure if she was ever going to get to this point. Now, without warning, she was thrust into racing and the spotlight. The press was there and the stands were packed, for a weekday. Had they all heard she was riding already? Did they all know? What did they have planned for her?

Her stomach burned as she changed into her husband's riding clothes in the bathroom. They were too big, but she could do nothing to make herself appear more like a man and, more importantly, less noticeable. Less obvious that she was going to cause a stir. Leaning on the sink, she looked directly at herself in the mirror. "What the hell am I doing?" Her reflection did not answer her, but instead reminded her of how feminine she was as she blinked her long eyelashes.

Was she tough enough for this? Were they going to bump her hard during the race? Would they cause a fall? Summer's running style afforded her the luxury of staying in the back of the pack for nearly the entire race, so she hoped to avoid as much trouble as possible. Apprentices were famous for going wide around the pack, losing precious ground, instead of trying to go through. She didn't want to look inexperienced. But she might not have much of a choice considering the other jocks were going to be out to get her.

Erick's valet helped her with her silks and saddle. Standing in the hallway near the silks room, she donned her stable's navy blue silks, and then covered her helmet with the blue cap. Gary came over to Aqueduct to help, and met them as the other jocks began coming out for the first race of the day. Rachel was happy she had him, but wished she had an entire flock of police officers, as Diane Crump did before her first race a little over a year ago at Hialeah. It had been the first time a female had ever ridden in a race where betting was allowed. Unfortunately for Rachel, one security guard would have to do.

She fought the urge to grab Gary's arm as they walked from the protection of the hallway into the paddock, now filled with horses, jockeys, trainers, and fans. As the first chorus of boos and Bronx cheers resounded from above, she made sure to divert her eyes away from them, hoping they would stop if she ignored them. However, it only made them work harder for her attention. Her heart pounded, flushing her freckled cheeks.

"Go get 'em, girl," she heard, and nearly laughed, as it was such a relief to have just one fan for her. And it was a man, too. That surprised her.

"Go back to the kitchen and make dinner," another yelled.

You do not want me to cook. Trust me.

"You should be making babies, not riding in races."

That one hurt.

"You can do it," one woman shouted over the men.

Finally, she made it into Chivalry's stall, behind the horse, and out of the view of most of the railbirds. Erick was there, along with her mother, and Summer's groom, Juan. It might have been Candy, had she not left town. But there wasn't time to think of that now. She had a race to plan. Not that she knew anything about this race.

Everything she had ever learned had seeped from her brain. It was replaced with stress as well as the evil comments and hatred coming from the fans. She shook her head and refused to give in.

Noting her glazed-over face, Erick took her hand. "Listen. You're going to be in back, anyway, right? As soon as you break, hold her back, let the others go. Don't let her get too far behind, and if you have to pass a straggler, do it. But once you hit mid-turn, let her go. It's not like Belmont. Shorter stretch here."

Rachel nodded. She knew all of this but it was good to hear again. She wanted desperately for Erick to hold her, which always calmed her down. But it was not the time to show any hint of what some might call "feminine" weakness.

"Rider's up!"

Rachel silently communicated with her mother, who patted her on the back, but said nothing. Rachel knew she was probably scared to death. Scared of losing her to an accident, scared someone was going to hurt her, scared they would gang up on her. "I'll be fine, Mom," she said, though she wasn't sure she believed it herself. Julia nodded as she reached for Rachel's ankle. Rachel gathered the reins, hopped up, and settled on Summer's back.

She wasn't sure, but there might have been more catcalls from the stands behind her as they walked toward the track. Somehow, she tuned them out as she kept her attention on her hands and her horse. Billy took over leading once they hit the track, and they were opened up to the entire grandstand, filled with even more angry men. She could almost taste the negative energy emanating from them. But only for a few seconds. That's all she would allow. After that, it was only her, her brother, and her horse.

"You know what to do?" Billy asked, speaking loud enough for Rachel to hear over the shouting.

"Yeah."

Billy nodded. "Okay."

Once they reached the gate, he handed her over to the assistant starter, who gave Rachel a disappointed glare, then pulled Summer forward. Attempting to seem unfazed, Rachel slipped her goggles down over her eyes as the starter led them into the third stall.

"Gonna knock you into the rail, bitch," the jockey next to her growled.

Thanks for the warning.

"Watch your mouth around the lady," another yelled.

"Shut up," the starter shouted from his vantage point in front as he supervised loading.

Rachel gathered her filly's mane into her hand, just as she always did whenever she broke a horse from the gate. *Just like a morning workout. Just like a workout.*

She knew very well that the chances of her finishing the race were slim, and winning was going to be next to impossible. She was ready for anything, even a spill. She had fallen before. Many times. Horses broke down during workouts every once in a while. Accidents happened in the morning, too, especially with horses running in all directions and speeds at the same time. She wasn't afraid of breaking a bone. In fact, it was a point of contention here at the track. The person with the most broken bones always won any fight concerning who was the toughest. If she had to break every bone in her body to prove she was as tough and strong as the guys, she was going to do it. Whatever it –

RING!

She wasn't ready as Summer bolted from the gate. She grit her teeth as she was nearly left behind. By some miracle, she held on, and kept her feet in the irons. However, the botched start was beneficial to them, as she leveled out and noted that they were in last place. Perfect.

She watched as a jockey twisted his whole body and glanced back toward her, knocking his horse off balance. "Under the arm, dummy," she mumbled.

Summer was pulling and asking for more rein, but the pack of horses in front of her kept her from moving her fastest. Dirt stung Rachel's cheeks as the kickback from the ten horses reached her. "Good for the skin," she mumbled into Summer's mane.

They had been released from the starting gate in the chute at the back of the track, and were now fast approaching the one turn in the race. She remembered Erick's instructions. *Smaller track*, she reminded herself, as she was so used to running on Belmont's mile and a half oval. Aqueduct's track was only one mile and an eighth around. It was already time to fire.

She clucked to her horse, loosened the reins, and guided her to the outside. She had to lose a lot of ground going wide, but it had to happen this way. Summer eagerly took advantage of her chance to run, surging forward.

"Come on, girl. Go, go, go," Rachel said into her horse's ear, hopefully not loud enough for anyone else to hear. She did not want to call attention to her higher pitched, female voice. Rachel urged Summer with her hands and voice, and wished she had her whip. However, as Summer brought her rider to the outside of the pack of horses, she knew she didn't need it. Summer was pushing herself, as if she knew she had to win the race.

They were flying, much faster than during morning workouts. The corners of Rachel's mouth inched higher and higher until she was nearly laughing with joy as they tore up space between themselves and the wire.

Then her heart felt like it fell from her chest. *Where is everybody? Where'd they go?* There was no one in front of her. No one. *Where's the pole? Where's the finish?* Panic washed over her as her mind went blank and she lost track of where she was. Fortunately, she caught sight of the black stripes on the rail fast approaching, and the giant pole that read, "Finish." *Whew.*

Suppressing the urge to scream and jump while still on her horse, she stood in the saddle and pulled on the reins. With one hand, she rubbed Summer between the ears. "You did it, girl. You did it." She patted Summer's neck as her brother and Indian eagerly galloped toward her. Sheer joy beamed like sunrays from Billy's bright green eyes.

"Yeah!" he shouted at the top of his lungs as he held up his hand. She smacked it in reply. Billy took hold of Summer's bridle, and they set off for the winner's circle. As they approached, they felt the hatred again. This time, they weren't mad at her for riding. They were mad at her for winning.

Hoards of men threw wadded up tickets and pages from programs in her direction on the track. Summer shied from the onslaught, pulling on Billy's grasp, knocking their lead pony off balance. "Wait, Billy, wait." Rachel gathered her horse's reins tightly again and made sure they stopped well clear of the falling debris. Policemen wielding giant black sticks came and pushed men back from the rails. She couldn't believe her eyes. *All this just because a girl's riding in a horse race.*

Finally, the coast was clear, and they moved into the winner's circle. Erick took Rachel's hand and excitedly patted her leg. "You did it."

"You doubted me?" she asked, and they laughed and stood still for the photo. It only took a second. Rachel slid down, took off the saddle, and weighed in.

"How much did we win by? I didn't even realize I had passed them, Erick. My brain was mush out there."

"Geez. Be careful with that mushy brain next time, kid," he joked as he messed up her hair. They were seated in the barn after she had emerged from changing in the bathroom. She tapped his arm and fixed her hair. "Nine lengths, I think he said."

"Nine. Nice."

"You didn't have to win by that much. Next time once you know you have the race in the bag, you can stop pushing."

"You know I didn't have a whip, right?"

"Yeah, but you were pushing her."

"I was?"

Erick laughed. "That's what it looked like to me. You were pumping on her neck. You looked good though, of course." He kissed her cheek and scooted closer, wrapped his arm around her and stared at her, taking in every detail that he loved so much.

"What?"

"You're beautiful," he whispered into her ear, prompting her to shiver.

***

"You can't go wide like that every race, you know," the angry voice growled from behind her. Rachel turned around to face the man. *Mario*. She nearly rolled her eyes.

"I know, Mario. Leave me alone," she started to walk away. He grabbed her arm, which she jerked free again.

"Listen. You think you're hot shit, don't you? You're just asking for it. I'm just trying to warn you. They're pissed."

"Who? The other jocks? Well, I don't care. They're going to have to accept that a female is riding a horse, *like they have for thousands of years,*" she added, leaning in closer for emphasis.

"Consider yourself warned," he answered simply, then stormed off. As strong and tough as Rachel tried to be, she was also scared, though she tried her hardest to hide it. She kept her jaw set, her eyes set straight in front of her. She squared her shoulders. She refused to let them know they were intimidating her.

Erick hobbled up to her as quickly as he could with his crutches. "What did he want? I couldn't get here in time. What did he say?" Erick glared in the direction Mario had gone.

"Just a warning, he says."

Still glaring in Mario's direction, Erick answered, "I really wish I could ride right now so I could have an excuse to be in the jocks' room and try to figure out what they're going to do."

"They'd hide it from you. Maybe by the time you get back, they'll give up. Don't they know the judges are watching? And there are cameras that the stewards watch. Are they that dumb?"

"Mario is."

Rachel chuckled. Still, Mario's words worried her. There was no way she was going to stop riding now. She had won her first race. Nearly unheard of with jockeys just starting out. Besides, her mom needed her now more than ever. No one else wanted to ride for her anymore.

***

With the crowd shouting jeers her way and the other jockeys glaring at her, Rachel did her best to ignore it. Again, her priority was to prove them wrong. Well, and to stay safe. She wasn't sure what the others had planned for her, but the horse she was riding today was not going to do well coming from behind and going around as Summer had done. Rachel and Groovy Guru were going to have to fight their way through the crowd today.

Once they were running, Rachel fought the urge to place her horse in the back of the pack. Guru had started well and was pulling on her full force. Somehow, she found herself in third and near the rail, boxed in by Mario.

Mario inched up next to her and Rachel groaned on the inside, dreading his move. Of course, Mario knew exactly where the judges were able to watch him, and where the angles were not the best. Coming around the clubhouse turn, Mario moved his horse closer and closer to Rachel, not with an immediate bump, but gradually moving over, crowding her horse. Guru grunted, annoyed with the other horse for invading his space. He surged forward without Rachel's prodding. Rachel was secretly thankful for his move. He had protected them both.

Thundering down the backstretch, Rachel peeked under her arm and found that Mario had fallen back. His horse was tiring. Rachel was relieved, but only for a few seconds. Now another horse and rider were next to her as they rounded the far turn.

With both horses swinging wide, Rachel knew she would be safe for the next few seconds. Then, as soon as the turn ended and the track straightened again, the rider next to her abruptly moved her way and slammed her into the rail. Rachel hissed in air and winced from the pain that shot through her left ankle. Her body tingled and she held her breath as she wondered if the other rider had broken it.

The other jockey laughed, but Rachel was able to refocus on the race and ignore the pain. However, Guru had faltered because of the bump, and the other rider continued on. Guru never recovered and came in third.

As Rachel stood in the saddle, she knew her ankle was working, and that this meant it was probably not broken, but it sure felt like it. Breathing hard, she tried to keep the pain under control. Once Billy took hold of the bridle, finally, Rachel relaxed and slipped her feet from the stirrups.

"Ow," she said simply.

"Did he hurt your foot?"

"Ankle. Slammed me on purpose." Rachel grit her teeth.

"You ought to launch an objection."

"Ha. You know they'll never let me hear the end of it."

"Might work. Might not. You're never going to hear the end of it either way. Might as well try it."

"You're right."

Rachel and Billy went to the outrider and had him call up to the stewards. Rachel dismounted and limped toward the telephone with the direct line to the men upstairs. The "objection" sign lit up the tote board, and the men in the crowd shouted non-stop as she tried to explain her situation to the judges.

"Sissy!"

"Wimp!"

They shouted a few other choice words, some of which Rachel had never heard before in her life. She chuckled and rolled her eyes as she sat down on a bench and took off her boot.

Touching it with her fingers hurt terribly, and she knew at the very least, it was probably black and blue under her black sock. She resisted the temptation to slide it down and check the severity, perhaps showing it to the crowd as if to justify her objection. But she knew it would do no good. They would probably cheer, glad that she was hurt. Rachel wondered why they did not see her as a human being. They saw her as an object, or some sort of monkey riding a horse.

When the objection sign disappeared and there was no change, the men shouted even louder, most laughing loudly at her as they leaned over the railing. Rachel marveled at how ridiculous they looked as she slipped her boot back on and limped back to return her silks.

***

There was one more hurdle for her, that if she could overcome it, it would make her feel like she had accomplished everything she had ever wanted. So far, anyway.

"Remember the address you got from Dr. Franklin?" Rachel asked Erick.

"Yeah."

Dr. Franklin had suggested several months ago that they go by the house where she was held as another way to face the fear and overcome it. She did not think she'd ever find the nerve to go back there. Now she had. "So, you want to try it?"

"Think you can drive? I'm afraid I'd go nuts and run into something if I drive."

"Yeah, my right foot is fine. I can drive. When do you want to go?"

"How about this afternoon? We don't have anything else to do."

"Okay."

They were soon on their way after looking at a map for directions. Erick didn't know his way around the city at all and had never been to this part of New York. Rachel wasn't all that familiar with Harlem, either. They marked out three locations on the map. Since she was going to go through with seeing the house where she was held, she figured she might as well see it all – Candy's house in Queens, the alleyway where she was taken, and then the monster's house.

As they passed the movie theater where Rachel and Candy had seen the movie, "Bonnie and Clyde," she felt her nerves trying to steal her breath away. Moviegoers stood in line as they waited to buy tickets, not even realizing that the last time she was here, a tragedy had happened. But she couldn't dwell, as Erick continued on.

Candy's house looked as though it had been renovated and had nice landscaping in front. Rachel knew Don had to be in jail and had probably lost the house. Her emotions swayed between feeling sorry for Don to missing Candy, to being happy that the house looked so nice now. Candy would love it.

"This isn't at all what it looked like before. It was so run down. Their parents had died, I guess about five years ago. Now, God only knows where Candy is." She bit her tongue to keep herself from crying. Erick patted her hand.

With a deep breath, Rachel admitted she was ready for step two – the alley.

Only a short distance away, on a quiet street lined with small businesses, Rachel's heart beat much faster as they neared the alley. She didn't even have to tell him which alley it was because Erick could tell from her reaction. Her face held terror and her violently shaking hand went to her mouth. Erick was having trouble as well, knowing this was the spot where, just a little over a year ago, something horrible had happened to her.

They stopped in a parking space on the corner, and Rachel's body shook with fear as she locked her door with her elbow. Then she scooted closer to Erick and he put his arms around her. Her whole body shook as though she was cold, and Erick held her tighter. With one trembling finger, she pointed into the dark alley. "Th-There's the door." Visions of herself banging on the door frantically, hoping someone would open it and save her, flashed before her, but she shook her head to rid herself of them. She repeatedly told herself that she was safe now, and that awful man was in jail. Finally.

It took several minutes, but she had finally calmed herself and told Erick she was ready to go to the house.

As they drew closer and closer, she felt that old familiar feeling of the blood wanting to rush from her head. However, she stayed focused and told herself she would be okay and that the monster wasn't there. A battle warred inside her mind as those memories wanted to attack her and take her back in time. She was determined to win this fight, though. It had been a long time since the kidnapping, and it was time to beat this thing once and for all.

Finally, Erick pulled over to one side of the road. The dark brick house on the right was boarded up and Rachel knew that was the one. Suddenly, and without warning, she was cast back into the past and was being carried from the van and into the house by a smelly man in a black t-shirt. Erick tried to hold her, but she wouldn't let him get near her.

"Rachel, it's me. You're all right. You're in the car. With me. Okay? He's not here."

She focused on her husband. Then tears started and she whispered, "This is harder than I thought it would be." She scooted herself to his side and clung to him. Erick waited. After a minute, she mustered up her bravery to look up at the house again.

Erick was shaking his head and trying hard to control his own emotions as anger and frustration swept through him at the sight of the house where his future wife had almost died. That monster had scratched her with a knife, leaving scars – physical and emotional. His disgusting actions replayed in Erick's mind as he remembered some of the things she had mentioned in her written story last summer. He pictured Rachel inside this place, tied to a sagging bed, a swarthy man at her side poking her with needles and knives before raping her, leaving her bloody, drugged, hungry, and thirsty. But she was strong. She was able to get away. He was proud of her for thinking so clearly despite everything she had been through, and rubbed her arms and kissed her head.

Meanwhile Rachel stared. She remembered things, then stared some more. She decided this was it. She was going to leave this behind now. The worst was over and now she knew it was time to let it go for good and move on. No longer would the fear scare her into having flashbacks.

Several minutes later, she felt it was time to go, and time to leave it behind for good. When she looked at Erick, he knew she was going to be okay, and it was the right time to leave. He put the car in drive and drove away as she stole one more quick glance, then looked back at the map to find her way home.

***

Though things calmed down over the next few races, Chivalry's next race seemed to reignite the flame of hatred as fans knew Chivalry's talent, but doubted Rachel's ability to ride him. What they didn't know was that she worked him every morning. They didn't know she took him out to graze from time to time, giving his groom a break. They didn't know she was able to ride this horse bareback, maybe even without a bridle. She knew him better than any horse in the barn, as she had latched onto him from the first time she was allowed to ride him a year ago.

As she and her brother marched in line in the post parade, she reminded herself of Chivalry's incredible speed. He would be able to win against these other horses easily, especially with her on his back. He liked her. He responded for her.

"This is a stakes race, you know," Billy reminded her, as if reading her mind.

"I know."

"Not gonna be as easy."

"Well, they're all at about the same level. Chiv's one of the best stakes horses around, though. He can do it." The purse in this race was larger and the competition was tougher than the normal every day races. This race, "The Gotham Stakes," was an important Kentucky Derby prep race.

"You planning on holding back at first?"

"Yeah. He's best at coming from behind. I'll try to do like I did with Summer that time. Maybe go around the outside."

Billy shrugged. "I guess."

This time, in the gate, she was ready, as she had run in seven races so far. She had won two, had come in second twice, third once, fourth twice, all despite the other jocks' attempts at ruining her. And this time, she knew she was going to win. She couldn't lose. Couldn't *let* him lose. She had to do everything right, think fast and be prepared for when the other jocks tried their tricks on her.

In the gate, there were jockeys and horses from out of town who had been travelling around the country racing and proving themselves before the Kentucky Derby. None of these riders had ever ridden with a female in a race before. Rachel found it amusing as they stared silently, some trying to give her a quick evil eye, some afraid she might get in their way, some just completely confused. They never said a word, but she knew that would change.

Bahama Dream was here, Delune, who was from California, and JackofallTrades, who seemed to be completely outclassed. She had done her homework, memorizing what each of these and the other horses had done in their previous races. She knew what to expect from each of them. She knew each of the jockey's strategies. But they also knew hers.

Chivalry chewed his bit as he waited, and she jiggled it to keep him focused. He tossed his head, and the assistant starter straightened him again. Rachel glanced down the line to find one more horse to load. She accidentally caught the eye of another jockey, whose anger burned through his layers of goggles.

With a loud ring and the clattering of the gates, they were freed, and the horses bolted. Rachel sank with the initial jump from the gate. It was as if the bottom fell out as her horse lowered, and he shot forward as if out of a cannon. His strong legs propelled them forward with a stronger kick than any sports car out there. She held on until the horse leveled out, then flattened her back and relaxed. The start is always the hardest part; at least that's the way Rachel felt, and, as she had heard from Erick, almost every other jockey felt the same.

Chivalry was smooth, gliding down the backstretch from the chute. The other six Derby hopefuls did exactly what she had expected, with Jack taking the lead, Bahama near the back, and Delune just off the pace. With a month to go before the Derby, each horse was out to prove they were the best. They each wanted to take Chivalry's spot as the favorite. Rachel knew that would never happen. Chivalry was the favorite, and always would be.

Rachel and Chivalry stayed behind the field, allowing themselves to avoid nasty moves from the other jockeys. However, she knew it wasn't possible to stay out of sight forever. They were approaching the time to fire.

As the horses rounded the turn, the crowd noise increased and whips sprung up and down. Rachel had enough races now to be allowed to use hers, and tapped him just a few times.

Then she waved it alongside his neck as she moved to the outside for their final push.

Chivalry swallowed up ground easily, much more so than any of the other horses she had ridden. Taking Erick's advice to heart, she stopped urging Chivalry when he reached the front. Rachel heard another horse coming from behind, but the finish line was steps away, and she knew she was going to win, regardless. As they flew under the wire in first place, she waved her whip in the air, and then pulled up her horse.

Surprisingly, the reception in the winner's circle was not entirely negative. They heard the usual nasty remarks about going back to the kitchen and having babies, but some clapped and cheered happily, encouraging her and her horse. Rachel rubbed her horse's sweaty neck.

CHAPTER TWENTY-SIX

The field of eight for the Wood Memorial at Aqueduct paraded by the stands, each horse carrying the Derby weight of one hundred twenty-six pounds. The start and finish lines were at the same spot on the track in front of the stands. Rachel rode her horse to the gate for the last time before the Derby.

Butterflies flew around her stomach as she thought about the Derby being only two weeks away. The Kentucky Derby – every jockey's dream race, and she was about to ride in it. Of course, she felt awful for her husband, who had been anxious to have his own chance at the big race at such a young age. But she had to step up and take over. This had to be done. No one else was able to ride Chivalry. Not if she had anything to do with it.

Chivalry felt her nervousness through the reins and saddle. He tossed his head and bucked as Rachel tried to straighten him out and get him inside the starting gate. The horse's behavior certainly didn't help her nerves.

"Easy, buddy. Easy, buddy," she repeated. "No need for this. You can do this. Let's get in there and go and you'll get to run all you want." Chivalry flicked his ears and was listening, but was still worked up. Two handlers came and pushed Chivalry into the fifth slot after turning him in circles a few times. While the other three were loaded, a normally well-behaved Chivalry stood still for a few seconds, but surprised Rachel by gathering himself and rearing up in the stall. The starter in the stall with them grabbed Rachel by the waist and pulled her to the side and off the horse. With the starter's help, they calmed Chivalry while Rachel sat back in the saddle. "What's with you today?" she asked the nervous colt.

"He can't wait for the Derby, I guess," answered the starter. She was amazed that the starter had been so helpful, and then had spoken to her as if she were human. Rachel chuckled, then grabbed some of the horse's mane and held on, prepared also for more acting up. A few seconds later, the bell rang and the doors flew open.

Chivalry had kicked the door as the starter pushed the button, and he wound up breaking out on the wrong lead. He quickly changed leads himself and leveled out, but was in last place now. Rachel shook her head. Things were going strangely today and she didn't like the sinking feeling she had in her stomach. She knew something was wrong. Chivalry wasn't pushing to catch up and wasn't pulling on the bridle. But since the race was long, Rachel decided to gradually move up and not push her horse too hard.

Going around the clubhouse turn, they stayed closer to the rail and in last place. Heading into the backstretch, she squeezed up between two horses and settled in behind Delune. Rachel had moved Chivalry up to third by the end of the backstretch, but they were still several lengths behind the frontrunners. She hoped the others were tiring themselves out and were going to fall back soon, but she gave Chivalry a tap to push him along as they reached the homestretch.

He didn't respond at all. He kept the same pace and refused to change leads. He wasn't trying to get the attention of his fans, wasn't trying to run with a friend, he simply did not push himself. Seconds ticked by as Rachel tried to figure out what was wrong. Then, she heard someone shouting her name and she looked back to find another jockey pointing at Chivalry's leg. He was yelling something in Spanish and Rachel couldn't understand him. She leaned over and saw blood dripping from his front right leg. It was running across his leg, mixing with dirt and drops were flying backward. He was bleeding, and bleeding heavily. Just then, they sailed under the wire in third place behind Bahama Dream and North Star. The crowd was silent as they witnessed the favorite coming in third. It was only his second loss, as he had won every race after his first career start last year. Rachel slowed Chivalry, her heart sinking.

He didn't seem to be limping, but his leg had to hurt. Rachel muttered under her breath, mentally slapping herself for not checking her horse's legs after he reared in the gate. Rachel knew she should have known better, but so should the starters. Or maybe the blood didn't appear until he'd kicked the gate and started running. Either way, she wished she would have known.

Billy rode up and pulled his horse to a quick stop "Oh, no," he muttered, seeing the blood up close.

The look on his face worried Rachel, and she leaned down to check Chivalry's leg again. Julia ran up on foot.

"What's...? Oh, no," Julia said with her hand over her chest. Rachel couldn't tell how bad it was, so she dismounted to check it closely. Chivalry was impatiently pawing at the dirt, making it cloud up and making his cut even messier. Blood was pouring down his leg quickly now. Julia and Rachel waved the ambulance down as Billy held Chivalry as still as possible.

The equine ambulance came, and a vet jumped out. He rinsed Chivalry's leg and bandaged it up enough to get him back to the barn.

The vet came to their stall, cleaned it out, gave him a shot, put ointment on it, and wrapped it tightly.

"If he were a person, he would need stitches. But I think we can avoid the trauma to him, We'll keep it tightly wrapped up and give him antibiotics. Try to keep it as dry as possible, put heat on it, and no running until I examine it again. I want an x-ray, though, just in case."

The Hanover team stayed quiet as they awaited the results from the veterinary team. Rachel and the others all thought the same thing – what now? They only had two weeks until the Derby.

Fortunately, the x-ray was clean, showing no damage to the tendons or bone. They kept his legs warm and kept the cut as clean and dry as possible, hoping for it to heal before Derby day. Or was it worth it to risk further injury by running in the Derby?

"I'm having flashbacks to several years ago," Julia muttered, referring to the last Derby horse she'd had, Midnight Star.

"Oh, yeah. Scratched because of a scratch. Was it this bad, Mom? Or was it worse?" Rachel asked.

"Well, it was closer to the Derby for one. He injured it two days before the race during a workout. So he didn't even have a chance. Chiv here... I don't know. He can't run until it heals. So I don't know how we're going to work him between now and then. I'm hoping in a week, he'll be ready for at least a jog around the track. If we take care of it right, I think he will heal up nicely."

Rachel shook her head. "No wonder he was running like that. I knew something was wrong. Even when we left the gate, I had a bad feeling. I should have trusted my instincts. I should have pulled him up from the start. I had no idea he was bleeding until Jose tried to tell me right before the finish, which surprised me, by the way."

"It's okay, babe. How could you have known? It's not like you can watch his feet as you're running the race," Erick said, putting a hand on her shoulder.

Julia tried to set her mind at ease. "You're so hard on yourself, honey. Don't worry about it. He'll be okay. Erick's right. How could you have known?"

"He kicked the gate just as the bell rang, too," Rachel remembered. "He was a nervous wreck before the race. But I was nervous, too, and I guess he was feeling my nerves."

"Why were you nervous?" Erick asked.

"Just thinking about how close we are to the Derby. We might actually have a shot. Although now, who knows?" Rachel groaned softly. "I should have been focusing on *this* race. Not one two weeks away."

Erick hugged her around her waist and kissed the side of her head. "It's okay, babe. Even if we scratch him from the Derby, he's a great horse and we all know it. Maybe he'll win the Preakness and Belmont and we will still have a great horse."

"Yeah, I guess."

Julia patted her on the back. "That's horse racing for ya. You gotta take the good with the bad, and accept it. Let's go home."

CHAPTER TWENTY-SEVEN

First Saturday in May, 1970

She stood in front of the mirror inspecting herself in the navy blue and white silks. Her shirt was dark blue and had a white Hanover family seal on the upper left corner. The same seal was on the back. She had a blue and white cover for her helmet, white riding pants and black boots. As always, she did her best to hide her small waist, and put her long curly hair in a low ponytail and bandana. Later, she planned to tuck her hair under her helmet for two reasons: she didn't want to look like a girl, and she had to make sure the silks could be seen all the way.

Officials added a pad of weight to the underside of her saddle as the valet held it, then gave it to Rachel. She stepped onto the scale. Exactly one hundred twenty-six. She handed the saddle back to her valet.

With a nervous gulp, she left the safety of the hallway and headed out into a crowd of people in the paddock. Fans lined the walkways and eyed her up and down. When they realized it was her, most only stared, but she surprisingly heard a few encouraging words. "Go get 'em, Rachel," and "You got this," resounded among several boos. One man shouted, "Jockeys are supposed to be men. You think you're a man? Go back to the kitchen where you belong."

Ah, the old kitchen thing again. She ignored him, trying to be positive and hold her head high, not letting anyone get her down. She was focused, and was going to win today to prove them all wrong.

Julia, Erick, and Willy met her in the paddock. Julia was inspecting the wrap around Chivalry's front legs. The weeks between the Wood Memorial and the Derby were spent watching him closely and putting heat on his leg to promote healing. The press hounded them constantly, each reporter trying to be the first to get the word on Julia's decision on whether to run him. However, she hadn't decided until that morning.

Rachel had jogged him every day for the last week here at Churchill Downs, and he had come back with no blood on his bandage. They knew he was able to handle running, but would he be able to handle running a mile and a quarter without any major workouts to prep him for two weeks?

Chivalry was ready to go, standing patiently in his stall as Rachel marched up. Erick left her alone, knowing she was thinking only about her horse and the race ahead of her, the biggest of her life so far. It was her first Kentucky Derby and the stable's first Derby horse in eight years. Last time they had a Derby horse Rachel had to stay in New York with her grandmother and missed the whole thing. Unfortunately, their horse scratched from the Derby, then lost the Preakness and Belmont. This time, though, Rachel hoped for a different outcome. She had always fantasized about winning this race, but never really thought she would get the chance. Now, here she was.

Rachel's valet handed the saddle to Julia, who put it onto Chivalry's back. Rachel stood at Chivalry's head, holding his bridle in case he became nervous and moved. She felt as if she had to do something too, or come apart from nervousness. She hadn't eaten all day, which may have been due to nerves or because she didn't want to gain weight.

Television cameras and reporters bounced from stall to stall, trying to get shots of every horse and rider. Rachel found the camera focused on her a few times and tried to hide from it. But the spectacle of a female jockey riding in such a prestigious race was too much for the reporter to ignore. Without asking permission, with the camera rolling, a reporter moved closer to her.

"Rachel Bennett, New York's first female jockey, holding her horse as she prepares for the race. Rachel, tell me what you are thinking right now. You must be nervous."

She had been interviewed several times today, once with a reporter who had sat her and Erick down in a quiet area for an extensive talk. No matter how many television reporters talked to her, each time, it had scared her to death to be on camera. She wasn't used to this. Reporters had interviewed Erick several times before the other big races, but they had never talked to her before.

She tried her hardest not to look at the camera or show her nervousness. "Kind of, yes. I suppose you can imagine."

"Why, yes, I can only imagine what it must be like for a young jockey, especially for a female jockey. Have you experienced any of the backlash against females that the other jockettes have experienced?"

"Yes. New Yorkers are quite vocal, and have expressed their disapproval. But New York women are tough, too, and I'm not backing down. I want to ride, I want to be a jockey, and I'm riding whether they like it or not. I have every right to."

"Yes, you do, Rachel. Tell me. What is your strategy for this race?"

"Chivalry's better the further he runs. He loves distance, and once he gets going, he will be able to pass the others easily."

"So you'll be coming from the back of the pack?"

"Somewhere around there, yes. There are so many horses this year that finding running room will be especially hard. If anything beats Chivalry, it would be me not being able to get him out of traffic situations."

"You're prepared to take the blame if he loses?"

"Yes. He's definitely fast enough to win. I just have to get him there, and I have to avoid the others doing everything in their power to block me in."

"Well, best of luck to you, Rachel and Chivalry. I hope to speak with you in the winner's circle soon."

"Thanks."

Once the camera was gone, she let out a huge puff of air as her shoulders relaxed. "How'd I do?" she asked Erick.

"You are a pro," he answered, then kissed her. The short kiss took a tiny bit of stress from her, and she wished she could kiss him for the next half hour, until post time. "You were right. They're going to do everything in their power to box you in."

"Yeah. Think I should go around like the other races?"

"I can't say until it starts. I mean, you have to see how it starts, where everyone settles, and what the pace is. If the pace is fast, lay low and pass the tiring horses at the end. There are so many horses that it may not be practical to go around. But you'll have to see once you're turning for home."

Erick saw that his wife's face was ashen white and she was quiet, just as he normally was before a big race. In a way, he felt bad for her and wished he could take over and do it for her. Then again, he wanted her to achieve the goal she set for herself and their team. She wanted to be a jockey. She wanted Chivalry to win the Kentucky Derby. She wanted the win for her mom as well. Mom would be setting her own record for females in the business as the first female trainer to win the big race.

Erick thought his wife was the bravest woman in the world. He was astounded at the amount of pressure she had on her shoulders right now. And those shoulders were able to carry the weight because of the adversity she had gone through in the last year. It seemed as though that rough time had prepared her for this very day.

***

Finally, it was time to mount up for the Kentucky Derby. Rachel was so relieved to hear the call for riders up that she sighed loudly. Erick gave her a soft kiss before giving her a leg up onto Chivalry's back. She blew a tiny kiss his way to thank him, and glued her eyes to his for several seconds, trying to draw strength from him.

"Here goes," she said, barely above a whisper, as she felt the sensation of her stomach crawling into her throat.

"Love you, baby. Good luck." Trying to give her a bit more self-confidence, Erick patted her shiny new black boot, one in the set she had recently bought for herself, and nodded. "You can do this. You and Chiv *can* win this, Rach."

His hand lingered for a few seconds as her feet dangled around her horse's girth. As Willy began to lead Chivalry away, Erick let go and hobbled clear of his path.

Willy led them around a crowded bush-lined circle, through the tunnel under the grandstand, and then handed them over to Billy, who had flown in for the big race. Billy and Indian led a quiet Rachel and an excited Chivalry in the Kentucky Derby post parade.

Billy tried making conversation with her, but she only nodded in reply. Rachel only thought about her horse and race strategy now. There was nothing else, despite the pageantry of it all. She never saw the thousands of colorful flowers, ribbons, and hats billowing in the spring breeze, rich folks in the grandstand, holding their mint juleps, discussing which horse they had bet on. She was not aware of the enormous party in the infield, with drunk people screaming and climbing on everything in sight, just to get a better look. Some fans hopped over fences and neared the rails, prompting security to gather and force them back. But she never noticed. Everything around her was a big blur of horses, jockeys, and lead ponies, and that was fortunate because it kept her mind off the fact that millions of people were watching on television and over a hundred thousand were in the stands and infield.

As the announcer named each horse in the post parade, Rachel was quiet. But the crowd reacted loudly when Chivalry's and Rachel's names came across the loudspeaker. To Rachel, it sounded of mostly cheers with a few boos scattered among them. This crowd wasn't the normal every day crowd of men, some of whom made their living betting on horse races. This crowd contained people who were here for the spectacle of it all, the grandeur, the hats, the dresses, the movie stars, and, of course, the big party in the infield. Rachel waved in reply and tried her best to appear jovial, but went right back to her serious face and demeanor once they mentioned the next horse's name.

The bugler played the call to the post, and then the University of Louisville Band played, "My Old Kentucky Home" as everyone sang along. The song meant the world to everyone in the beautiful state of Kentucky, and many people were too choked up to sing it. But they stood and acknowledged it with their hands over their hearts as if it were the Star Spangled Banner. Everyone who was able to, sang. From the Queen of England and movie stars in Millionaire's Row to the drunken guy in the infield wearing only shorts and tennis shoes. The sound of tens of thousands of voices singing overwhelmed Billy and Rachel as they each tried to hide their emotions from the cameras.

There were so many horses starting that they had to get an additional starting gate tacked onto the end. There were eighteen running that year. It was going to be extremely hard for the horses in the outside positions to get to the rail for the turns. And those along the rail were probably going to get stuck in a pocket or squeezed back, forcing them to slow down. With this many horses, it created more chances for things to go wrong, and more chances for accidents.

Some owners and trainers had threatened to scratch their horses in protest of Rachel riding in the race, but they decided instead to do everything in their power to keep her from winning. Rachel was expecting some dirty play during the race but hoped to avoid as much as possible. For a fleeting second, she considered leading the race gate to wire. But Chivalry was not that kind of horse. He enjoyed firing and taking off like a rocket in the homestretch, not leading from the beginning. He probably wouldn't have had the stamina to go gate-to-wire in this onslaught of horses anyway.

And staying behind the large field would make it next to impossible for them to find a clear path through it at the end. The other jockeys, once they figured out she was trying to get through the pack, would work extra hard to keep her trapped. Her mind swirled as she tried to make some sort of a plan, though she knew it could all be tossed out the window at any point during the race.

The other jockeys sent the evil eye her way so many times, she had almost become immune to it. As the parade of thoroughbreds doubled back toward the gate, one particularly angry jock passed her, eyeing her the whole way. This time, instead of trying to ignore him, she winked, making him even more angry. She almost scolded herself for doing that, but decided it may be more beneficial for her to have him concentrating on her and not on winning the race.

As Billy continued to lead her, he tried to calm his sister's nerves by going over their plans and the what-if situations. She glanced at him occasionally and listened. "You're ready, Rach," he said with confidence. She nodded as their matching green eyes connected.

Finally, Billy let the horse go, and Rachel and Chivalry were handed off to the gate crew for loading.

They were number two in the large field, an unbelievably bad starting position. It meant with almost complete certainty that they were going to be smashed into the rail at the start. Rachel hoped Chivalry would start slow, as he did most of the time, though not always, which worried her.

Any of the riders in this race could bump her into the rail at any point, possibly injuring her foot, maybe causing a fall. They could keep her in a pocket with horses on all sides. They could put her between horses and squeeze, forcing Chivalry to check his speed, or maybe even clip heels and fall. But it was a chance she was willing to take. She was prepared to accept whatever happened, even if it meant losing the race or even breaking a bone. She just hoped it wasn't Chivalry's bone.

She kept her horse still and quiet in the starting gate while the others were loaded. Unfortunately, the scowling jockey from the post parade was right next to her in the gate. "Scowling man," is what she called him in her head, though his name was Diego. She felt his icy cold glare as she tried to focus ahead of her. *Pretend he doesn't bother you.*

She pulled a lock of black hair from her horse's mane into her hand. The horses were almost loaded up now. *This is routine. You've done this at least a thousand times. It will be just like back home, but with a few more horses around.*

"Good luck, kid," the assistant starter in her stall said softly. She was completely surprised by his well wishes, but Rachel only nodded in reply. Ready for the jump, she focused on the track ahead of her. Then she listened for the announcer in the top of the grandstand to her right. "The horses are in."

RING! The bell sounded and the horses took off. Rachel reacted quickly as her body was already tense, and she held on tightly as her horse bolted from the gate. He started well and settled near the rail in fourth place, which was not at all what she wanted. Chivalry ran comfortably but Rachel knew that any moment now, she would be slammed into the rail. So far, she was surprised that it hadn't happened. No one touched her, unlike most of her other races.

The first eighth pole flew by, and Rachel had felt that the pace of the race was fast. Too fast. She lowered her hands, slowed her horse a bit, and fell further back in the pack. She didn't want to run her horse into the ground. It was a long race.

As she slowed, she found herself among different horses and jockeys. The horse next to her moved in her direction, which scared her a bit, as she was expecting to be slammed into the rail. But he only moved close and didn't touch her. Now in seventh place, she found herself amongst a pack of wolves, or, horses. She had wanted to avoid it, but in recognizing that the pace was too fast and slowing down, she fell into a trap. Pretty much jumped into it herself. *It's okay, I'll get out soon. Something will open up. Plenty of time.* They rounded the clubhouse turn with every jockey staying as close as possible to her, keeping her trapped.

At the three quarter pole, she was still in seventh place, content to stay there for the time being. But in order to move up, she was going to have to go wide if no one moved from the rail. She decided to go a little wider now and try to find a hole. She tried to work her way around to the right, but found herself blocked in tighter instead. *Ugh, I knew it.* She might have to slow down even more and go around. With an internal groan, wishing she did not have to do this, she pulled harder on the reins.

However, as she and her horse slowed, she found that the others were also slowing down. Would she have to stop completely in order to go around them? How far are they willing to go to make her lose? Would they ruin their own chances? They were even yelling at each other in Spanish as they coordinated their speed to keep her trapped.

But, surprisingly, no one was touching her at all. It had to be that they were trying to avoid the scrutiny of the judges. Maybe the stewards had warned them not to touch her. *Hm...* She could use this to her advantage.

After thundering down the backstretch, they headed into the far turn. There was a hole forming between the two horses in front of her as they started the turn and one lugged out just enough for her. Rachel loosened her hold, and then whispered, "Come on." Chivalry surged forward as soon as he was given more rein. She barely had enough room but each jockey predictably moved over to make room for her, making sure they did not touch her.

She was still in a bit of a box with one horse on every side of her, but at least there was only one in her way now – Bahama Dream. She knew he was not able to handle the distance, and wasn't worried about him. But there were also three more further ahead. Chivalry was going to have to speed up, and the others were going to have to slow down, which all horses do in long races. But not Chivalry. For him, longer races were more fun, and he loved the chance to run almost to his heart's content.

At the mile, and still with a quarter of a mile to go, she was in fifth place and comfortable. There was no chance of getting boxed in again. She just had to get around the stragglers, who were now tiring and faltering. The horse along the rail to her left was exhausted, and he weaved and slowed drastically, making an opening near the rail. It was her chance.

But, just as she thought she was clear to move over and take his spot, "scowling man" came up on her inside, passing her in two huge strides as he violently whipped his mount. For a split second, off her left shoulder, Rachel found terror in poor Allegro's eye as he tried his best for his rider.

As "scowling man" was just in front and to the left of her, she watched him glance her way as everything became slow motion. The hatred in his eyes told her this was it. He was going to do it, whatever "it" was. She watched as he grabbed a tight hold on his right rein and yanked it hard. Rachel felt that an accident was imminent and sharply checked Chivalry, who became furious with her for doing so. But it was for his own good. Allegro swerved in front of them, pushing Bahama Dream over in the process. Diego risked his horse's safety and career and Bahama's to knock her out of the race. Was it worth it? She almost yelled out in anger, but decided to remain quiet and focus on getting her horse running again.

Just as she and Chivalry recovered from the shock, she found daylight on the rail, and swerved Chivalry in. They were in the end of the turn now, and she let her horse choose his own footing as they both realized that the finish was near.

There was under a quarter of a mile to go when she decided to hell with staying quiet and yelled at her horse, urging him on. "Go buddy, go. Go!" She hadn't had to bring out the whip yet and she decided to save it for an emergency. So far, Chivalry was responding well, excited to have his chance to run. At last.

However, "scowling man" wasn't finished with them and his horse's sweaty and dirt-caked head appeared on her horse's right flank. She lowered herself in the saddle, leaned forward, and stayed as still as possible, with her head so low it was seemingly buried in Chivalry's mane. Rachel clucked and her horse responded with additional speed and strength. "Scowling man" and Allegro were unable to match Chivalry's burst of speed and fell behind.

She never heard the deafening roar of the crowd as they were on their feet cheering for her. Only the sound of her horse's rhythmic breathing and hooves pounding the dirt resounded in her ears now. She was tiny in the saddle, balanced perfectly over Chivalry's withers, and hardly moving. They were soaring down the track and increasing their lead with each stride. The other horses were exhausted, but her horse had energy to burn.

The sounds of thundering horses behind her grew further and further away but she didn't notice. She only thought of her horse, running as fast as he wanted. Four quick thuds and silence, over and over, was music to her ears. Her favorite sound on earth was that silence between strides as her horse floated over the track. His mane whipped her face, reminding her of his incredible speed. She wanted to run forever. Stride after stride, they pulled further and further ahead of the others. The record-setting crowd was on their feet in a tumultuous roar as they were excited to witness history being made. But Rachel paid no attention to the crowd. She never heard the roar. Her focus was on her horse and loving life as they ran full speed down the track together. Too soon, she found the black stripes on the inner rail, then the finish pole and her horse sweeping under the wire in first place.

She didn't raise her whip as she had done in her dreams from childhood. She was having too much fun letting Chivalry run to his heart's content. He was running so easily, so beautifully, so effortlessly with his long strides, but she knew she had to slow him down. She waited a second or two past the wire to stand up in the saddle, lowering her hands and slowing her eager horse to a canter as they reached the clubhouse turn, where thousands of people stood cheering and waving at them. She told Chivalry that he had done great and he had won, but it still hadn't hit her fully yet. Her mind was in another world, enjoying the ride. *Did I just win*? She was so focused on the fun of it that she forgot she had helped their team win the Derby.

The Kentucky Derby!

She lowered her head and laughed at herself as Billy galloped up pumping his fist in the air. Meanwhile, the deafening roar of the crowd never died down.

"Rachel!" Billy shouted at the top of his lungs and over the crowd. She laughed again in reply, still unable to talk. "The Derby, Rach. You did it."

"I'm dreaming, Billy," she said, barely loud enough to be heard over the crowd. Billy grabbed her hand and raised it in the air, prompting even louder cheers.

In the owner's box, Erick, his parents, and Julia were cheering, jumping for joy, and celebrating with the Hanovers. The patriarch of the family sat in his chair with the biggest smile Julia had ever seen on his face. It was his first Derby winner. Without a word, Julia took his hand, as she was too emotional to speak. A police officer approached and escorted them from the stands and onto the track. Erick hobbled along with his crutches as they sank into the dirt. He wasn't able to keep up with the quickly moving crew, so Willy picked him up over his shoulder and carried him as Erick cheered wildly to those behind him.

Chivalry's owner, William Hanover, full of pride, and tears in his eyes, did his best to straighten his hunched back as he led Chivalry to the winner's circle, with the rest of the staff following behind. Julia walked next to Chivalry with her hand on the colt's shoulder. Erick was back on his crutches now that they were in the infield, and limped along next to Julia.

As he looked up to his wife, Erick was surprised at the expression on Rachel's face. She was happy, but he could tell it hadn't sunken in yet. He wondered how stressful the race had been for her, though she had made it through the race with no serious incidents, and she had won by about eleven lengths.

As Rachel eagerly patted and praised her horse, Erick patted her leg. "You did it, baby," was all he could say. She was unable to speak at all, so she nodded silently and then leaned over to wrap her arms around Chivalry's neck as they reached the rose-themed winner's circle. They heard applause. *For them*. Rachel beamed.

A group of men placed the blanket of roses over Chivalry's neck and the Hanover team gathered around while holding the large silver trophy. It took everything in their power to stand still for as long as it took to take a few pictures. They all wanted to jump up and down in celebration.

"Here you go, baby," Rachel said as she handed a rose to Erick. Erick took the flower and laughed as he took her hand and kissed it.

When Rachel was finally able to hop down, she immediately grabbed Erick and they held each other so tight they might have been one person. Surprisingly, a few of the other jockeys congratulated her on her ride. "Scowling man" wasn't in sight and never congratulated her. Not that she expected him to. He was probably upset with himself that he had left the rail open for Chivalry, which was a move that had cost him the race. Rachel didn't care. He did it to himself, and she won, and that's all that was important. Besides, he was completely disqualified from the race for that stunt. Rachel just laughed.

Finally, she took the saddle off and weighed in, making it official, then came back to the celebration to be included in more pictures.

"You won by eleven lengths. Eleven," Erick told her while standing still, having their picture taken again.

She could not believe it. "Eleven? Eleven. Wow." It took a moment for that to sink in. Then she looked at Erick and said, "I wish you had a chance to ride, though, baby. I..."

"No, you don't," Erick interrupted with his hands on his hips.

Rachel burst into laughter, as did her mother, who had overheard, and had remembered those same words just over a year ago the day Rachel was first scheduled to ride Chivalry for a workout. That day, Rachel would have never even dared to dream she would be riding in the Kentucky Derby, let alone winning it.

Just then, reporter Tim Simmons, the television reporter who had interviewed her before the race, appeared to her right and shoved the microphone in her face. "Rachel Bennett, congratulations on the ride of your life." He was truly excited for her, displaying a wide and toothy newscaster smile, and shaking hands with everyone. He could hardly contain himself. She giggled at his reaction.

"Thanks, Tim." Erick's arm was over her shoulder as she helped him stand up straight while Julia stood on the other side of her. Tim talked to Julia for a minute, then Rachel for the race recap.

"We broke well, almost too well. I backed him up a little after the first eighth because the pace was too fast. I wanted to save some speed for later. But that put me into the pack. Here I'm thinking I'm stuck, but I waited for an opportunity." She paused as the replay of the run down the backstretch played out on the monitor. "Then I decided to squeeze up. There was a small hole but there was room, so I took it. I have cooties and no one wanted to touch me, so they let me pass." Everyone laughed as she continued, "Allegro appeared on my left as Cronus fell back. He passed me, but look. Here, Allegro's jockey decided to help get me out of the pocket by swerving and pushing Bahama over. See? That was nice of him, wasn't it? He left a huge hole for me. So I took the rail and... There we go. To the wire."

"What were you thinking as you sailed under the wire?" Tim asked.

"Wow! Look at him go," she shouted as she watched Chivalry pulling ahead with every stride. Then she laughed as she remembered that she had to answer his question. "Oh, I was having a blast letting him run as fast as he wanted. It was so liberating and he was so happy. I wanted to keep going. See? I didn't even slow him right away. It took me a second." Rachel laughed again out of sheer happiness.

"This is amazing, Rachel. Congratulations on your first Kentucky Derby. Hopefully not your last," he said as he shook her hand.

"Thank you," Rachel said gripping Tim's hand tightly with her strongest handshake.

Then she remembered something. "And Tim?"

"Yes?"

"I need to thank two men who saved my life a little over a year ago and I have no way of finding them. I hope they're watching today. Two garbage pickup men from Harlem saved my life one evening in the middle of the night. I had been kidnapped, but I escaped by jumping out of a second story window and was knocked unconscious when I fell. But those men saw that I needed help, and they wrapped me in a coat and took me to the hospital. I can't go into many more details about it, but since they never gave their names when they brought me to the hospital, I was never given the chance to thank them for saving me. So," looking directly into the camera now, "to the two brave men that saved my life that night...Thank you."

EPILOGUE

The after-race ball held in the clubhouse was the most attention Rachel had ever received in her life. Julia felt much the same, even though she had received plenty of attention simply for being a female trainer before this.

It was overwhelming, though, for Rachel. Reporters stood in line in front of her, some even asking for autographs, which she never expected. Some stood in a semi-circle as they held microphones in her face as she recounted the race repeatedly. Erick reminded her that she had to speak to each reporter as if they were the only reporter to have asked her those questions.

"How does it feel to win the Kentucky Derby?"

"How did you know Diego was going to cut you off?"

"Did Chivalry feel as strong as he looked at the end?"

"How have the other jockeys been treating you?"

"Do you think you'll be riding for the Preakness?"

Once she had answered these questions several times, she had come up with the perfect wording, and merely regurgitated those words whenever prompted by a question. It became automatic pilot for her, and it was almost as if she were watching herself speak to reporters.

They tried asking about her statement at the end where she thanked two garbage men for saving her life, but she refused to talk about it. She only said that she thanked them for saving her. One reporter had found out about her kidnapping, which released a flurry of questions, but Rachel answered none of them, choosing to focus only on today's race. That discussion was for a later day.

Reporters also asked Erick many questions, but he spent most of this time seated at a table with the others from the Hanover Farms team. Meanwhile, Rachel stood in one corner, surrounded by reporters.

"Excuse me. Mrs. Bennett?"

"Wait your turn," shouted a short and stocky reporter as he waved his notebook at the man who had just walked up.

"Mrs. Bennett, there is an emergency phone call for you."

"Huh? Who..."

"This way, ma'am," he said, then held out his arm and helped open a path through the reporters for her to walk.

"Who is it? Everybody I know is here. They don't want to talk to Julia?" She hated referring to her mother as, "Julia," but that's how everybody else knew her. She couldn't call her "Mom" though everybody knew it was her mother.

"No ma'am. It's a woman, and she sounds upset about something. She insisted I interrupt your interviews."

"That's crazy. Who could it possibly be?"

"Here we are." He led her into an office, where they were protected from the loud sounds in the nearby ballroom. "I'll leave you alone." He closed the door behind him.

"Hello?" Rachel asked, tentatively holding the phone close to her ear. Muffled laughter and loud chatter resounded through the door behind her.

"Rachel?"

"Yes?"

"Rach. It's me, Candy. I saw you on television, Rach. I saw you. You're alive." Candy broke down in tears, sobbing into the phone, and in hearing this, Rachel followed suit, completely forgetting about her makeup.

"Candy, where are you? Where did you go? What happened?"

"I left, Rach. I was stupid, but I couldn't stay there anymore. I couldn't face it without you. I thought you were, well, you know. I thought you were gone. So I'm in Miami."

"Miami? What on earth possessed you to go there?"

"Long story, Rach. But I need to get out of here. I'm...sort of...in trouble." Candy's voice lowered. "I need help."

"What happened?"

"Well, this guy, he's my boyfriend, he's um, well, not a good person, Rach. He's sort of, well, mean."

"Does he hit you?" Rachel shouted into the phone.

"Um..."

"I'm coming down there right now. You have to give me the address." Rachel searched the desk for paper and a pen. "What's the address?"

"I um, I think I have an idea. He's out cold, drunk, and I think I can just..." Candy lowered her voice to a whisper that Rachel was hardly able to hear over the long distance between phones. "...drive away."

"Yes. Do it. Why didn't you do this before? Why have you stayed there?"

"I don't, well, it's hard to explain, Rach. But I can't stay on the phone, okay? This is going to cost him a fortune."

"You are worried about a damned phone bill when the son of a bitch beat you?" Rachel heaved a sob again at the thought. "Get out of there. Now," she shouted into the phone in a panic.

In a way, she almost wished this jerk of a boyfriend could hear her. She wanted to yell at him so badly that her blood was nearly boiling. "Candy, drive away. Leave him. Get on a plane. Do you need money? Cause –,"

"I got it. I have money now. I guess that's what I'll do. I'll, um, get on a plane. But you're in Kentucky."

"We're going home tomorrow. We'll be back at night. We'll be there for a week before heading to Maryland."

"Tomorrow?"

"Tomorrow. Get on the next flight out of there, even if it's a red eye or whatever. Get out of there now, Candy, and go to the track or wait at the airport. I can meet you when we get back. Get out of there."

"I will."

"Do you promise me? You wouldn't go back on your word to your best friend, would you?" Rachel suppressed a sob as she tried to stay brave for her.

"I promise, Rach."

"Do you have my phone number at the track? Or at my house? Do you remember?"

"No. I forgot. Give them to me, quick. I have to get off here before... Go ahead, Rach."

After giving Candy her phone numbers, one at the track and one at her house, they hung up, and Rachel stood in the office with her arms wrapped around herself. After a minute, she remembered her makeup as it ran down her face. "Oh, God," she muttered as she searched for tissue. There was a small starburst decorative mirror on a wall nearby, and she used the reflection as she cleaned herself up, then took some more tissues, and opened the door. The man was still standing there, and she knew he had probably heard her entire conversation.

"Not a word," she said, just in case. *Just in case, what*? She had no idea. If she was now a celebrity, she knew celebrities had no way of keeping secrets. And if this one caused harm to Candy in any way, she could never forgive herself.

Enjoy an excerpt from the next book in the series:

WOUNDS INTO WISDOM

February 1969

"How despicably I have acted!" she cried; "I, who have prided myself on my discernment! I, who have valued myself on my abilities! who have often disdained the generous candour of my sister, and gratified my vanity in useless or blamable mistrust! How humiliating is this discovery! Yet, how just a humiliation! Had I been in love, I could not have been more wretchedly blind. But vanity, not love, has been my folly. Pleased with the preference of one, and offended by the neglect of the other, on the very beginning of our acquaintance, I have courted prepossession and ignorance, and driven reason away, where either were concerned. Till this moment I never knew myself."

"Love does silly things to people." Candy folded down the edge of the page, worn with excessive use. Pride and Prejudice was one of her favorite books, though she had no idea why. She didn't believe in all that romance stuff. Though, she did sort of hope for it. One day. Maybe.

Longingly, she gazed at the poster on her wall of Bobby Darin. If only she could find someone as romantic as he. Musicians were the most romantic of all men. They were so deep. She suppressed a sigh of pining by pressing her lips together. Guys like that weren't real. But they sure were cute to look at. Candy fancied herself as an old-fashioned girl when it came to music. Darin's nine-year-old "Mack the Knife" was her favorite song of all time, and that record was always on her record player, ready to go.

Laughter from downstairs rang over the sound of the annoying rock music from the record player blasting in the living room. *Jimi Hendrix again.* He was her brother's hero as a drug-using guitarist. To Candy, the music was tinny and almost painful to listen to. It was wild, screeching, eerie, almost. And loud. *That's not music.* The only reason her brother and friends could stand it was because they were high. The sweet smell of marijuana smoke slipped under her door in soft waves. Candy let out a breath of air, hoping none of it got into her lungs. She was just about to grab a towel from her hamper to cover the crack under the door when she heard shouting.

"Can Can!" It was her brother. "Get down here! Now!" The music stopped as someone dragged the needle across the record, scratching it. *Good.* She dropped her head into her hands and groaned. What could he possibly want from her? "Hey! Can!" She heard footsteps running up the stairs and her heart thumped. Any minute now his arrival would be announced by a loud bang as the door hit the wall behind it, sending the doorknob further into the hole in the wall.

She tensed. *Bang!* She jumped anyway. "What?" With her exclamation, her hands slammed onto the side of her bed as her long, ginger hair shook with frustration.

"Rachel's on TV!"

"What?" Candy stood. A glimmer of hope shone in her eyes. Did they have a stakes winner today? On her day off, too! Ugh, how frustrating that she wasn't there to see it.

"It's bad, Can. Come on!"

Her hope vanished in an instant. The two ran down the stairs together in a rush that might have been the scene on a Christmas morning in any other house. Not theirs. That thought was the furthest thing from her mind, though, as she turned her head so she could see the television as she ran. Once at the bottom, she pushed Don out of the way and jumped right to the television. One of Don's friends slapped the side of it and the black and white picture became clearer.

"She was wearing a dark blue pea coat and mittens. Jeans and a green blouse. Boots." The woman on the screen paused to take a breath and compose herself as a man patted her back in encouragement. "We are offering a reward of two thousand dollars for any information...," It was Rachel's mother. Candy's skin crawled with fear and every hair stood straight up on her arms. Her bony hands covered her mouth as she noted a small picture in the corner of the screen. Rachel's eleventh grade yearbook photo.

Julia, Rachel's mother, had her arms wrapped around a notebook as it covered her chest like a shield. This woman, also her boss at Belmont Park, was the strongest woman Candy had ever known, but now... Now, she was a mess. Candy could almost see her quivering with fear. To see Julia this way, someone who had always been dauntless in Candy's eyes, scared her to death.

"No," she whispered, her voice husky with emotion. Fortunately, the others in the room let her watch the rest of the story. When it was over, the talking head went on, speaking as if the world had not just ended. It certainly had. "No. No," she continued with huge tears drizzling down her face and over her cold hands. The warmth did little for that chill. Nothing could. Nothing ever would.

"Can, you went to the movies with her last night, didn't you?"

She almost didn't hear her brother's question as she continued to stare at the television. Now the reporter was talking about the Beatles, but she didn't hear a word of it. The question finally registered with her and she nodded.

"Oh, my God," she whispered.

"Didn't you walk her to the station? Did she get on the train?" Don's voice rose with every word.

"I don't know!" Candy couldn't take another question from him and ran back up to her room. She slammed the door behind her and paced the floor in her small room. Fortunately, there wasn't much furniture on which to stub her toes. Only a twin bed and a small dresser. One of the drawers had no handles, was crooked and unable to close all the way. The dresser was the same shade of wood as the paneled walls of her attic bedroom. The red carpet remnant was worn, so thin in places that she could see the wood floors beneath. She almost tripped over one wrinkle, but didn't, because she knew where it was without thinking. It had been there for so long.

"What do I do?" she asked herself, but had no answer. Only seconds later, it hit her. *Look for her!* It was cold. February. Icy. She had to get to her quick. If Rachel were outside somewhere, maybe in an alley, still in Queens, Candy knew she could find her. She knew this borough like the back of her hand. It was noon, the sun was up, lighting the way, maybe melting some of the ice that had formed overnight. Maybe it was warm enough for Rachel to survive. If she were out there somewhere, Candy would find her.

She grabbed her coat and tossed it on as she ran down the stairs.

"Where you going?" Don shouted as she barreled through the front door then slammed it behind her. Her brother's demand for answers was her last concern. She had to find Rachel. Her best friend. Her only friend. Her rock.

Every alley was an opportunity to Candy. She thoroughly searched behind trash bins, cans, bags, kicked aside rats as she asked them where her friend was. They weren't telling, the filthy beasts. Behind every trash can, in every corner, she just knew she would see her friend lying there, half frozen. Despite that, she would still be alive and Candy would take her home, warm her up, give her some soup... Well, if she had any soup. She probably didn't. The house was usually void of food. They didn't even have mice because there was never anything for them to forage. They had all gone next door. One good thing about being poor.

Once she had thoroughly searched all of the alleyways between her house and the subway station, she ventured on to other alleys. Just in case. Maybe Rachel had gone a different way. Why would she do that? Didn't matter. If there was a remote chance of finding Rachel, Candy was going to take it.

Her adrenaline, along with her hope, faded over the next two hours. With each step, her shoulders sagged a little more, her head drooped. And finally, she stopped and looked around. Her heart burned as she turned around in a full circle. Just one more look.

She had to admit the truth. Her friend had vanished.

WOMEN IN RACING

In the 1930s, there was a woman named Wantha Davis who won around one thousand races before women were even allowed to hold a license. How? She wasn't allowed to race in pari-mutuel races, so she ran mainly on small bush tracks in the south. She was occasionally allowed to ride in match races and even beat Johnnie Longden in one match race. Later, she rode at Pimlico for the ninth Pimlico Classic, which was only for female riders. No betting was allowed on this race because none of them were licensed. Six women rode that day with Wantha winning, going away by twelve lengths.

In 1964, the Civil Rights Act opened doors for women in any field of work, allowing men and women, no matter what race, to work wherever they wanted. Despite this, men fought hard against women, trying anything they could to keep women out of horse racing. It didn't work.

In 1967, Kathy Kusner repeatedly applied for a jockey's license and was turned down every time. Finally, she sued the Maryland Racing Commission, and after a long court battle, a female judge decided it was unconstitutional to exclude women from racing. Unfortunately, Kathy was injured and was unable to ride for a while, but she did eventually get her license.

In the meantime, other females scrambled to get their licenses as well, with Mary Ryan being the first licensed woman, and Diane Crump being the first woman to ride in a pari-mutuel race, and later, the Kentucky Derby (coincidentally in 1970). Several others followed suit and were soon known as "jockettes," a name that somewhat annoyed the women. Despite threats, acts of violence, and acts of aggression during races, many of them had great success as they broke stereotypes and proved that women were just as good at riding, if not better.

Amazingly, and despite prejudice against her race *and* sex, in 1971, Cheryl White became the first black female jockey and rode for over twenty years before an injury sidelined her. This opened up a chance for her to work as a racing official in California where she currently works.

In the 1980s, Julie Krone came along and demanded respect for women like never before. She proved to the racing world once and for all that women could ride. Even in the 1980s, though, nearly twenty years after women were able to obtain licenses, she was victim to acts of aggression and violence during races. One man even whipped her ear, causing her to need stitches. However, eventually, she rocked the racing world, earning her way into the Racing Hall of Fame as the only female jockey to do so thus far. Hopefully soon, more will be voted in as well. Current riders such as Forest Boyce and Rosie Napravnik are well on their way to becoming Hall of Fame nominees.

ABOUT THE AUTHOR

Raised in Southern Maryland, Kristie Higgins grew up as a horse lover, riding friends' horses whenever possible. Short stories written as a horse-obsessed teenager have stuck with her and are now emerging as novels.

She is a graduate of Indiana University, Bloomington and a retired instrumental music teacher. She taught in various elementary schools in Maryland for twelve years before retiring. No musician can ever give up music, so she plays keyboards in her church, with her two teenage sons playing guitar and bass alongside. At the end of the day, she relaxes, watching horseracing and writing with the help of her two cats, Shadow and Cookie.

43316306R00189

Made in the USA
Lexington, KY
27 July 2015